BREATH

By Jean Lowe Carlson

First Novel in the Three Days of Oblenite Series
Copyright 2015 Jean Lowe Carlson

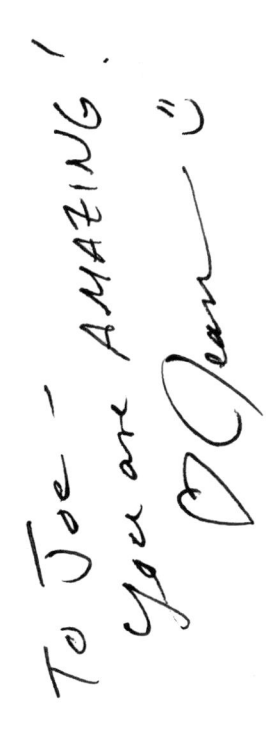

COPYRIGHT

Copyright 2015 Jean Lowe Carlson. All Rights Reserved. This book or any portion thereof may not be reproduced or used in any manner whatsoever without the express written permission of the publisher except for the use of brief quotations in a book review. If you would like to share this book, please purchase an additional copy for each recipient. If you're reading this book and did not purchase it, then please return to your favorite retailer and purchase your own copy. Thank you for respecting the hard work of this author.

First Paperback Edition, 2015

ISBN 978-1-943199-01-3

Createspace:
https://www.createspace.com/

Cover Design Copyright 2015 by Jean Lowe Carlson, Creative Commons modified with permission from photograph "Gold and Red Mask" by Julija Mazhora, https://www.flickr.com/photos/109927353@N07/ - model credit to Inga Balode, http://vk.com/asjkaaa. All Rights Reserved.

This book is available in print at most online retailers. Please remember to leave a review for *Three Days of Oblenite, Book One: Breath* at your favorite retailer!

OTHER WORKS BY JEAN LOWE CARLSON

Three Days of Oblenite Series
Breath
Tears (Coming May 2015)
Blood (Coming June 2015)

The Key of Fire Series (Coming Fall 2015!)
Triumph of the Undoer
Brotherhood of the Abyss
Key of the World Shaper

The Kingsmen Chronicles (Coming Spring 2016!)
Kingsman
Kingswoman
Kingskinder

ACKNOWLEDGEMENTS

To my sister Stephany, a constant inspiration in my life, let's travel this road together and grow to be feisty old ladies. To my mom Wendy and my dad Dave, who always encouraged me to be just who I am and told me they loved me, "just because you're you." To my grandparents, I'm so lucky to have you all in my life, providing such support when I need it most. To all my friends who have buoyed me through this journey, some near and many far, I think of you with joy in my heart. To all the doctoral students out there - there is a life afterwards, and it doesn't always look how you think it will!

And to my beloved husband Matt, who has sat through how many hours now of out-loud reading? I couldn't thicken the plot and draw all the twists together without you. Thank you for pushing me forward in this, and all the research you've done to bring every facet of writing alive in my life, and for all your boundless, beautiful love.

And last of all, to Athenos. Couldn't have done this without you, soulfriend. You challenge me constantly to be just who I am, and I love each and every moment of it.

So be it.

TABLE OF CONTENTS

PROLOGUE	6
CHAPTER 1	8
CHAPTER 2	26
CHAPTER 3	34
CHAPTER 4	48
CHAPTER 5	63
CHAPTER 6	78
CHAPTER 7	89
CHAPTER 8	100
CHAPTER 9	111
CHAPTER 10	127
CHAPTER 11	145
CHAPTER 12	154
CHAPTER 13	164
CHAPTER 14	178
CHAPTER 15	188
EPILOGUE	194
ABOUT JEAN LOWE CARLSON	196
PREVIEW: TEARS	197
PREVIEW: KINGSMAN	203

PROLOGUE

Time passes, as all things do, Death to Life, and back into Death.

He was cursed, they say, as a little boy, when he became fascinated with old bones upon the porch of his manse. Inside an ancient coffin of wrought-iron there slept the bones, dry, brittle, and nearly sand, and he was enamored of them as a child. He would steal away from his mother's watch and go to the bones, to visit them, and to play near them.

Then one day, when he was no older than three or four, his mother caught him staring at the bones, and she scolded him, saying, "Come away."

But he looked up at her with his blue eyes and said simply, "I miss her, mère."

And then she scolded him by name and reached through the wrought-iron fencing and again said, "Come away."

But he did not. Instead, the boy reached through the ornate iron of the coffin and touched the bright yellow day-flower that grew up from the bones' ribcage. And then he touched the bones themselves. Stroked them, really, as if stroking a lover's long-forgotten heart. And the bones fell all to pieces, siphoned away from his touch into nothing but shimmering sand, as beautiful as pebbled crystal.

His mother had screamed.

And the boy had felt a strange wind come through him, like a breath.

Frightened, he had run back through the bars of the iron railing to his mother. And she had coddled him and kissed him upon the cheek, frightened for him and cooing his name sternly but sweet, petting his hair. In relief, the boy had lifted up his lips like he had done a thousand times, to kiss his mother's cheek.

And at the touch of his lips, her breath had choked in her throat, and she spasmed, and died.

When it was finished he had been left there, in the cold with his mothers' cold body, and he had begun to cry. But when the boy needed a sweet caress of comfort, he did not lay down in the loving, dead arms of his mother. Instead, he went to the bones, all sand now, and curled up in them. Inside the cage of iron, he curled around the single yellow dayflower, which he stroked with one finger.

And that's how they found him, when someone finally came. The milkman, perhaps, no one really knows who it was.

And that's how the curse began.

Or so some say.

* * *

CHAPTER 1

"Gryffine! Come away!"

Her mother scolded her sharply, and Gryffine Toulunnet turned her head with a sharp hiss of breath. She had been enjoying the old Gypsun woman's tale, and none of the other young men and women hearkening to the raglady's fire were being scolded and fetched away by the arm like they were barely out of swaddling. It was embarrassing, and Gryffine's cheeks reddened as a few youths her age turned and snickered, and the old Gypsun woman scowled at the interruption. But Gryffine's mother pulled her on like a little girl in braids, ignoring the old Gypsun woman and everything else she didn't want to see.

Gryffine allowed herself to be hauled away from the bright sparks of the Rollows-eve fire, and back to the main avenues of bustling trade in the brisk autumn evening, booths and tents already being packed up so their proprietors could be free to enjoy their own revelry his heady night. Glancing at her mother, Gryffine felt a familiar curl of unease in her belly, concerned not that she'd been caught and hauled off, but what it was going to cost her mother. And indeed, her flighty mother was nearly in a fit that Gryffine had been meandering about the colorful Gypsun booths, this night of all nights, when the dead danced their bones to the rancor of Rollows with the living, the first and most terrifying night of feasting and celebration of Oblenite.

The First Night of Oblenite had always been special to Gryffine, with its mysterious and devilish parades of costumed men and women shaking their bones like the dead were said to do. Her eyes drifted to the Gypsun booths and all their ready-made wares for the occasion, as her mother seized her roughly by the hand and drug her along faster, murmuring feverish chants to the Immaculate and fingering the rose-beads around her neck. Her mother's eyes darted almost frantically at all the hubbub and press of gaily and darkly-arrayed folk now in the streets, the fantastic revelry of Rollows just beginning as the sun flashed out over the rooftops and beyond the city of Julis. Torches and fires had been lit now, not just the braziers and lamplight of a typical evening in the cobbled streets of the Gypsun Quarter, but real bonfires. And around them, folk danced and caroused, played instruments and drank their wine, and displayed their gaily-macabre costumes to one another by the fire's light. Masques were being donned, laughter and cheers to thwart Death were raucous in the air now, and Gryffine had begun to tingle with anticipation, aching to join the revelry.

But her mother tugged her along, Gryffine still slight enough at sixteen and constrained enough by the corset and slim ankle-length skirt of her taupe and brown striped day-dress, that her fine-boned mother could. Their evening's shopping dangled from the basket upon Marionne's arm as her delicate face beneath her chignon-constrained black curls went more and more pale, fiercely whispering her prayers to thwart the Beast of the Inferno and the Infinite Lust that Padrenne Henri Coulis frothed at the mouth about from his austere pulpit. Marionne's thin, nervous fingers alternated between the long string of rose-beads about her high-collared neck, and brushing themselves off on the black twill of her corseted day-dress. Gryffine lingered at the end of her mother's grip upon her hand, watching a tall man pass that looked surprisingly like the gaunt Henri Coulis. But this man was arrayed in a Jacque-bone suit striped in dazzling color, with a masque like an eagle of death burst into flame.

The tall man caught Gryffine looking, and he surged swiftly forward with a hiss, shaking his mane of red and orange-dyed eagle feathers at her. Gryffine met his true eyes beneath the beaked, black-eyed masque, a pale blue as perfect as the sapphires upon Padrenne Henri's midwinter robe. Gryffine challenged his bright gaze, ready for the headiness of Rollows and all the lasciviousness it brought, when her mother gave her a swift jerk with a near-fainting shriek of terror. The man's blue eyes laughed along with his beautiful mouth as he swirled his long red and black cloak to move off. But not before surreptitiously running a daring finger beneath Gryffine's chin and down to the demure lace of the high collar of her corseted day-dress. Gryffine knew that she flushed, ready and desiring to be touched by a man so. He winked one pale blue eye as she was hauled off by her mother, and then swirled his devilish cloak away into the throng.

***

A sharp slap stung Gryffine's face.

"What were you thinking, young lady! Stealing away from me like that! And on *Rollows*! Don't you know what the Beast and all his demons will *do to you* if they find you out tonight?!"

Gryffine's mother shook her viciously by the shoulders, then hauled the wrought-iron gate of the yard closed behind them. She tugged Gryffine up the stone porch-stairs of their manse with such force that Gryffine almost tripped in her brown low-heeled boots, constrained by the narrow fit of her striped twill skirts. Marionne unlocked the door with a woeful wail that she had such a wayward daughter, and then pushed Gryffine in, locking everything behind them quickly.

Home at last, the tirade fizzled out in the dark, lamplit hall as Marionne shuddered in the dregs of her fear. She shrugged out of her black ladies' dresscoat and dark scarf in an exhausted haste, then unpinned her cormorant-feather and black lace hat. Her bird-fine fingers fussed to assist Gryffine with her own brown and cream pinstriped dresscoat, though Gryffine was long past needing such childish attention. But she knew her mother liked to fuss, and though it was Gryffine's bane, it was also her joy. Her father had passed nearly three years back, and it had been just the two of them ever since, and Marionne was a sweet mother despite her piety and fears. Marionne sank to the bench beside the door, trembling violently and pale as fine silk, running through her rose-beads with one hand.

And Gryffine knew that another fit was going to take her if she didn't do as Dotorre Fausten had said.

"Mère," Gryffine sat beside her mother upon the ebony hall bench and reached out, touching her mother's face gently. Marionne startled, her eyes coming back into focus, though her breathing was still fast and shallow. "Mère, do the breathing the dotorre said you must do. Come now, practice with me."

Gryffine took a long slow breath in through her nose, then out through pursed lips, modeling the breathing for her mother. Reaching out, Gryffine grasped the ever-worrying hand with the rose-beads and placed it upon her chest, letting her mother feel her own slow breath. Marionne shuddered, but her fretting fingers stilled, and she began the breathing. Gryffine's breath sighed through the hall. She could feel it moving out and around her mother, soothing Marionne at last.

"That's it," Gryffine encouraged in a mesmeric, low tone just like the dotorre had taught her three years ago, though the man had no idea whom he showed such breathing to. "Slow and deep, mère. Slow and deep, just like Dotorre Fausten said."

Her mother was finally immersed in the breathing, and had closed her eyes, her head sinking back against the wall with fatigue, dark curls escaped from her chignon below her modest black hat in disarray. Gryffine felt shame at what she had done tonight, what she had caused. As much as she craved Rollows, she knew such nights frightened her superstitious and delicate mother nearly to fits, and for her to have slipped away during the shopping at the market stalls in the Gypsun Quarter of all places was inexcusable.

Gryffine should have simply waited to go out, like she'd done last year.

And the year before.

Gryffine's cheeks flushed at that, wondering what would happen if her mother found she went out alone on Rollows, seeking the excitement and permission of the night, the attraction of Death dancing side-by-side with Life. That she stole the key from her mother's bedside table and let herself out the back porch by the sepulcher when her mother was deep in laudannie to block out the noise and terror of the streets. As Marionne slept like the dead, Gryffine rejoiced with the dead in all their dire finery and their raucous, hedonistic pomp. And that for two years Gryffine had defied her mother this way, ever since father had died.

Defied her in this way and so many more.

But Marionne was only getting worse, despite everything the good dotorre had done for her. And Gryffine thought perhaps she shouldn't go out this year. It knifed her heart to think that she would miss Rollows, the one night of all the year that she could do as she wished, and be as she wished like all the other revelers did every night of their lives. But her mother was so much worse this year than she had been last time Oblenite came around. Gryffine left the question unanswered as she stroked her mother's thin fingers, still pressed to her own chest in the semi-dark of the entry hall.

Marionne had a bloom of color in her cheeks now, and the fine wrinkles in her forehead had eased, her breathing gentle and slow. Gryffine knew she was beautiful. Few girls had mothers as beautiful as Marionne, with her raven-dark curls and her silk-fine skin. She was bird-boned and frail, and Gryffine knew father had loved that fragility. But when he had died, the fragility had overtaken Marionne, and she had let her pious superstitions and fears run riot. It saddened Gryffine to know that her mother would never take another husband, though many men appreciated and tried to come calling.

"Mère." Gryffine pressed her mother's china-fine hand between her own slender fingers. Though slight and bird-boned like her mother with the same wayward ebony curls, Gryffine had always possessed a heartiness and lust for life that only her father could have given her. Roulen had been a debonair man, and had imparted to his daughter the same strength of will, along with his pale green eyes.

Almost too much will for her poor mother.

Marionne opened her dark eyes, and a wan smile grazed her features, otherworldly and fey. She reached out, stroking Gryffine's cheek, then petting back a few ebony curls that had escaped Gryffine's long braid, straightening it over her shoulder. "Gryffine. Such a good girl. Come here, come here. I'm not mad, my love, I was just... so frightened for you! So many *demons* out tonight...Come here." Marionne reached out and pulled Gryffine close, still stroking her fine-china hand over Gryffine's ebony curls.

"You're getting tall, my love," Marionne whispered into her ear. "Even though you have my bones and not your père's. Would you like to help me start supper? I bought us eggs and couthonne, and fall-cress, and fresh ginger. How would you like couthonne-pie for dinner and ginger creams for dessert? I know you enjoy the markets on Rollows, but let us stay in and make a night of it here, shall we?"

Gryffine couldn't help but smile. Many nights her mother wasn't strong enough to cook supper and would retire to her solar to take a few powders and tinctures to calm her nerves. It was a rare treat that she made something as ornate as couthonne-pie anymore, not to mention ginger creams. More than half the cooking would fall to Gryffine, as Marionne would weaken as the night wore on, but for now, Gryffine was touched by her mother's intent. In a rare bout of energy, her mother tickled her about the ribs and Gryffine shrieked, bouncing off the ebony bench and snatching up the basket.

"I'll whisk the eggs and chop the cress!"

Gryffine moved quickly down the ebony-paneled front hall, past the darkened solar, the morbidly dark entertaining-parlor, and the family parlor, is somber recesses lit by only a single gaslamp. She tossed the basket upon the center block-table in the back kitchen, turning up the low-burning gaslamps and setting the gas alight in the broad iron oven to warm the autumn-chilled kitchen with a cheery glow. But Gryffine couldn't help but notice how slowly her mother moved from the bench in the hall down the dark corridor to the kitchen, and how the lamps' light made her look more skeletal than the costumes of the revelers now cheering and yelling outside the wrought-iron fence on Rue Coullard.

Marionne stole up slowly as Gryffine began to crack eggs in a bowl and whisk them, and her hand was like the brush of a sad ghost down Gryffine's ebony locks.

***

Gryffine had thrown her windows wide from the second story, to afford the best vantage of the revelry down below upon Rue Coullard. Supper was long finished and the ginger creams sat extravagantly in her stomach, and she set her chin upon her crossed arms as she took in the throng now gathering all along the broad avenue in anticipation of the Rollows-eve parade. Marionne was long asleep in her laudannie-drenched dreams, and Gryffine had tucked her in over an hour ago and turned down the gaslamps throughout their dreary city manse. Now she sat upon a patterned stool by the bay-window in her own darkened room at the front of their manse and imagined herself below in the raucous, colorful hedonism upon the street.

Gryffine could smell the caramel-nuts in their gay red-and-black papers from the vendor at the corner in his Jacques-bone suit with an ibis head. She could hear the parade coming, the boom of the drums and the clack of the scatter-bones and the shrilling of pipes and the howling of the performers. Incense was in the air already from masked men making their way through the crowd with musk and opium-censers. A man and woman embraced against the manse's wrought-iron fence, masques askew as they fevered each other with drunken need. Gryffine watched it avariciously, fingering the iron key in her hand, chin still settled upon her forearms. She watched the man's hand steal up to unhook the woman's corset and bare a breast, heedless of others in the street. Gryffine flushed to watch the woman bend like a willow branch, baring her throat as he clutched her close and suckled at that beautiful white skin.

A low moan escaped Gryffine's lips as the woman cried out, and fire raced through her as the man stopped that cry with a kiss. Gryffine could feel that kiss, every furious pressing of those lips, over her entire skin. Her eyes tracked the lovers as they scooted to the side, now partially concealed from the revelrous throng by the immense regalia-bush at the corner of the fence. Gryffine watched the masqued man hitch the masqued woman's skirts up and turn her, watched them take each other, his hand at her throat and hers upon his hips and the iron bars of the fence, tucked into that heady nook of red regalia-blossoms.

Gryffine's fingers turned the wrought-iron key over and over in her hand.

* * *

The heady promise of Rollows had won out, as she knew it would.

Gryffine wore a black cloak of pure silk, deep hood pulled up to hide her face as she slipped through the throng towards the sound of the parade. A low-cut silk dress could be seen beneath, the corseted bodice trimmed with red lace, and only lace covering her shoulders like the harlots and the Gypsun tumbler-girls wore. A ribbon of black silk choked her throat, and Gryffine had pinned her hair up in the twisted waves of the Gypsun girls, letting a long, thick curl drape over one shoulder and between her breasts. She had inked her eyelids and rouged her cheeks and lips before donning the black, red, and gold silk demi-masque trimmed in red lace and gold sequins to obscure her visage.

The dress itself was close-cut, clinging black silk, and so was the bodice, trimmed in long bone-suit stripes in bloody red and fiery gold that followed the lines of her corset. Slashed to mid-thigh, the scandalous dress bared a tight garter of red lace upon Gryffine's bare thigh as she walked. The black boots had cost Gryffine much from her trading of laudannie from her mother's apothecary, but their well-polished leather was fine tonight, and their hourglass heels made Gryffine sashay as she maneuvered quickly through the crowd.

Gryffine's mother would have died from a fit had she seen her daughter. And so, everything had been sewn in the late hours, when Marionne was drugged asleep, and then stored in the hide-nook behind the ebony bookcase outside Gryffine's door in preparation for this night. Her mother didn't know about the hide-nook in their ancient, dark manse and she never would. Gryffine had found it when they'd moved in three years ago from their manor home in Lousoutte, when they had needed to come to the city as their fortunes failed and Marionne struggled to find work. Roulen Toulunnet's pension from the bank had been enough to reopen the long-shuttered three-story city manse owned by his cousin, but little else, and it did not pay for the expense of Marionne's apothecary or regular visits to Dotorre Fausten. The Toulunnets weren't destitute, but they weren't of wealth any longer, and so Gryffine had traded for her silks and lace tonight and stashed everything secretly away over time.

Some part of Gryffine felt guilty as she threaded through the throng, following Rue Coullard around the sprawling Saint Sommes Park until it met Rue Veline, then turning left out of the Saints Commons and towards the heart of the Quarter, and the revelry. Stealing her mother's powders and selling them in the Gypsun Quarter was deceitful, trusting that Marionne wouldn't remember how much she had or had not used despicable. But another part of Gryffine raged that her mother used those powders, and felt no guilt at all in ridding them from the manse.

But tonight was a night for revelry and not guilt, such as could not be indulged at any other time of year. A night when the dead danced with the living and Light became Dark and Dark became Light. Gryffine pushed her mother from her mind and guilt from her heart, and wove deftly along Rue Veline towards the sound of the drums and scatter-bones. Masques sneered and roared around her, dizzying her with their fanciful designs and bright colors, not to mention the bone-striped suits and fanciful dresses beneath. Here was a lion, golden-maned and proud with the bones showing through his lower jaw and immense fangs. To her left suddenly appeared the Old Hag, crooked of nose and red of eyebrow with her ferocious ruby lips that dripped blood. A woman in the Secret Face passed, her gay, tinkling laugh obscured by the cherubic white full-face masque with its white eyes and white lips. Gryffine spun, taking in everything with scandalous delight behind her own silk masque.

The drums thundered, nearer now, and she stepped briskly to the lift of the sidewalk pavers, near the lamplit cart of a caramel-nut seller. He hailed her garishly from beside his roasting-cart with its red lantern, in showman's nasal tones.

"Ten for a penny! Ten for a penny! Small bag for six! Pacanne, welthonne, or almonne, all rolled in caramel!"

Gryffine stepped over, her stomach churning. It had been a long time since supper, and these were her favorite treat on Rollows, before the evening truly began. "Small bag of the pacanne, good *chevronne*," she called, breathless from the excitement, counting out a few coins from her boot-purse. "And do you have drinks?"

Gryffine saw the nut-seller sway, and knew it was from the coursing of her own breath, excited and uncontained tonight, from her curse that was a gift but one night a year. His eyes brightened, and he gave her a lascivious grin from beneath his cockatrice masque as he served her nuts into a small red-and-black chequed bag. "A little young for drinks, aren't we, *madamme*?" They traded the bag for coins, which he whisked away into the purse at his belt.

Gryffine smiled, enjoying his mistake, that he thought she wanted something alcoholic, but now that she thought about it, she did. "Oh, but I *always* have markou on Rollows!" She quipped, blustering her way through the ostentatious lie. She had seen her father take markou, though Gryffine had only been allowed it once. But the bittersweet almonne aperitif was the favored drink of the demons upon Rollows, and suddenly, she longed for its heady delight.

He chuckled, admiring her spirit, and his brown eyes flashed in the light of his roasting coals. "Now I don't know about markou here, *madamme*, but if you ask for Jessup Rohalle over at that establishment

15

there," his finger pointed across the crowded throng at a little bar absolutely packed with laughing revelers spilling from its wrought-iron tables, "he might see what he can do for a slight fae in silk and lace. Tell him Rolf sent you."

"My thanks, *chevronne*." Gryffine sampled his wares from her chequed paper, and smiled in bliss. He saw it and laughed.

"Off you go, dark fae! Before Rolf gets tempted by those slight little bones and those pretty manners! Shoo!" He turned away with a laugh, and went back to his hawking, ready for a pair of tawny-costumed revelers in leopard masques who stepped up counting out coins.

Gryffine turned and pushed her way through the burgeoning throng, munching caramel pacanne, the press of bodies seething as the drums approached. The parade would arrive in minutes, and she wanted a good vantage point by then, and the bar across the street looked like just the thing. Hung with red lanterns and long strings of black, gold, and red glass beads for the celebrations, the bar glowed like the Inferno that Padrenne Henri preached against every week. The drunken creatures that spilled from its porch and open-air balconies with their wrought-iron railings had just the right vantage for the parade. Incense-smoke charred the air, and a bang concussed her ears, and Gryffine turned to see the annunciatory fireworks of the parade far down the crowded street, yet blocks away. The pipes cavorted and the drums thundered as she shouldered faster through the throng and tripped lightly through the wrought-iron fencing around the bar's outdoor tables.

The brightly-lit bar was packed, and Gryffine quickly maneuvered her petite, slender form through until she was facing the stout mahogany bar. A tall, slender man in black shirt, black silk waistcoat, and black trousers with the masque of the Infinite Lust stood pouring drinks behind it. Red with glittering golden and black tiger-stripes from cheek to its four corkscrewing horns, the masque was one of the cleverest Gryffine had seen, with little ridges of horn all along the high cheekbones and brow, each tipped with a dot of gold. Its strong lines and luscious design accentuated the fine jaw and dark stubble of the man beneath, whose dark eyes widened when he turned from making an order to see Gryffine at his bar.

But his slow grin was teasing and lascivious, and there was a twinkle in his dark eyes to match his very white teeth. "Such devilish lusciousness as has come to my bar! What'll you have? A pepper-gin? Limone? Sweet-hush?"

"Are you Jessup?" Gryffine shouted over the din. "Rolf sent me! He says you have markou?" She was bold tonight, aroused by the revelry and the tempting, teasing manner of the man before her. Emboldened, Gryffine shouldered one side of her silk cloak back so the tall, slender bartender could appreciate more of what lingered beneath. The barman pursed his lips and exhaled, his long-fingered hands deftly preparing another order. He glanced down at his work for a moment, then glanced slyly up.

"I am Jessup!" He shouted back, but leaned in, managing to make it conspiratorial for her ears only and loud enough for her to hear. "But markou?" He shook his head with a sly grin. "Never heard of it." He hailed a barmaid in a white leopard demi-masque, who whisked off the drink he'd made with five others, her pretty pout in the packed bar one of the few irritated faces Gryffine had seen tonight. Gryffine slid into a suddenly-vacated mahogany stool immediately before the barman and leaned over the bar upon her bare elbows, décolletage artfully presented.

"You just made a drink with markou! I saw it!" Gryffine shouted over the din.

"What, this?" He lifted the small white and gold bottle of the aperitif in question. "This is not for pretty fae! They drink such things and then dance wild, tempting men nearby into disaster! Fae should only drink the first morning dewdrops, not markou." The barman Jessup's white grin teased, his dark Gypsun eyes glowing with mischief.

Gryffine leaned closer. "How do you know I'm a pretty fae at all? And not some *demonne* come to eat your heart if you don't libate me with markou?! What if the markou upon my lips is the only thing that will keep you safe?"

He leaned in close upon his elbows and slid a finger out, tracing her flesh above the lace at her décolletage. "Such pretty soft skin," Jessup murmured, his face mere inches from hers, his dark eyes admiring from behind his clever masque. "*Demonne* don't have skin like yours. And those pale green eyes and ebony hair could only be fae…drowning in the Darkness to reveal the Light."

Gryffine trembled beneath his touch, the din of the bar fading around her as her body heated and her cheeks flushed. This was what she wanted. This was the meaning of Rollows. The barman Jessup leaned closer, to whisper conspiratorially in her ear. "Give me a kiss, pretty *demonne*, and I'll give you markou. And if you want a good vantage to watch the parade, come with me and I'll show you. They're nearly here…"

Gryffine leaned closer, turning her lips to his and running them carefully across his own, ready for her revelry, as she could do on no other night of the year. "I'll give you a kiss, but I'll find my own vantage for the parade," she whispered. "All I want is markou…" She breathed out, long and slow, and watched carefully as Jessup trembled from it, the call of her breath too strong for any man to ignore this night. But the barman was no boy at the bonfires, to be taken by Gryffine's tricks and rolled by her beauty. His lips lingered over hers, taking her breath and exhaling it back to her, tempting and teasing.

He knew her words for the lie they were.

"Why? Why not watch the parade with me, pretty *demonne*?"

"Because you're Death, aren't you?" But Gryffine Toulunnet was trembling now as the barman's lips whispered over hers and the drums thundered the glasses suspended on a rack behind the mahogany bar and set them to chiming.

Jessup leaned closer, stroking long, clever fingers down her neck. "I am the Infinite Lust. But Death I could be, for the right one who asks for it. Death for Life, Life for Death tonight. Light to Dark and back to Light again, all night… until the light of the Blessed Renewal comes at dawn…" He turned his head slightly and took a sip from a glass nearby, then moved his lips back, trailing their sweet softness over Gryffine's once more.

"Here's your markou, pretty *demonne*…"

His lips pressed hers gently, boldly, his tongue licking out to taste her mouth, and Gryffine moaned, feeling her face flush scarlet beneath her silk lace masque, committed to her revelry at last. It wasn't the first time she had kissed, nor the things that followed, having enjoyed her revelry before upon Rollows-night with the boys in the Gypsun Quarter.

But having a man to revel in was another thing.

Jessup's lust carried Gryffine away, and the markou upon his lips and tongue was bittersweet and tasted of the almonne from which it was made. Their isolation in the crowded bar stretched as the drums thundered, though it was but a moment. And though the moment yielded to her breath and his, and Gryffine reveled in the deep hedonism of kissing a man she'd just met, she didn't breathe the moment to perfection, not yet. It wasn't the right moment, not with the crowded, seething bar all around.

Not just yet.

Long fingers stroked the silk over Gryffine's breasts and then her collarbones as Jessup kissed her across the bar, and went up the side of her neck, cupping beneath her long black curl as his lips pulled away to move down her jaw. Gryffine moaned again, and felt him shudder as she did so, his longing rising to meet hers upon the tide of her breath.

"Dark's mercy, pretty *demonne*..." Jessup's breathing was ragged at her neck, his lust nearly unbound by Gryffine's heady breath. "Come upstairs with me... I have a room on the third level overlooking the street."

Gryffine pulled back, trying to control her breath, considering the barman a moment. Jessup's dark eyes were merry beneath his masque, Gypsun eyes, but with a knowing that caused Gryffine to drown in them. He was not so very old, perhaps twenty, trim with a goodly height. His black shirt was open at the collar above his finely-woven black waistcoat, baring a strong chest of caramel Gypsun complexion that fit his general leanness. His sleeves were rolled up to the elbows, to keep them clean at his work, and his hands were long-fingered and elegant.

He was an excellent choice this night. More than excellent.

"Bring the bottle," Gryffine whispered.

Jessup's dark-stubbled chin dipped in a nod, and his white smile broadened. His other hand claimed the markou-bottle, and he gestured to the side of the bar, where a mahogany staircase was packed with revelers swaying to the thunder and rattle of the night. Gryffine slid off her barstool, and pushed her way through to the stairs.

* * *

The view from Jessup's balcony was superb. Absent the pushing, seething throng, they could watch the parade entirely at their leisure, and Jessup poured markou for them both, the golden liqueur totted out into tiny crystal aperitif glasses, one of which he handed to Gryffine. His dark eyes glittered behind his gold-and-red horned masque, the very embodiment of Infinite Lust incarnate.

He saluted with his aperitif, and Gryffine did the same.

"To the Dark, and the Death, bones come now to sand," Jessup intoned. It was an old saying from the Gypsun Quarter, oft-repeated around the fire, and the traditional call of Rollows.

Gryffine followed it with the customary reply. "To the Light, and the Life, bones rise now and stand."

Jessup nodded solemnly, raising his glass a touch higher, and then they both drank back at once. The markou burned like fire racing down Gryffine's throat, but liquor was no stranger to her. The sweet-bitterness of charred almonne soon drowned out the fire, and afterwards her lips could taste nothing but the cloying, lingering sweet of the thick syrup. The drums were making the old building dance from its very bones now, and she saw Jessup's dark eyes flick over her shoulder through the turned-up holes in his masque.

"It comes! One more."

He poured quickly for the two of them, and they drank without words, then Jessup tugged Gryffine along by the hand to the wrought-iron balcony with its wealth of potted plants. Fascination lit his eyes as he stared out over the throng, and then he was pulling Gryffine into his arms, turning her towards the scene so they could both watch as he stood behind her, his long-fingered hands twining about her corseted waist. Thunder slit the night as the barman's deft fingers danced over her collarbones, as he teased the lace from her shoulders. Her cloak was long gone, Gryffine realized, and his hands were at her throat and her bodice now, fevered by the call of the drums, working the clasps open one by one.

The parade finally tumbled into view as he touched her, gently and deftly, arousing Gryffine's ardor to the raging of the drums. Lit by fireworks in every hand, the parade slithered forward with the magnificence of the Beast incarnate, red-and-black beadstrings and confetti tossed over the heads of the revelers to litter the night with a living Inferno. Gilded tumblers drove a wedge through the crowd with the sparkling fireworks. Fire-blowers came, and fire-spinners, too, and then a chariot that spewed flame from a tall spout, drawn by six naked strongmen painted silver with chains around their necks. Behind the fire-chariot was the first wave of drums and scatter-bones, with the shrill pipers carried high upon platforms hefted by teams of strongmen in costumes of the Beast.

Jessup's hands were all over her now, stroking up Gryffine's bare thighs beneath her silk skirt, slipping down her half-bound bodice to cup her breasts, cradling her neck as his smooth lips and stubble whispered over her earlobe, all the while drawing his energy from the parade and from Gryffine's rapidly-quickening breath. Gryffine melted into his arms, her mind losing focus upon the parade and all its delicacies, and sharpening upon the man growing hard behind her and the promise of tonight. Her hands slid back as her breath came fast, touching him, pulling his hips closer. He moaned in her ear and pressed her to the wrought-iron railing of the balcony. Gryffine touched the waist of his trousers, pulled his belt, and had his clasps quickly undone, rubbing her palm down upon him. Jessup pulled her back by the neck with a groan, his breath hot upon her ear, his hand up her skirt and between her thighs, sliding his long fingers beneath her undergarment, slipping his fingers inside her. Gryffine arched with a gasp and pressed back as another wave of drummers passed, shaking the balcony, thunder in the street and in her veins. Jessup moaned again, and then his fingers were out, teasing down her undergarment as he slipped the silk of her skirt aside. Gryffine found him, hard and ready, and slipped herself upon him, arching in his arms.

He gasped in her ear. "Pretty *demonne*…!"

And then Gryffine was lost upon him, screaming her ecstasy out to the thunder of the drums and the cacophony of the throng below as the barman gripped her by the hips and throat, kissing her neck and pulling her back as she gripped the wrought-iron railing and pushed herself upon him, deep in the true revelry of Rollows. When Death became Life and Life became Death and her breath entered his lips as he entered her, flaming them both to unfathomable heights.

Like she could do but once a year.

* * *

Naked upon the bed, Gryffine was draped over Jessup's lean frame, his energy and hers long spent to lethargy and the drums pounded out to drunken laughter and bawdy singing down below upon the street. Jessup reached over with one arm to the decrepit side table, pouring them each another measure of markou with a satisfied rumble, his other arm snugged around Gryffine's waist. He passed along one glass to her, and saluted her from his place reclining among the ratty pillows.

"*You* are a wonder, pretty *demonne*."

Jessup's masque of the Infinite Lust was long gone, and Gryffine watched him a moment as he tossed the liquor back. No older than twenty or twenty-two, perhaps, Jessup was lovely to look at, all lean lines and light-caramel skin, and Gryffine felt pleased with her conquest. His cheekbones were high like his masque, and his almonne Gypsun eyes mimicked the graceful lines she had admired those dark eyes through earlier. His black curls were in disarray, pulled from the tight, short tail he had slicked his hair back into earlier, and he tousled them with one hand with a satisfied sigh, his head resting back upon his arm against the headboard with dark eyes now closed.

On her belly and half-draped over him, Gryffine came to one elbow and sipped at her aperitif, savoring what could only be savored but once a year, taking Jessup in by the dim lamplight. Her skin drank in his warmth and his closeness. Her nostrils savored his musk and the clean sweat of their lovemaking. Gryffine opened her lips slightly, inhaling him in long and slow, tasting the breath and the scents of a man, and a kind man at that, not some callous boy at the bonfires. Eyes closed, he felt her

21

breath and shuddered, snugging her slightly closer by his arm about her waist. At length, he felt her watching and opened his eyes.

"What do you see, pretty *demonne*, with those pale green eyes?" The barman's hand slid up her neck, a clever finger fishing for the edge of her masque. Gryffine twitched away, and his hand fell back with a rueful smile, to stroke the side of her breast instead.

"I see the Infinite Lust, incarnate." Gryffine dipped her head, kissing the thin curling of dark hair upon Jessup's chest, and his smooth lean muscle beneath. "I see my Death come to Life, only so I can die again in his arms. And again. And again. And again."

Jessup made a rumbling sound, his head falling back against the plain wooden headboard and tattered pillows. "And do I not even get to enjoy the pleasure of your name?"

Gryffine shook her head, and kissed his chest again. "One night of revelry. Just one night a year. Only one night to turn Death into Life."

He peered down at her, almost sadly. "Just one night, pretty *demonne*?" Jessup's long fingers stroked her spine now, languid and imploring. "Is that all we get? Stay with me, and it could be hundreds of nights every year. We could have Rollows every night… if you wanted to."

Gryffine's mouth quirked at his cheek, but there was a raw honesty beneath it that caught her and held her motionless above him. Something about this man drew her, something about him had called her to be reckless, even more so than any previous Rollows. He could have killed her, raped her, hurt her up here all alone. And yet, there was such a tender sweetness beneath his bright cheek, which pulled at Gryffine and demanded that she stay. But she could feel dawn coming upon the autumn breeze now, and just as soon as she smiled to feel Jessup's earnest plea, her smile died into wistfulness.

Gryffine stroked back a lock of his lovely dark curls. "You already get hundreds of nights a year, I'm sure, from whomever you please. But this night… you'll remember."

"Will I?" His artful eyes teased. "And what makes you think you're so memorable, my *demonne*?"

Gryffine pushed up to her hands, considering the man beneath her, naked in the dim lamplight of the shabby room. Her fingers splayed out over Jessup's lean-muscled chest, and his teasing smile died, absorbed in her sudden wistfulness. His callous teasing had been a bluff, a masque, and the unspoken plea between the both of them lengthened, stretched, then erased his bluff completely. His dark eyes considered her as she touched him, slow and sad, and he reached out, gathering Gryffine atop his long nakedness and holding her close. The moment had come at last, and as Gryffine gazed into his eyes, she saw he knew it, too.

Rollows. When Death became Life and the bones walked.

One moment to live forever, as Gryffine could do but once a year.

One perfect moment.

Gryffine lifted her lips to kiss him upon the mouth, deep and slow. Jessup's tongue found hers as she breathed in every inch of him, making everything about the moment last. She tasted the markou upon his mouth. She breathed his musk from his heat-furnaced body, and the sweat overlaying it. She reveled in the smooth contours of his lips and tongue, drawing it lightly from his mouth. She teased the breath from his body, feeling its ethereal light dance upon her lips. And she breathed into him, diving down his throat and rushing to his heart, her breath cascading deep with a life all its own, her curse under Gryffine's control no longer.

Time stopped.

Everything stopped, expanding, perfect and endless around them and through them and between them, absent of time, absent of reason. Just one moment, going on and on and on, primal and ancient and unknowable. And then Gryffine felt Jessup's heart stop beneath her hand, before it raced frantically on.

Death had become Life.

Like Gryffine could do but once a year.

Jessup's breath choked in his throat, and his whole body shuddered. A low moan took him, and his eyes rolled up and back, ecstasy in his every movement. And then he shivered and pulled away, dark eyes blinking wide.

"What did you just *do*?"

Gryffine gazed at him solemnly from behind her masque, unblinking and steady, her pain and pleasure mingling together to form the sweetest ache. "I stopped time for you. I stopped everything for you, all this…" she whispered at last. "You'll remember it as I will. Perfect. Forever."

Jessup blinked a few times, stunned, his breathing fast, his heart thundering hard beneath her hand now that it beat once more. Gryffine nuzzled his nose, wanting to stay with this beautiful man, then pulled away with a sigh, sliding off the bed to standing. The revelry of the night was dying, and the air smelled ever more of dawn, the streets silent below. Gryffine began collecting her things, putting them back on one by one. She was nearly clad, raising the lace of her dress up over her shoulders once more, when a gentle touch from behind her slid them back down.

"Stay." Jessup murmured in her ear, his soft lips kissing her neck.

"I can't." Gryffine adjusted her bodice, but his hands reached around her middle to clasp hers.

"Why?"

"Because all we have is but a moment, and that moment has already died."

"I don't care. Stay," he pressed. "Give me an eternity of moments. Let me give them to you." Jessup was kissing her neck now, soft and seductive, kind and generous.

"I *can't*." Gryffine pulled away reluctantly but with firm determination, and fetched her black silk cloak from a fraying cane-woven chair, pinning it at the throat. She turned, to see Jessup's merry dark eyes ravished with woe.

"Why won't you stay? I can feel that you want to. Take off the masque, tell me your name. Stay. *Please*."

Gryffine pulled up her hood, regarding Jessup from its depths. Something deep within the barman had riven because of what she had done, some lock that had remained ironbound in a woman's arms, and his heart spilled open before her, naked and raw. It was beautiful, and painful, and honest, and it smote Gryffine's heart as deeply as she had knifed his.

She wanted to stay. With all her life, all her breath, she wanted to stay.

Jessup was a man worth staying for.

Gryffine took a step closer and lifted her hand to touch his stubbled cheek.

"You'll understand once I'm gone."

His breath caught, almost a sob, and with that, Gryffine slid past him and out the door, closing it firmly behind her. She leaned a moment back against its rickety wood, breathing hard, tears choking in her throat. With one hand she dashed them away, and fled down the stairs and out of the bar through the sleepy throngs of late-night drunkards.

***

Hours whittled slowly by, a latent red dusk lighting the street before dawn. Gryffine had stowed her dress, boots, cloak, and masque carefully away in the hiding-nook, but not before smelling every inch of them for Jessup's sweet musk. Her tears were long dry, and her heart closed once more as it had to be. Rollows came but once a year, and now the night was over for her, and Life was turning back into Death with the rising dawn.

Gryffine leaned upon her elbows at the windowsill, clad in a long nightgown with a modest neckline and prim lace, something her pious mother had chosen for her. Her window was wide, and she breathed deeply of the chill autumn air, still feeling Jessup's long fingers all over her body. He had been beautiful tonight, their last moment more perfect than any she had yet created, and time had truly stopped for them. That last kiss lingered upon Gryffine's lips, perfect, the draw upon Jessup's heart and soul and breath the sweetest gift anyone could ever give her. She ached for it now, and buried her face in her arms, resisting the misery.

But it came anyways, and soon she was sobbing.

"Why can't I have every night of all the year, just like the rest of them do?" she whispered to the quiet pre-dawn. A drunkard stumbled slowly past upon the sidewalk below, singing a mournful tune, his fingernails sliding over the bars of the wrought-iron fence. Gryffine turned from the sorrowful sound, unbearable, and stepped to her bed, burrowing deep into the feather duvet in her dark and forbidding prison of a room. Try as she might, she could not get Jessup's touch from her skin, nor the heat of their lovemaking from her body.

But the eyes.

The eyes Gryffine saw as she touched herself beneath her nightgown and made her imagined lover take her again in the darkness of her room were pale blue. His eyes were perfect as sapphires as he kissed her, on and on and on.

***

CHAPTER 2

Gryffine stood beneath the black umbrella, numb. Rain pattered upon its peak and dripped off its ribs and onto her fine black boots. Everything was black today. Her gaze lingered upon her black gloves, and the black lace at the wrists of her sleeves. The gabardine of her corseted dress was tight and itchy, and she longed to be rid of it, but it was proper and respectful mourning attire, she supposed, as it had been for father.

Her eyes flicked to the open sepulcher, and then away. And lighted upon the filigreed wrought-iron casket with its opaque vellum that allowed one to view the body within. Marionne looked so beautiful, done in her spring best, a high-collared dress of yellow with white lace at the throat and sleeves. Her skin was so china-white it was almost translucent, and her fine wrinkles smoothed in repose. Her ebony hair had been artfully arranged over one shoulder, her curls misted with resin so they wouldn't fray like they had on a rainy day in life.

A light hand patted Gryffine's shoulder. She nodded to a few soft words murmured from a relative she didn't know. Another hand fell to her shoulder and stayed, comforting and kind. She blinked and looked up.

"She is at peace now," Dotorre Krystof Fausten murmured, his kind blue eyes peering out from behind his wire-round spectacles. "Come, Gryffine. Would you like to walk with me? The internment is not for a few hours, and there is food inside."

Gryffine nodded, mute, but then shook her head quickly. "Can we go to Saint Sommes? I'd like to take the air in the park."

"As you like." Dotorre Fausten nodded and offered his arm. Gryffine placed her black-gloved fingers lightly upon it, and they stepped away from the mourners around the sepulcher, and turned their backs on the dark and dreary manse, now thronging with people Gryffine mostly didn't know, the tables inside laden with food she didn't want to eat. They passed Padrenne Henri with his gaunt frame and fevered eyes, who had the decency to only nod as Gryffine passed on the arm of the good dotorre. It rankled that he was here, but Marionne would have wanted the Padrenne of Saint Sommes Cathedral there, and so Gryffine had let him stay, though she hadn't allowed him to deliver the service.

But Dotorre Krystof Fausten was calm and generous, a balm to Gryffine's tired heart, and together, they strolled through the open wrought-iron gate, and took to the pavers of the sidewalk. They turned left towards the broad greensward of Saint Sommes Park, ambling past stragglers hurrying through the drizzle and huddled beneath their umbrellas on this damp spring day, as the occasional hansom carriage rattled and splashed down Rue Coullard.

Dotorre Fausten led her carefully around a puddle, standing like a gentlemen to the right, so that his long double-layered coat was splashed by passing carriages and not Gryffine. "Your mother would have been proud of you," he began. "You have grown into a fine woman, Gryffine. She was lucid for a bit at the end. She spoke fondly of you."

Gryffine nodded, nothing touching her emotions today, but thankful for the dotorre's calming, grandfatherly presence, and his kind words. "I didn't have many letters from her in the past two years. I tried to visit once, but..."

"Yes." Dotorre Fausten nodded serenely. "She was not very lucid for a long while. Three years at least."

"She was raving," Gryffine whispered, watching the tall oaks drip water was they passed beneath, "when I last went to see her. Raving of demons and the Beast. She saw me... and she pointed at me. Her eyes... she called me harlot, and *demonne*. She called me the Breath of Lust."

"Yes. Marionne had many such words for the nurses and the dotorres, and any visitor. And many words for myself, also. Do not blame yourself, Gryffine. You did the right thing, bringing her to the Sanitarium when you did. Such a person is far too much for any sixteen-year-old girl to handle. You do not need to blame yourself for the decision you made back then."

The day was bright despite the wet, the edges of the early-spring leaves crisp and clear, every drop of rain falling from Gryffine's umbrella standing in crystalline relief. "I cannot help but feel guilt, dotorre. Did you know that Padrenne Henri blamed me for a time? He said I was a wicked girl, and that I drove my mother to madness."

Dotorre Fausten nodded serenely, his comforting presence keeping easy pace at her side. Krystof Fausten blew a long breath from beneath his grey-streaked mustachios and combed his grey-streaked short beard with one hand absently. "Padrenne Henri is not an easy man, either. He is tortured by his own troubles."

Gryffine nodded, her eyes skipping to the emerald of the rain-bejeweled grass as they turned from the street onto the crushed gravel promenade of the park. They strolled in silence for a while, past the white marble fountain of Saint Sommes with her flowing locks and her doves upon each upturned wrist. Dotorre Fausten relieved Gryffine of the umbrella, holding it over them both as they strolled. The spring holofenne were in bloom, their tall, rangy limbs trained over time into artful twists and weeping bowers. Gryffine stopped at one, and Dotorre Fausten reached up to coax a trailing limb down for her to smell. Gryffine breathed deeply of the tiny buttery blossoms, her lips just brushing a miniscule collection of petals, fixing it within her mind and upon her breath in one everlasting, perfect moment. As Dotorre Fausten leaned in with eyes closed to smell a racime also, Gryffine saw that the one she had inhaled had withered and died.

But the good Dotorre had not noticed, and he let the bough go with a sigh. "How go your studies at university?" He took Gryffine's arm once more, and they ambled onwards, leaving the withered branch, but not Gryffine's anguish about it, behind.

Gryffine nodded. "Well, I suppose. I am a diploma candidate now, in Anthropology and Ancient Studies of the Near West. I'm focusing on Gypsun folklore."

"Very good. A modern woman. I approve." Fausten patted her hand in a grandfatherly manner. Though only in the late-prime of his years, Dotorre Fausten had always assumed a softspoken manner with his patients, and it had put Gryffine at ease since she was a little girl. "And your prospects?"

"Everything is provided for. I entered with highest merits and am on full scholarship. Messir Henowe you recommended has made some very keen investments on my behalf, and the manse deed is fully mine now that both mother and Cousin Benoit have passed on. And I have extra, thanks to Henowe's rigorous investments, far more than I've had since father's time."

Fausten gave a chuckle. "Very good. But truly, I meant your *romantic* prospects, child. I saw the deeds when I signed off everything from your mother to you. I knew Gabriel Henowe was taking good care of you, as he does me. But do you have a man in your life? You've always been so solitary, Gryffine…"

Gryffine smiled wryly, hiding her true pain, the bitter truth of her self-imposed isolation from human love, human joys, and even as little as human contact. Every day of every year, except Rollows. "I don't have time for such things, dotorre. I am quite busy with my studies." They turned down a side-path, ambling deeper into a wild section of the vast parklands, passing beneath untrained racimes of holofenne and the higher spreading branches of oak and vinter, only just starting to bud.

"I am sure. I am sure." Krystof Fausten patted her hand again. "But still, every young woman ought to try out a man in her life. They are distracting, yes, but the company can also be…enjoyable. When one is not so alone."

Gryffine smiled a little. "Find me a man who studies as much as I do, and he'll be a perfect fit."

The dotorre regarded her sidelong from behind his spectacles, now lightly pattered with rain, then chuckled, but his clear blue eyes were piercing and keen. "If I do that, you'll never even have dinner together, much less court one another."

"He sounds perfect…" Gryffine tried to hide the woe in her voice, opting for forced gaiety.

Fausten chuckled again and let the subject drop. They strolled along in amiable silence for a while, listening to the rain patter upon the oiled canvas of the umbrella. But at last, Gryffine had to know. It had been lingering since that last letter and visit, what her mother knew about her only daughter.

And what she'd said.

"Dotorre? Will you tell me of my mother? At the end?"

Fausten's sigh was long, and it blew his mustachios the smallest bit. "There is not much to tell, really. Marionne was mostly as you saw her that day, either in a state of wilting catatonia or raving and having her trembling fits. But she did have that moment of lucidity, at the very end. I came in to check her pulse, she was in one of her catatonias, you see, and had been for many days, when suddenly she sat up in the bed and simply looked at me."

"Did she say anything?"

He nodded slowly. "She did. Calm as calm could be. She said you were a good girl, and that it wasn't your fault that you are the way you are. She said she was proud of you, for resisting Lusts' temptation for so long. And that was why you had to continue to see Padrenne Henri Coulis. That she still had hope Henri could cleanse you, and you would at last be free. It was rambling, really, not far from her usual tirade of demonsand the Beast and such, coming to steal the breath from her little girl. But what struck me was that it was really quite lucid. And she was very tender, sorrowful almost."

Gryffine had gone very still upon his arm, her steps measured and focused so she would not stumble upon the gravel path. "And then?"

Fausten sighed again. "Then she laid back, and whispered your father's name. She whispered, 'I tried' with her very last breath. And then she went. It was all very peaceful, Gryffine. Know that she went in peace, and she loved you and remembered you at the end."

Gryffine had stopped walking, the day's light too bright around her now, the outlines of everything the rain touched crystalline in her vision. Tears began to fall, slipping slowly down her cheeks.

"Oh, I'm sorry my dear, I shouldn't have said all that just now."

"No," Gryffine shook her head, "No... it's all right. I lost my mother years ago. But dotorre..." She glanced up into his kindly blue eyes behind their wire-rimmed spectacles. "What do you know of demons?"

"Well, my dear," Dotorre Fausten patted her hand again, "That's really a question for Padrenne Henri. I am a simple man of science. There are troubles that the mind creates when it has undergone a shock such as your mother had when your father died so suddenly. Having survived being apart for years and years of war as they did, and to suddenly lose him the very day he came home... it left her troubled. Your father's death was not your fault, nor was it anyone else's."

"But what if I am a demon? What if my father's death *was* my fault?" Gryffine's voice was a mere whisper, her very breath stolen away by her fear.

"Come, now." Fausten patted her hand again. "Your father's death was an accident of his heart, sweet girl. It simply seized in his chest as hearts of men and women sometimes do. Any thirteen-year-old would do as you did, blaming themselves for the sudden death of a parent right in their very arms. But it was *not* your fault. You are fatigued. Let's get you back to the house and get you something to eat. A fully belly and some wine does wonders for the soul."

But as they turned and walked back, Gryffine saw none of the lush spring verge of the park or along the avenue. All she could see were her father's eyes, misted over in death, after he had gasped his last upon the floor of their manor-parlor. It had just been a kiss, a quick kiss on the lips after he had returned from being at war. Gryffine had missed him so while he was away. She could remember her excitement; her fervent hope that this time, he had come home to stay. And that this time, their love and their togetherness would be forever, and their family would be perfect, every moment perfect for her and mother and father from then on. She had simply kissed her father upon the lips in her excitement, but she had felt her breath draw from him, spinning his doting embrace out into one endless, perfect moment, to fix it within her heart and soul forever.

And then Gryffine's father had choked, his breath halting in his throat and his heart stopping beneath her hand. And then Roulen had fallen.

And then he had died.

***

With a last groan of the stout ironwood front door, the death-revelers had abandoned the manse. Gryffine sank with a sigh to the ancient ebony bench by the coat-tree, and let her head fall against the dark wainscoting of the wall. All was silence in the manse, and after so many voices and whispers and furtive glances all day, the dark-walled cavernous structure now seemed crowded with ghosts. Dim colors of the ancient wood enhanced the shadows around her. The burning of the gas-lamps in the hall were sooted and filthy, casting an eerie and uncertain light that spoke of Death in the house. High ceilings were lost above Gryffine, stirring drafts and beckoning with turbid moroseness. Silence pressed against her ears, calling, calling with voices long gone and never to be heard again.

Before she knew what she was doing, Gryffine was up, shrugging on her dark wool day-coat and stepping out into the rain. She had gloves in one hand, she realized after a moment, stepping down the silent path in the rain-washed near-dark and pushing through the wrought-iron gate, but not an umbrella.

She didn't go back for one.

***

Gryffine walked purposefully towards the Gypsun Quarter, crossing Rue Coullard and then Saint Sommes Park upon unfamiliar gravel paths in the choking wet of the miserable rain. At last, she exited the park and stepped across another street, spying at last the bright red and gold lanterns of a gay little bar upon the corner, nowhere near her manse in the Saints Commons. No one could possibly know her here, to gift out solemn condolences or make furtive glances and uneasy small talk, and the bar's close confines and deep scents of mahogany and cooking were just what she sought. Gryffine sank into a close booth near the massive stone fireplace with a sigh of relief. She shrugged her black wool dresscoat to the seat of the bench behind her, then brushed her unbound curls back with one hand, arranging them over one shoulder of her black dress to dry. She leaned her head back, smelling the fragrance of the various smokes in the lamplit bar, and closed her eyes. The lace of her gabardine was itching up beneath her chin, and Gryffine unhooked her dress to the bodice and spread the lace collar wide, baring her long throat and breathing deeply.

"You know, your coat will dry faster if you hang it by the fire."

Her eyes blinked open as the barkeep set a glass of water to her table, his dark eyes glinting merrily, an amiable smile upon his lips. But as their eyes met, he blinked suddenly, and the smirk wiped away, replaced by astonishment. And suddenly, Gryffine realized her vast mistake, noting her cozy, brightly-lit surroundings for the first time. And the man before her. His almonne eyes turned up at the corners, and his dark skin was smooth, his white sleeves rolled to his elbows, his long-fingered hands artful and careful. His black curls were bound back, and his soft lips dropped open in wonder as they recognized one other.

Their heady Rollows-night and their moment of perfection so many years ago flooded Gryffine, and she flushed scarlet.

The barman's caramel cheeks colored also, and he blinked again, his long fingers sliding slowly away from her glass. Without looking, he set his tray down upon an adjacent table, and slowly sank to the bench across from her. His fingers stole out across the table, reaching for her hands. Gryffine flinched back, flushing more. His smile changed from wonder to a wry bitterness as he leaned back against the paneling of the booth, regarding her.

"Was I really that much trouble? That you had to leave so suddenly, pretty *demonne*? You were right. I never forgot that night. Or what you *did* to me…" His dark-eyed gaze went long with the memory of their mutual rapture.

"I'm sorry… I should go." Gryffine bundled her damp coat close and was about to rise when long fingers settled upon her wrist. His touch thrilled her through and through, the memory of his kiss still crystalline and perfect within her mind. She froze beneath his touch, eyes flickering up to his, breath caught in her throat.

"Stay." His dark eyes were imploring, the smirk banished and replaced by the same earnesty she had felt that night. "Please."

Everything within Gryffine screamed at her to go, to wrench her wrist from his fingers and flee to the rain and never return, but some pull held her motionless. She let her coat fall to the bench.

"Stay," he implored again, "have a drink. At least tell me your name. You could give me that much, after everything…"

And though Gryffine knew it was wrong, she found her lips whisper, "Gryffine Toulunnet."

His dark eyes lingered upon her, and he shivered a little at her whisper, relief and bliss within them to even hear her name. "*Enchalle,*" he whispered, lifting her hand up to kiss her damp black glove, his long fingers stroking her bare wrist. "I am Jessup Rohalle." His dark eyes took on a wistful and slightly bitter flavor. "Was that so hard?"

"I can't stay," Gryffine found herself mumbling in a rush. "You can't be near me... we can't...I have to go."

His fingers gripped her wrist firmly, and something sparked between them. A small sigh escaped Gryffine's lips, and a lance of pure fear was fast upon it. "There's been too much death today..."

"Death?" Jessup's straight black eyebrows arched, surprised. But then his gaze seemed to take in her attire, and he pursed his lips and exhaled, slowly. "Ah... I see. Forgive me. I press you to distraction upon a most unfortunate day. Would you like a drink, then? Markou..."

Gryffine nodded wordlessly, and he made to rise, then thought better of it, pinning her with his gaze. "Stay. Please. Warm yourself by the fire. I will not press you, Gryffine Toulunnet, but if you flee... I will find you." The dark glimmer is his eyes spoke of the surety of his promise, and Gryffine found she was pinned where she sat.

She shook her head a little, then slowly removed her damp black gloves and laid them out upon the table. "I will warm myself at the fire. I welcome a glass of markou, *chevronne*."

Jessup's lips quirked at her reply, and he gave her a considering gaze at the formality of her words. But at last he nodded, then rose, sliding off the bench and maneuvering smoothly to the bar to pour her drink in the quiet of the rainy late-afternoon. But he kept an eye upon her all the while, and even as Gryffine rose to warm herself closer to the roaring flames in the ample riverstone fireplace, she could still feel a tingle at her back where his gaze lingered.

* * *

CHAPTER 3

Jessup Rohalle was back quickly, after a few low words to a stout man behind the bar, who glanced at Gryffine with shock plain upon his round, mustachioed face, and then motioned Jessup swiftly on with an encouraging nod. Gryffine watched from her place before the fire as Jessup settled the bottle and tiny aperitif glasses at her mahogany table, along with a trencher of lentil soup with chevre and parsley, buttered bread, and a side plate of toasted pacanne. He poured for them both, then approached her at the fireplace, handing a glass to her with solemnity.

"To the Dark, and the Death, bones come now to sand," Jessup intoned once more, throwing Gryffine right back to the heady revelry of her night with him almost six years gone.

"Is it bad luck to give the Call when it's not Rollows?" Gryffine murmured uncertainly.

Jessup's dark eyes twinkled with mischief and amusement. "I don't think so. My grammère never had anything against saying that phrase whenever she was drunk and throwing the tell-bones. Which was practically every night."

"Your grammère was Gypsun?"

He lifted his glass in a tiny salute. "And so is her grandson. Full-blooded and fully entrenched. Where do you think I learned to mix and pour beverages? At grammère's wrinkly brown teat."

Gryffine smiled a little, charmed by his easy manner, her tension and fear easing somewhat. Jessup Rohalle was as good as his word, and wasn't about to press her into something rash, something that she would utterly regret. Gryffine followed with the customary reply of the Call.

"To the Light, and the Life, bones rise now and stand."

They both drank, and Jessup gestured to the table, preceding her to gather her coat and hang it by the fireplace before he came to seat himself upon the mahogany bench of the cozy booth across from her once more. They stared at each other for a long while, speechless, before he at last cleared his throat and poured another round with his long-fingered hands, then gestured to the soup.

"Please, eat. Marnet will be furious with me if I did not encourage a drenched young woman to warm herself from within... with soup." He flushed, and dropped his dark eyes for a moment before they snapped back up, curious and fascinated.

And suddenly Gryffine found she was ravenous, having not eaten anything in her grief all day. She took up the spoon and inhaled the sweet spices of the lentils, noting a sour twist of lemon among the rosemary and fresh parsley, and lifted it to her lips. Jessup watched her silently, letting her eat for a time. At last, Gryffine's hunger abated, and she looked up.

"Marnet? Is he the other fellow at the bar?" Gryffine saw the shorter barman with brown hair and twirled-up mustachios glancing at the two of them occasionally with amusement upon his face between his serving of orders.

Jessup looked around and chuckled. "Marnet is the first one I told."

Gryffine's eyebrows raised, and she colored. "You *told* him about me?"

Jessup's grin was wolfish, a masque that covered the rawness beneath. "The most beautiful, most agile and dangerous young woman comes into the bar and takes me all night upon Rollows? Then stops my heart, literally *stops* it, with a kiss that I can't possibly forget... and you think that's the kind of thing a man never dreams of? Never tells anyone of? Really? That's the stuff of Gypsun tales!"

Gryffine felt her flushing spread wide over her cheeks and neck. "I just never thought... it was the sort of thing anyone would ever share..."

Jessup reached out, long fingers tracing her jaw lightly, and his touch speared Gryffine to her very core. "So you *were* just a bit naive, then... And see how you blush now..." His eyes roved over her skin. "Like you've never been touched by a man, despite everything I know to be true..."

"Please stop," Gryffine whispered, shivering now with her need and her arching fear, trying to hold it all in with a desperation she'd never had before. Something about Jessup's touch flared her, made her curse sing with desire, and made her breath reach for him, lusting and implacable. She saw Jessup enjoy her reaction to his touch, but Gryffine's fear flared, and she shivered violently, pulling away from his hand though everything in her longed to press his fingers to her skin and never let go.

She saw he was about to come up with some clever and biting retort, but then something in her demeanor struck him, and his hand fell away. "Are you afraid of me?"

Gryffine looked away to the fire, then sipped her drink. "I'm not afraid of you."

"No? Then why blush when I touch you?"

Gryffine paused, watching the flames of the fireplace, both wanting and not wanting to bare her soul to him. "It stirs me."

"You? Such a simple touch stirs a woman like you?" Jessup's voice was incredulous and slightly bitter, and when Gryffine looked back she found his dark eyes confused and slightly angry. "But you took me in... such a wave of hedonism years ago. Tell me a woman like you cannot have any man she wants, at any time. Tell me!" Jealousy flickered in his eyes, and hurt. "Or are you married?"

"No... I'm not married. But I'm... unavailable."

He snorted. "Unavailable. So you're engaged to be married, then. And where is *he* when you've been mourning all day and come to a smoke-bar in the Gypsun Quarter drenched and sorrowful?"

Gryffine's eyes flicked back to the fire. "There is no he."

"No he?" Jessup's tone changed suddenly, to amazed, and then apologetic and stricken. "Do you mourn a *husband's* death today? Ah, Inferno! Forgive me... Dark's Love, but I have been a callous cur... Gryffine, gods forgive me, I didn't mean to..."

Gryffine looked back hastily, suddenly in need of apologizing herself, in distress that she had caused this beautiful man pain, both today and so many years ago. "No... no! I did not lose a husband. It was my mother who died. She was in an institution... for a very long while. I've been a horrible daughter... and I was so horrible to you... I was so horrible to you, Jessup, please forgive me... can you ever forgive me?"

Tears welled up from deep within, the tears Gryffine had been holding back all day, compounded by the bitterness and anger now before her of one she had so desperately wronged. Hating herself, tears spilled down Gryffine's nose, dropping into the dregs of her soup, and she clutched herself in vast misery. And when Jessup reached out to touch her hands, she cried all the harder, turning heads now in the quiet of the nearly empty bar, unworthy of his kindness. Jessup slid from his side of the booth and over to hers, and before Gryffine knew it, he had gathered her into his arms, gentle and immeasurably kind. He held her close, just held her, and stroked a hand down her still-damp locks, soothing her, allowing her to cry. One arm around her waist, she felt him nod to the barman as he guided her up off the bench and led her around tables and up the stairs, carefully assisting her up step after rickety step as she sobbed.

And when he had finally shut the plain wood door of his room and guided her to the moth-eaten bed, Gryffine collapsed with her arms twined around his neck, weary and sobbing. Jessup scooted back upon the bed and stretched out, pulling her into his arms and throwing a ratty feather duvet over them both. It was a long while before Gryffine's sobs dwindled, but Jessup simply held her, smoothing her wet locks and holding her close until the great misery within her eased at last.

***

"Thank you."

Gryffine felt Jessup startle a little beneath her. "For what?"

"For just… holding me. I don't know why I… it was all too much, all of a sudden."

"You lost your mother today," Jessup murmured, fingers gently brushing Gryffine's now-drying ebony curls. "I remember when I lost my own mother. She was a lovely woman, she had the brightest voice, like birds. I was just a boy at the time. Was your own mother lovely?"

"She was lovelier than I will ever be."

"Preposterous." Jessup kissed her hair lightly. "Nothing is lovelier than you." His fingers stole up under her chin, raising her face so he could look in her eyes. Gryffine startled at the devotion she saw there, and the raw pain. He stroked her hair gently back from her face. "Nothing is lovelier than you, Gryffine."

Jessup's body tensed, and he drew her closer by one arm about her waist. Gryffine felt herself heat, wanting him with a suddenness that shattered her careful control. Lust found her in a riotous wash, and Gryffine's breath came fast, drowning them both with desire. Jessup moved against her with a needful sigh, and Gryffine heard her own moan as his hand came up to caress her neck.

"Kiss me… stop time for us again…" he whispered, his nose brushing hers, his lips barely held back.

"No… I can't…" Gryffine's heart was beating hard with fear. And with the shattering tirade of her own powerful lust she trembled in his arms, wanting him and knowing with a terrible certainty what would happen if she indulged that desire.

"Please…" Jessup breathed, lips whispering over hers as he gathered himself, molding himself to her body, pulling her close. Gryffine was drowning in her lust now, motionless, senseless, breathing hard and not daring to close the distance. But suddenly, in a powerful wave of need, Jessup did, and their lips locked for the sweetest of brief moments before Gryffine shrieked into his mouth and pulled away, struggling out of his arms and sitting upright upon the bed.

"*Why?*" Jessup was stricken, confused, and a bitter anger brewed deep in his dark eyes.

"*I cannot kiss you!*" Gryffine felt herself shattering, one breath from what she feared every waking and dreaming and nightmarish second of her bereft life, and this one had come too close, far too close. Her hands flew up before her lips in prayer, as if that could stop their need. "You cannot kiss me…" she whispered fearfully, her pale green eyes round with torture.

Jessup sat up against the headboard, confused now, and reached out to stroke her face, then her neck. Gryffine moaned, her head falling back slightly but her hands still protectively before her lips, as Jessup's long fingers trailed over the bare skin of her chest where the black gabardine of her mourning-dress was undone.

"Why? I know you want me to," Jessup pleaded. "Let me ease you. You don't have to love me, you don't have to stay… but please…let me take away this pain that fills you…let me do that for you at least… just tonight, and then you never have to see me again."

"I cannot make love to you…" Gryffine whispered, eyes slipping closed at the ecstasy of his touch. "I cannot give you such a horrible death."

"Death?" Jessup's fingers stilled. "You speak again of death today. Why do you think kissing me will bring my death? I will mourn if you leave me, all the more if you never take me in your arms again, Gryffine. But death? You left me once, and I survived. I survived staying here six more years, all in the hopes that I might see you again, might find you. I survived that grief, and if you choose to leave me like you did before… I'll survive that, too."

His last words were bitter, and Gryffine opened her eyes to see Jessup Rohalle's dark beauty stewing before her. "Jessup, no… you don't understand…"

Jessup snorted, fingers toying with one lock of her unbound ebony hair now. "Maybe I do. Maybe this is who you are. Maybe you're one of those religious women who find a Gypsun man to fuck by the heathen moon and then pray away your sins by day, never bold enough to take the ecstasy you've been given and make it last. Maybe you're just a *demonne* after all. You told me you'd devour my heart that night. I should have believed you."

Jessup Rohalle struggled out from beneath her and rose from the bed, going to the cold fireplace and kneeling with his back turned to kindle a blaze. His shoulders hunched, Gryffine could feel the anger upon him, and her heart clenched in misery.

"Jessup. If I could... I would have given up everything to stay with you that night. You didn't see the tears I shed, to have to leave you. You didn't hear what I whispered to the morning winds. You don't know the curse I bear."

"Curse?" Jessup Rohalle eyed her sidelong, settling into a crosslegged seat before the hearth as he fed the stirred flames another log. "Loving a man isn't a curse. Wanting a man isn't, either. Letting someone love you and longing to be loved isn't a curse."

"No but... stealing someone's soul and their very life through their breath is."

"*What?*" Jessup's dark gaze sharpened upon her, confused and concerned. "That's *not* what happens when a woman kisses a man, Gryffine! What pious monster of the Immaculate settled that into your brain?"

Gryffine fixed him in her gaze, growing angry that he would shame her so. "No one had to tell me. I figured it out on my own. And when you've seen six men die in your very arms, and you *know* it was your own fault, then you can judge me like you do!" Gryffine rose from the bed, trembling with anger, something that pushed the lust away. It was all she could do.

"Goodbye, Jessup." She flowed towards the door.

But he was there before she could reach it, his back pushing it shut, gripping her face gently in both hands, his dark Gypsun eyes smitten and woeful and befuddled. "Ah! Gods Dark and Light, Gryffine! Don't leave me this way! What do you mean? Did six men truly die in your arms?"

Gryffine gazed up into Jessup's lovely dark eyes, wanting to drown in them and fearing it. Wanting to tell him and fearing it.

"Truly," she whispered.

"Gods," Jessup breathed, his dark eyes incredulous. "*How?*"

"I..." And suddenly Gryffine wanted to confess, wanted to tell someone as kind as Jessup the horrible secret that had slaughtered her heart for nearly nine long years. "It just happens. I don't exactly know how. When I kiss someone... when I want them, when I *truly* want them, I draw something upon their breath. I don't know what it is, but it... creates a perfect moment. One blissful moment that stretches on and on, and flows through my whole body. But if I... indulge in it... they die. Whomever I kiss... they *die*, Jessup."

His eyes were round with wonder now, and a touch of fear. "So what you told me, that night... when my heart stopped? But if it is as you say, why didn't it kill me?"

"I told you already. I get one night a year. Just one. Rollows. It never kills anyone on Rollows-eve. And no, I don't know why."

"Gods of the Dark have mercy," Jessup whispered. His hands fell from Gryffine's face and slid down over her shoulders. "So you can only kiss a man on Rollows. That's what you meant that night. You can only... love someone... on Rollows."

Gryffine nodded, another tear leaking from her eyes.

"Are you certain? Is this true?"

"Six deaths say its true. Eight lives say its true."

"Six deaths," Jessup breathed, "eight lives. Eight men you've kissed on Rollows, who lived. And six you didn't." He gazed at her a long moment, then lifted her hand gently in his own. "Come. Sit by the fire. Tell me."

Gryffine blinked. "You're not going to accuse me of demonism? Condemn me?"

Jessup's dark eyes were solemn. "Gypsun never condemn another for acts of the Wilder. Gifts of the Light and Dark are seldom given, but... we keep the tales of them. Unlike the Immaculate faith. Who would rather call it all demons and the Beast and be done with it." He stroked her cheek tenderly, kindness and understanding upon his face. "Some Gifts are harder to bear than others. Please. Come sit. Tell me."

Stunned, Gryffine allowed herself to be led to the fire. Jessup pulled old pillows and blankets from the bed until they had a cozy nest before the fireplace, and then reclined, pulling Gryffine gently into his lap where he sat. His dark eyes rested upon her for a long moment, as if pondering something.

"Is it all right if *I* kiss *you*?"

Gryffine nodded. "Yes. But not upon the lips, and I cannot kiss you back. Not anywhere upon your skin."

"And what about other things?" His eyes took on a darker simmer in the fire's light.

She took a deep breath. "We cannot... do that. Something about lovemaking is the same. Every night but Rollows."

"But I can do this." Jessup pulled her closer, trailing his lips over the side of her neck, and planting there a gentle kiss.

"Yes," Gryffine breathed, her heart racing in her throat.

"And I can do this." His lips traced along her jaw to the corner of her mouth.

"No!" Gryffine breathed, her terror surging, "You mustn't!"

"I *won't*," Jessup whispered. "We Gypsun trust the old tales. Every Dark and Light gift has a boundary. Every curse has a blessing woven inside of it, and every blessing a curse. Find your blessing and your boundary, Gryffine. Let me help you find it."

It was something Gryffine had never considered. She paused, her lips nearly touching Jessup's. "I don't want to risk your life."

"Shh…" he played his lips expertly along hers, touching so lightly that Gryffine moaned, but he did not kiss her. "Let me help you find the woven blessing within the curse. Lay back. Let me take away your pain."

Gryffine found herself sinking to the pillows before the fire, helped down by Jessup's strong hands. He braced himself above her now, leaning over in the fire's light, brushing his lips softly over hers, barely touching, almost a kiss but not quite. Gryffine ached deep within, the need for his kindness and touch swallowing her whole and spitting her out raw by the light of the flickering flames.

"What if there is no blessing?" Gryffine murmured, fear gripping her heart.

"Don't you listen to old Gypsun-wives? There is always a blessing within every curse…" And with that Jessup's lips moved to the side, kissing her softly upon the neck as his hand slid slowly up the bodice of her mourning-dress, undoing the hooks one by one.

* * *

Gryffine was slick with sweat by the heat of the fire, and thoroughly exhausted by the time Jessup gathered her in his arms and they stretched out on their sides upon the pillows, watching the fire. He kissed her shoulder gently from behind, and Gryffine sighed, utterly spent. It hadn't been quite the same as laying with a man completely, but it had been close, and she still tingled in an exquisite way from his clever fingers and tongue. Jessup gathered her close, one hand settling over her bare ribs to cup a breast. It was the safest Gryffine had ever felt in anyone's arms, and the most loved.

She sighed, and he kissed her neck lightly again.

"Good?" Jessup asked softly.

Gryffine turned her face up, and Jessup nuzzled her with the tip of his nose, then whispered his lips over hers in what had become an unspoken rule between them over the course of the past few hours. It was tender like a kiss, but not quite, and even in her exhaustion Gryffine felt herself quicken again. She let her head fall back over his shoulder with a moan, and Jessup stroked her throat with a soothing touch.

"I never knew such pleasures could be indulged…" Gryffine sighed. "I was so afraid to even try anything like this, except for upon Rollows when I knew it was safe."

41

Jessup's chuckle was low and amused. "Then you haven't lived yet."

"No. I haven't," Gryffine murmured, realizing the solemn truth of those words. "I've spent so much time and effort denying it... turning away from looks and glances, holding myself rigid and aloof because of the danger I pose to any who might court me. Immersing myself in my studies and turning down any and all requests for dinner or even coffee. I haven't allowed myself anything like this, Jessup... ever. Except on Rollows. And then..." she paused, then sighed. "Well... you know how it has to be, then."

"So that's why you blush when I touch you. A body starved of life... longing for it with every breath...every touch... every kindness..." Jessup's long fingers played out over Gryffine's collarbones, tender and serene. A long pause stretched between them, comfortable and easy as the fire crackled on.

"Jessup?"

"Hmm?"

"Why didn't you run, when I told you what I was?"

His fingers paused. "Because the Dark is nothing to fear."

"How so? My curse can kill, and it has. Have you ever heard of anyone so cursed as I am?"

"Curse? Or a benefit?" Jessup chuckled knowingly. "Seems to me *you* got quite the benefit tonight." But he chuckled again before she could reply. "No, no... I am quite satisfied, believe me. Watching you was one of the greatest experiences of my life. Seeing a woman so starved be pleasured, doing it for her, feeling her surge... I believe I can die now. Please kiss me."

Gryffine made a startled sound, but realized he was jesting as he chuckled again.

"No, but certainly," Jessup continued, "I do not mean to make light of what is yours. A terrible thing, to have a Dark gift blossom to life like that so young, and to have killed so many unknowingly. And to hold yourself back from living for so very long."

"My father died because of it. When I was thirteen. I kissed him when he returned home after the war. I was so excited to have him home, and it... stopped his heart."

"It wasn't Rollows."

"No. It wasn't Rollows."

A long silence stretched, Jessup's kisses gentle and kind upon her shoulder. But at last Jessup broke it. "And how did you find out about Rollows?"

"By mistake," Gryffine murmured to the low-burning fire. "When I was fourteen, I slipped out for the Rollows celebrations for the first time. Father had been dead a year and I was angry and rebellious. I made my way here to the Gypsun Quarter to watch the thick of the celebrations."

"Dangerous."

"I didn't know it at the time. I found a group of others my age, watching the parade. They let me join them. And then I followed their antics, reveling in being terrible. We stole money from the crowd and bought sweetnuts. We lit fireworks. We thieved drinks and stole off to imbibe around the Gypsun bonfires. I was trying to be careful, not touching anyone, not giving anyone the eye. But I wanted to be free, to try it out, what Life felt like, what it smelled and tasted like. And when a boy who had been watching me all night snuck up behind me and spun me around for a kiss, I was too drunk and foolish to pull away in time. But when our lips locked, I felt that deep breath come into me, engraving the moment. I sunk into it, drunk, wanting Life and to forget what my kiss could do. And when he did not die, merely had a brief moment of death, like you did, I thought my curse was lifted. I celebrated that night with him, all night. And come the dawn I still had not returned home, but lingered in his Gypsun-tent, kissing and touching, not caring what my mother would think. But as the sun first touched his tent and he swept me down for another embrace… the pull on his heart came again. And this time it didn't stop. He died in my arms. I fled."

Jessup didn't speak, didn't make light of her terror or her curse, merely kissed her shoulder, comforting, and at last Gryffine spoke again.

"I knew then that I was wrong. The curse hadn't lifted at all. There were a few more times I was sure the curse would be gone. I prayed for months, cleansing myself with rigors and fasting, and then tried again at All Saint's Feast at midwinter. I killed another boy, a beautiful, pious boy with tawny hair, in the cathedral eaves. I tried each other night of Oblenite. Just the same. The dead began to pile up around me, and by my sixteenth year, when I met you, I was certain Rollows was my only night of freedom. And so it's been… ever since. I've never tried any other days. I couldn't bear it."

Jessup's gentle hand smoothed her hair back from her neck. "You were *sixteen*?" Jessup's voice was incredulous. "When you wore that black silk and red lace and came for me? Gods of the Light… I knew you were young, but… you looked at least eighteen. And the way you held yourself…and demanded from me… gods of the Dark."

"How old are you, Jessup?" Gryffine smiled a little, amused by his astonishment.

43

She could feel his grin behind her ear. "Guess."

"Twenty-four?"

He shook his head and chuckled. "Would I be as scandalized as I am having just learned I slept with a sixteen year old girl when I was eighteen? No. Guess again."

"Twenty-seven?"

He chuckled. "Wrong. Scandal, scandal. Let's put it this way. If Marnet had known, he would have tanned my hide and kicked me out with chamber pots dumped on my head."

"Thirty?" Gryffine glanced back over her shoulder, incredulous.

Jessup chuckled again, his hand rubbing her ribs. "I'm thirty-two. Six years ago I was twenty-six to your sixteen. Now I'm thirty-two to your twenty-two. Scandal, scandal, scandal! I'm a dirty old bastard..." He chuckled once more, completely amused, his dark eyes shining with mirth.

Gryffine's eyes widened. "But you look so young! And you did then, too. I thought you were only twenty-two that night, at most!"

Jessup's lips brushed her ear. "We Gypsun age well, especially the men. It was a pain in the ass when I was younger. I looked eighteen until I was about twenty-five, and I looked twenty-two until I was thirty. And I'll look twenty-five until suddenly I'm eighty. At which point I'll have a frightful scowl and long eyebrows and berate the children for being too noisy." He laughed again, amused at his own joke.

"If you keep pursuing me," Gryffine murmured, sober now, "you won't make it to eighty."

Jessup chuckled darkly and rubbed her ribs. "We'll see."

"When did you start working here?" Gryffine change the subject, not wishing to dwell on the bitter.

"Marnet is a family friend. He offered me a job at sixteen. I took it. I've been working here ever since. He's a generous sort. I don't pay for my room or my board and I get money besides for the work I do. It's comfortable."

Gryffine frowned down at the threadbare pillows. "Not *that* comfortable."

"I don't get paid *that* much." Irritation was in Jessup's voice now, and Gryffine turned to her back upon the pillows now to gaze up at him.

"Forgive me. I didn't mean to pry."

Irritation flickered over Jessup's features again, and then it was gone. "No. Forgive me. It rankles, sometimes. Being here this long, doing what I do. I do enjoy it... but the Gypsun blood is to travel, and I long to see the world, or do other things with my life. I've never amassed enough money, though." He shrugged fatalistically. "I suppose I don't know the right kind of people."

Gryffine reached up, trailing her fingers over his bare chest. "I have an investor that has secured some of my fortunes. Perhaps he could help? Do you have any extra you could invest?"

Jessup chewed his lower lip a moment, thinking, then lifted an eyebrow and grinned. "Wouldn't grammère just turn in her grave."

"Gypsun don't approve of investing?"

He frowned. "Not like that, no. Buy a good horse, breed some fine colts, sure. Buy a wagon or a merchant booth or a shop and invest in turning it into your livelihood. But property, oil, gold? No. Well… only gold if you can wear it."

Gryffine stroked his chest again. "You don't wear any gold."

He arched an eyebrow again. "I don't have any. Except for a gold ring and pocketwatch from my grammère. They were my grampère's."

"Oh."

"And your grammère? And parents?"

"Dead, dead, and dead." Jessup smiled ruefully. "At least I think my father's dead. I imagine him so. I'd kill him if I ever saw him. I was a Fortune's Child, they call us. But really, my father slept with my mother one night and ran off with her money before dawn."

"Haven't you done just the same, sleeping with women?"

Jessup Rohalle's dark eyes glinted in the firelight. "*You're* the one who ran out on *me* that night. Not the other way around. And your estimation of me was wrong back then, and it still is. I've had my share of lovers, but I *always* made sure to take the proper herbs so I didn't get them pregnant and didn't catch or pass on some ghastly disease. And I *never* stole from them." He lifted one eyebrow. "In fact, I've had fewer women than you've had men, assuming each of your Rollows trysts were separate men, which I'm sure they were, as eager as you were to see me again. Though I've had my women for far longer a time, generally."

Gryffine was ashamed at her judgment of him, and she flushed. "But… on Rollows… you just…"

Jessup rifled a hand through his black curls, and flushed also, then glanced at her sidelong. "Seduced you? Like a crazy man? I know. It's not generally my style. Marnet and I get along so well because I *don't* generally sleep with the clientele, and I always stick my post on Rollows. But you…" Jessup's fingers smoothed over her ribs and belly and shook his head. "Gods of the Dark… there's just something about you. It pulled me that night. *Physically* pulled me. I'd never seduced a woman that I'd never met before. But when I sipped the markou and tasted your lips…" he gave her a rueful smile. "There was no going back for me. Marnet was furious in the morning, but after I told him the whole story… he just sat there. Confused. Looking at me. Like I was some new species of dog he'd never even thought possible."

Gryffine laughed at the expression upon his face, the perplexed confusion in imitation of the portly bar owner. Jessup grinned, then dove upon her, smothering the side of her neck with kisses and pressing her to the ratty pillows. Gryffine shrieked and laughed, and soon he had her pinned by the wrists, covering her face with kisses, everything except her lips. She shrieked again, but as he began to suck at her collarbones her shrieks turned to moans, and soon she was writhing against him. Jessup slid a hand down, undoing the buckle and clasp of his trousers. He gripped her wrist gently as he continued to kiss her chest, then suckled her breasts. Gryffine moaned.

"Take me as I take you." Jessup slid her hand along his flat belly, and then down upon himself.

"I don't know if…"

"Shh… It's safe… I haven't died from the touch your hands yet…"

And then Gryffine gripped him hard, needing to feel his pleasure along with her own, and Jessup moaned in his throat, sucking her breast harder as he slipped his hand down her own naked belly and into her cleft. Gasping, Gryffine arched with pleasure as Jessup took her again with his long-fingered, skilled hands, and his lips came away from her breast with a moan as she took him in the same fashion. Gryffine could feel his thrusts as he pressed against her, his urgency after such careful composure all night, and she arched up, seeking his lips. Jessup bent to her, making her writhe, keeping himself carefully away, just the barest touch of his lips upon hers. And she gasped in his breath without fear, and he breathed in hers without worry, until in a bright moment, they climaxed together. And a force of such magnetism gripped Gryffine that she surged up in that moment, locking her lips upon his.

And Jessup turned his head quickly away with a gasp, kissing her neck instead.

"Not yet… don't kill me just yet. We have so much more of this to enjoy."

***

Gryffine woke, curled in a ball, her head resting in the crook of Jessup's shoulder. He gave a sleepy mutter, and pulled her naked body closer in the tattered bed. She smiled and rubbed her nose against his ribs, inhaling his sweet, bed-warm musk. He sighed. She snugged the threadbare duvet closer up over her shoulder and drifted off again.

※ ※ ※

And woke to long fingers smoothing her bed-tousled ebony curls away from her face.

"Good morning." Jessup was on his elbow, looking down at her, a pleased smile teasing his smooth lips.

"Good morning." A delighted smile blossomed over Gryffine's face, and she sighed as Jessup bent down to kiss her neck, and then laughed as he nibbled her nose like a rabbit.

※ ※ ※

CHAPTER 4

An embarrassed flush crept across Gryffine's face as she descended the rickety wooden stairs behind Jessup, who wouldn't let go of her hand. The portly bar-owner Marnet was polishing glasses, and his ruddy face lit in a broad smile that turned his well-waxed mustachios up even further at the corners when he saw them come down. His dark eyes danced with a merry pleasure as Jessup led Gryffine to the bar and sat her upon a mahogany barstool right in front of him.

Marnet positively beamed at her, and gave a conspiratorial wink. "Breakfast?"

"Starving!" Jessup agreed heartily, and Gryffine flushed crimson.

"So I *heard*." Marnet gave Jessup a clever look and Gryffine decided she wanted to hide behind the bar for the rest of the morning. But Marnet only gave a hearty laugh and clapped Jessup on the shoulder, then reached out to take Gryffine's hand solicitously, pressing it with a light kiss.

"Marnet," Jessup grinned. "May I present miss Gryffine Toulunnet, a student-fellow at the University. Gryffine, this is Marnet Lousit, owner of this fine establishment and creator of excellent breakfasts."

"*Enchalle*, lovely *madamme*." Marnet lifted her hand again and pressed it with another kiss. "Any friend of Jess is a friend of mine."

"Not that friendly!" Jessup gave the older barkeep a teasing, warning glance.

"*Mais, non!*" Marnet held both hands up, conceding, then laughed. "So! Food. I have chantrelles omelette, or pork rondelles in broth."

"One of each," Jessup nodded to a steaming pot at the end of the bar. "And what's in the hot-pot?"

"Beignets." Marnet gave a clever grin. "Gents and ladies who exercise need a little fat and butter in the morning. Not to mention sweets to round out the sweet. And she is so skinny," he reached out, patting Gryffine's cheek. "And so are you!" He slapped Jessup's shirt. "But I am fat!" He double-slapped his own slight paunch around his middle. "And so you two must eat them all!" With a brash laugh, he poured two glasses of fresh-squeezed orangine, and then slapped his rag over one shoulder and retreated into the back area through a door hind the well-polished mahogany bar.

"Mmm…beignets…" Jessup rose and ducked behind the bar, then whisked quickly to the hot-pot and fished out a few steaming, already-fried buns with tongs. He flipped them quickly in powdered sugar in a bowl, then shook a tin of seasoning over them and whisked them back to Gryffine. He slid the platter across the bar with a waggle of his straight dark eyebrows and ducked under the bar-access again to re-settle at his stool.

"Here, try," Jessup lifted one confection and moved it to her lips. "Marnet makes the best beignets from the Gypsun Quarter to Haslen."

Gryffine panicked for a moment. "Your fingers! I can't touch them with my lips."

Jessup gave her a roguish grin. "Then eat *carefully*."

Gryffine was very careful as she bit the confection from his fingers, and reveled in delight as the doughy pastry melted in its buttery splendor across her tongue. She chewed slowly, eyes closed, letting the sugar and cinname and cardamom roll through her mouth before swallowing. She made a little pleased sound in her throat and opened her eyes at Marnet's coarse laugh.

"Ha! I can see how she wooed you, Jessup!" He winked again. "She likes my beignets. I might have to spirit her away and marry her."

Jessup was happily devouring his own confection by this point. "*Everyone* likes your beignets, Marnet. That's why I stick around."

Marnet laughed again, and lifted two hefty platters up from behind the bar, one with a steaming pile of omellette with chantrelles and cress upon it, and the other a wide shallow bowl of broth and scallions and pork rounds. He set surprisingly clean cutlery and nicely pressed white napkins upon the bar, and poured two glasses of water. He wiped his hands upon a rag, then slapped the mahogany bar twice.

"Eat, eat! Before it gets cold! You will excuse me, Jess, I have the lunch quiche to prepare."

"You sure you don't need any help?" Jessup was already tucking into the omelette with a healthy appetite, but the question was sincere.

"No, no! Take the day off. Gods of the Light, take two! Go do what young people do, *enjoy* each other. It's been so long since you've had someone in your arms, Jessup, I thought you'd sworn off women altogether! Go. Eat. Play, young ruffian. Good morning, lovely *madamme*." And with that, Marnet bowed himself backwards and retreated through the strung beads that separated the kitchen from the bar.

"Well," Jessup eyed Gryffine again, both curiously and

appreciatively as he sipped his orangine. "Marnet likes you."

Gryffine blinked, then took a spoon to the pork rounds and broth. "I didn't even get to say two words to him! What do you mean he likes me?"

Jessup shrugged and grinned. "He likes you."

"How can you tell?"

"Because..." Jessup reached out and ran a finger under her jaw. "He's usually a big fat grump in the morning. And he *never* makes beignets mid-week."

Gryffine blinked, and then smiled, lingering over the heartiness of the broth and pork. "What did he mean, he thought you'd sworn off women altogether?"

Jessup tried to smooth his unbound, wayward black curls back, and a flush crept to his face. "Believe it or not... I haven't even courted a woman in... over a year. And even that was short-lived."

"Well, that's..."

"Not what you supposed?" His lips quirked as Gryffine nodded. "That's what everyone thinks. Debonair barman, libator and purveyor of fine liquors, takes any women he charms and leads them straight to his rooms upstairs. Not so. I'm really a fairly private man, Gryffine, though I enjoy the familial aspect of my people. And for all its faults, I do enjoy my work, and it's easy for me to smile and laugh here. And so I do. And so that's what women see when they gaze behind the bar. But that's *all* they get to see. In one night... you've seen far more."

"Two nights."

"Two nights," he agreed, and then smiled again. "Eat up. Marnet will be furious if we don't finish it. And then the day is ours. That is... if you want to spend it with me." This last was said with such vulnerability that Gryffine reached out and took Jessup Rohalle's hand.

"There is nothing more, that I would rather do."

* * *

The morning began with a stroll around Saint Sommes Park and Jessup scandalously trapping Gryffine behind a large oak and slipping a hand up under her black mourning-dress, just out of sight of the gravel path. She'd had to bite her lips together and press her face to his waistcoat to keep from crying out, and when it was done her cheeks were flushed and her undergarments hopelessly wet. Jessup had only grinned at her like a rogue and kissed her neck, then helped her straighten her black mourning dress and re-pin her hair. They stepped from behind the oak to follow an elderly couple strolling in their spring finery, and Jessup snugged her close around the waist.

"What next?" He whispered jovially in her ear. "Behind that fountain?"

"Scandalous!" Gryffine muffled a laugh in his shoulder. "Do you think they heard us?"

"Who cares? Those old codgers could use a little, too, I think."

Gryffine laughed in shock, and slapped him lightly across the chest with one gloved hand. "You rogue!"

"Always," Jessup grinned. "What next?"

"Well... I should like to change my clothes, I think." Gryffine gazed down at her mourning attire, not wanting to go home to her dark and dreary manse but needing a fresh garment all the same.

"Ah... Yes." Jessup had the decency to look slightly chagrined. "How long will you wear the mourning colors?"

Gryffine shook her head, a certainty rising in her heart. "Not a day longer. I've mourned my whole life, mourned this wretched curse, and I've mourned my mother for years. I'm ready for something new, Jessup. And it's about time I began it."

He turned and walked backwards before her, fingers in his shallow waistcoat-pockets. "So you're taking *me* home with *you* now. I suppose we can do that." Jessup smirked jauntily.

Gryffine laughed aloud, a bright, carefree sound she hadn't made since before her father had died. "This way!" She turned down a path that she knew would cut through the park to Rue Coullard near her manse upon the far side. Jessup bounced in her wake, nearly skipping as he caught her arm once more, then tugged her forward in a run. Gryffine shrieked, then stumbled and ran also, which turned into an uncouth sprint to a giant blouelle-tree, while hauling her black gabardine dress up to the knees of her heeled boots. She was breathless when she arrived, just behind Jessup's long legs, and he caught her about the waist in delight. They came together in a rush, and again, lips brushed lips before Gryffine pulled back in alarm. Jessup blinked, their sweet moment nearly bursting, but then bent and scooped her up, throwing her over one shoulder and packing her off down the cobbled walk.

Gryffine shrieked, pounding his back with her hands and kicking her feet under her skirts, giggling like a schoolgirl. Jessup only hefted her more securely upon his shoulder and strode on, chuckling. The elderly couple behind them on the adjacent path stared and made disapproving clucking sounds like chickens.

***

"You live in one of these?" Jessup had taken her arm like a gentleman as they emerged upon the opposite side of the grand park, and began pacing the pavingstones of Rue Coullard towards Gryffine's manse.

"Mmm, one block up. Can you see it? The three-story with the red gables at the very top."

"Beautiful. I've always wanted to live in one of these old manses." Jessup was gazing around, noting each and every detail of the three-story city manses behind their wrought-iron fences as they passed. "This is one of the oldest quarters in the city still standing, you know. Over four hundred years and more. These manses were built to test time's wrath, and they have at that. They all have sepulchers in the back yards, plots where the families laid their dead to rest even though the cemetery was originally near Saint Sommes Cathedral."

"I know," Gryffine murmured, "They laid my mother to rest in ours yesterday."

He glanced at her sidelong. "Is the manse a family house?"

Gryffine nodded. "It used to belong to some great-great-aunt of mine, on my father's side, but she died suddenly and the house was taken back by the city. It was empty for a long while. My mother's wealthy great-cousin bought the deed from my father's cousin, who had bought it back from the city, knowing my mother liked to have a place closer to the bustle of Julis than where father lived when they married. Mother and Cousin Marlene were close. They used to go the town together, one hopelessly ancient and one boisterous and young. Mother used to like the noise and the gaiety, the balls and fancy parties, before father passed. Afterwards, when we had to sell the manor in the country, it was different. I think she saw this house as more of a prison. And now she'll never leave. Here we are."

Gryffine pushed through the wrought-iron gate into the yard, and paused as Jessup gazed upwards, admiring the ancient structure. Gryffine looked upon her manse with his eyes, noting the wearing of the red paint around the ornately-tooled eaves, how the gables still stood firm though a number of shingles were missing now from the spring storms. The blackiron of the fanciful front-door grille was starting to rust again, and the yard hadn't been trimmed in a season, the regalia-bushes run riot. Everything spoke of a shabbiness and neglect that had rolled over from year to year and owner to owner. But still, it was a lovely house, and Gryffine felt ashamed that she hadn't invited workers to attend it in some time, mostly because she couldn't stand living in its bleak depths alone. She stayed in the dormitories of the university more often than not, only coming home on week-ends to air the rooms and run the furnace so nothing would molder.

"Beautiful," Jessup whispered, gazing upwards. "May we go inside?"

Gryffine gestured him up the stone steps before her, then paused to unlock the front door, the wrought-iron grate of flowers and vines already latched open. But finding the door open, Gryffine suddenly remembered the haste with which she had left her manse after the funeral.

"I don't think I was entirely within my mind yesterday," she murmured with chagrin as they entered and she ushered Jessup inside into the dark-wainscoted entry hall.

"Maybe you were *too much* in your mind. It happens when people die."

Gryffine shut the door and locked it, and the light in the hall was disastrously dimmed, swallowed by the dark paneling and ebony furniture. It gave the manse a ghostly feel, the ebony balustrades of the ornately-carven staircase to the upper levels looking like snakes underwater. "Maybe." Gryffine shucked her coat and hung it upon the coat-tree, and Jessup did the same.

Jessup glanced towards the openings that led off the forbidding entry hall to the various parlors, then up the dust-thick grey-carpeted stairs. "Would you like me to check the rooms for intruders? It's a bit dark in here." It was a gentlemanly offer, and Gryffine brightened a little.

"Let's check them together. I'm sure you would like a proper tour, no?"

Jessup smiled, warm and pleased. "Indeed. That I would. Lead the way, *madamme*."

Gryffine walked Jessup all the way back to the kitchens, then halted when she saw the spread of foodstuffs still sprawling out over the counters and the center block. Most of it had been covered and carefully packaged up by her leaving funereal guests, but still there were things out upon the tiled counters that should have gone in the icebox. Gryffine was certain much of it had ruined overnight.

"You keep a tidy kitchen." Jessup smirked winsomely. "Well, at least there's lunch for after our tour."

Gryffine shrugged. "Help yourself. I don't want any of it. I'd rather have my meals at Marnet's."

Jessup turned her gently by the elbow, wrapping his arms around her waist. "Why?"

"It smells like death in here," Gryffine whispered, not meeting his eyes.

"Did she die here?"

"No. At the hospital. But she was dead the moment we moved here."

His fingers stroked her hair back from her face. "Was it really that awful, Gryffine?"

"I would burn this manse to the ground if I could," Gryffine whispered. And then choked, her eyes welling with tears, knowing what she spoke was true.

Jessup pulled her close, and Gryffine rested her head upon his shoulder. "I tell you what," he whispered. "Let me bring some people over to redesign it for you. Give it a month, Gryffine, and we'll see if we can't brighten it, make some better memories here."

"We?" Gryffine looked up, hopeful for the first time in years.

Jessup smiled down and kissed her forehead. "We. Unless you have some other man you'd rather bring home?"

She shook her head, tears of relief welling in her eyes. Jessup leaned down, brushing his lips lightly over hers, but not kissing, not quite. "Show me your room. Let's start there."

Gryffine clasped him by the hand, and nuzzled her nose against his chest, then guided him towards the stairs.

* * *

"You know, it's really not so bad."

"What?" Gryffine opened her eyes, tucked in close under Jessup's arm in her own bed.

"Your manse. It's a little shabby, and frightfully dark, and most definitely not in the *haute couture*, but that's all."

"Shabby?" Gryffine sat up with the duvet pressed to her naked chest and grinned at Jessup, her spirits markedly elevated after the last hour. "After *your* rooms?"

He grinned back, still reclining upon her bed with his hands interlaced behind his head, showing his immaculately white teeth in that lovely caramel skin. "Well, I have an excuse. I spend all my time bartending and helping Marnet cook, not decorating. And besides, I have better things to spend my money on."

"I thought you didn't have any money."

He grinned wider. "I don't. But I'd happily spend yours."

"On?"

Jessup gazed up and around at the eaves from where he lay, Gryffine followed his eyes, noting the cobwebs thick in every vaulted corner, the dust scattered across the ornately-carved ironwood sills and upon the sconces, and layered in the dark panels of the wainscoting. It was a dreary room, actually. After the bright colors and homey feel of Jessup's bar, Gryffine realized how muted and dark her entire manse was. It all looked like a prison, really, rather than a house. Someone long ago had invested in a dark brown stain for the wood that was nearly black, and the walls throughout most of the manse were painted a drab, dirty cream or dark brown. Iron was the only fitting in the manse. Iron rods for the curtains, iron chandeliers, iron grilles for the fireplaces, iron runners for the carpets on the stairs, and twisting, filigreed iron for every balcony and gate. The furniture, most of which had come with the manse also, her mother not having had the energy to see everything from the country moved to the city, were dark wood and iron, also.

Gryffine thought it seemed more like a torture-chamber than a house.

"Well…" Jessup sat up, duvet dropping to his narrow hips, still gazing around. "For starters, we could give it a good cleaning. And most of the furniture needs reupholstering, with brighter colors. I know a fellow who makes that his trade. He works for a number of upper-class families. This wainscoting could be sanded down and stained brighter, or simply painted. Cream would look very nice. And the walls should *definitely* be brightened. The iron and the ebony and ironwood accents will look lovely once you get the colors brighter here, like at the bar."

Gryffine blinked, thinking of the gay reds and homey yellows and rich purples of Jessup's bar, and how it all blended so nicely with the wrought-iron and dark wood already present in that old building. But the looming expense made her fret. "How much will all that cost me?"

Jessup smoothed a hand over her bare shoulder, and followed it with a kiss. "Not much. I know some people who owe me favors, and I can do the rest of the work myself."

"You?"

He grinned at her, sliding a finger along her jawline. "You don't think I stay this handsome tending bar and cooking, do you? I'd be as paunchy as Marnet! No, I do work for my friend Rennet on the side. Rennet restores these old beauties. He does the designing and organizes any tricky parts of the restoration, like rebuilding rooflines and re-setting foundations and chimneys, or designing new carpentry. I do most of the rest."

"And does Rennet owe you a lot of favors?"

Jessup grinned wider. "*Tons*. That man is simply drowning in the favors I've done for him over the years. It's part of how he keeps his costs down for bidders, is that I don't ask for much for my labor. I've never really needed it. Until now. It's time to call in some of those debts." But Jessup glanced at her sidelong then. "Unless you just want to sell it. I'd understand that."

Gryffine set her jaw. Unseen fingers tugged at her everywhere she looked, and suddenly she felt that selling the manse would be a betrayal of some kind. She didn't know why, but some deep part of her urged her to keep it, that it belonged to her, dreary or no. "I think I have to keep it. It's been in the family for generations."

"Has it?" Jessup rested his elbows around his knees. "You told me about your great-great-aunt, but how long has your father's family held this estate?"

Gryffine shrugged. "Ever since it was built. When I had the deeds transferred to my name, the city sent a property auditor to reassess its value. He had the original documents from the city of when it was built and who built it. This house is actually the oldest on the block. The rest of the block was its grounds, once. An ancestor of my father's built it, one Gerald Toulounne, five hundred and seven years ago. It's been passed through his family ever since. In one way or another."

"In one way or another?" Jessup rose from the bed, tugging on his trousers and belting them, then shrugging into his white shirt and tucking it in. Gryffine rose and went to the armoire to select an outfit of twill split-pants with a high waist in spring beige, and hooked on a fresh corset with a plain cream silk shirt over it, belting the high waist of the wide-legged trousers over the shirt and corset. She picked through her jewelry in the mahogany tray upon the armoire, finding a few demure pieces in gold as she answered Jessup.

"There were apparently a number of broken lineages in my father's family. The auditor showed me the deeds. Every hundred or so years, the family who lived here had sudden strange deaths, effectively ending the main branch of the family that owned the manse, so it had to be sold to distant relatives. He explained that the city tries to offer the manses in this quarter to relatives first, because of the sepulcher issue. No one really wants to purchase a house with someone else's dead relatives in the backyard, and no one wants to uproot the dead and move them to the cemetery at Saint Sommes Cathedral."

"Fascinating." Jessup came up behind her, running his hands over the high waist of her beige slacks as Gryffine pinned her dark curls up in hasty, artful twists. "So your father's line was quite interrupted."

"Quite. And the strange thing is that the deaths didn't coincide to any of the plagues that swept through. More often than not, there was the notation of *death by accident* as the reason for the deed sale. But the auditor told me very frankly that he'd dug into the death records and found that there were recorded suspicions of *death by misfortune* of the owners, and a record of children who subsequently were found missing."

"Misfortune? And the stealing of a child? Sounds more like foul play."

Gryffine sat herself in a chair and started buttoning up a pair of cherry-brown hourglass-heeled boots, and shook her head. "No. There was never any ransoming of the lost child, and never any sign of them. They simply disappeared. And the parents were found dead without any marks upon them. Back then, *misfortune* was just another word for early death by natural causes."

"You sound like a dotorre."

"I have a very good friend who is one. Krystof Fausten. He helped me look into what the language of the deeds meant concerning the deaths. He explained that it was basically a seized heart, like my father experienced."

Jessup whistled, soft and low.

Gryffine didn't meet his eyes.

"So this curse…"

"Comes back in my father's family every hundred years or so. Yes." Gryffine gave a heavy sigh, and gazed out the filthy window. "I think my mother knew. Perhaps father had found something out about the family manse's history and told her, and when he died the way he did… She used to call me horrible names, when she was raving. And when she was not, back when she was still mostly sane, she would constantly be praying for my soul and fervent that I had to avoid contact with demons, especially at Rollows. We used to go to Saint Sommes Cathedral every week, sometimes twice a week. She'd make me pray under Padrenne Henri's sole guidance for hours. They both agreed I had the Infinite Lust within me and needed to be cleansed somehow, even long before my father died, but especially after."

Jessup shook his head, admiring her with sympathy. "How horrible. I'd never let any child of mine go to one of those cathedrals of the Immaculate. Beautiful they are to look at, and the services are often serene, but the Padrenni have more wanton superstitions than any Tale

Woman I know. How was this Henri fellow?"

Gryffine stood and tugged her corset straight under her shirt. "Devout. Fervent. He used to froth at the mouth when he gave the weekly service. He put me through every kind of penance he could think of, from scrubbing marble floors on my knees for weeks to starving me of food, to saying a thousand Immaculate Rights every evening before bed. It took me hours." Gryffine waved her hand. "Anyway. Let's speak of better things. What can we do about this awful house?"

"Well..." Jessup put his hands on his hips a moment, and then suddenly went to the window and threw it wide. "Air it out, first! Even the damp of the spring is better than the bone-dry scent in here."

Gryffine sniffed at the air. "It smells like bones?"

Jessup turned with a curious lift of the eyebrows. "You didn't notice?" Gryffine shook her head. "It smells... not musty exactly, not moldy, but ...exhumed? Like bones that are so old and dry they've turned to dust, and someone opened the sepulcher door and dust swirled up into the air."

It was Gryffine's turn to raise her eyebrows. "I suppose we had better check the sepulcher, and make sure it hasn't cracked. There's an underground passage between it and the manse. That might be open."

Jessup gave her a curious look, but motioned her on. "Lead the way."

* * *

They checked the ironbound door from the kitchen to the cellar, which was securely shut and not sporting a draft. Gryffine lit a branch of candles and descended into the arched underground cellar with Jessup behind her, and together they checked the stone door to the sepulcher-passage. That was shut tight, too. They took the sepulcher passage and wandered through to the low-buttressed dome of ancient stone and mortar, to have a look around from the inside and search for cracks that might show daylight. Gryffine noticed the musty-bone smell down here, but she knit her eyebrows to think that Jessup could smell that upstairs.

"Did you come down here often?" Jessup was gazing at Gryffine curiously, and she smiled, realizing that to someone who had not grown up here, the sepulcher might seem macabre.

"I used to come here to be alone, to just sit or peruse the wrought-iron coffins. I was fascinated with their vellum. I couldn't imagine why anyone would want to see the dead, but I found I always tried. Though, as you can see, most of the vellum has aged to the point that it obscures the desiccated bones behind these wrought-iron grates."

"And what would you do while you were down here? Play?" Jessup chuckled sarcastically.

"I used to love thinking about who these people were in life," Gryffine murmured as they continued walking from casket to casket. "It helped lave my soul when I accidentally killed. It gave me the strength to resist my urges, to see the plain face of Death, daily. Mother never understood it, of course. She would have fits when she found me down in the sepulcher again and again, and always her fear would cause her to retire early to her powders and her bed. And then I would simply wander back down, to sit with the dead in all the late hours and feel their comfort, begging their forgiveness for what I had done."

"Gods of the Dark."

Gryffine shrugged, stopping to admire one of her favorites, a particularly ancient casket where the vellum had completely decayed, adorned with doves twining though baskets of vines all through the iron filigree. She ran her fingers gently over one wrought-iron dove. "I still feel that comfort even now. Down among the bones. It's the only place in this manse I truly enjoy."

Jessup stepped closer, wrapping an arm about her. "Time to change all that."

Gryffine nodded and smiled, moving close to Jessup and inhaling his sweet musk before they walked on.

Together, they wandered from niche to niche, admiring the carefully-wrought iron coffins with all their fanciful twists and foldings, and the mummified creatures within. The funereal vellum of Julis was stout stuff, thick enough to protect the aging bones but translucent enough to be seen through. Lined with vellum beneath the wrought iron, the older coffins had taken on a yellowed appearance, the vellum beginning to crack and flake from time. In some of the oldest, like the dove-casket, the vellum had disintegrated altogether, into a fine powder that dusted the wrought-iron and piled around the bones. These bones had far more wear, breaking down quickly from exposure into desiccated lumps.

"In the cathedrals," Jessup said suddenly, "they must replace the vellum."

Gryffine nodded. "They do. I saw priests doing it once. Every few years, they'll take a survey of the caskets that are starting to crumble, and schedule them for replacement. There's a special ceremony to consecrate the bones of the displayed saints and old families when they're moved into a new vellum-case, and then replaced within the original iron coffin."

"But not so here."

"I don't think most families have any reason to replace the vellum in manses like mine. These sepulchers are not for public perusal, only for private entombment and contemplation." She ran her fingers along the stone kneeling-bench that graced the far end of the chamber and faced a plinth with the crossed circular sigil of the Immaculate upon it for contemplation, and a double-row of candelabra to either side. A small votive for incense sat at the base of the plinth, old ashes scattered around it, with newer sticks in a wooden case by the candelabra.

Gryffine opened the wooden case, and selected one stick of incense that didn't look too dried-out, then took a phosphor match from the box and struck it alight upon the stone floor. It flared and she applied it to the incense, blowing it carefully to a coal, then placed the stick in the votive. A curl of smoke drifted up into the dry air and she sighed with a strange contentment.

"Did you come here often?" Jessup was kneeling beside her.

She nodded. "Often enough. When my mother was bad. Or when I killed."

"It wasn't your fault."

"It was. I should have been more careful."

"You couldn't have known your family's curse."

Gryffine turned to look at him. "No. But I should have suspected. My father's family had an old tale, that the Infinite Lust hounded Toulunnet children. Father thought it was nonsense, a bedtime story to scare children into being good. But mother believed it. She was nothing if not superstitious. She tried to cleanse me. And Padrenne Henri. But I was too stubborn."

Jessup brushed long fingers over her cheek. "I don't think any of this is your doing."

Gryffine sighed, watching the long curl of incense smoke weave up towards the dome. "Part of me knows that. But part of me still feels I am this way because of something I did."

"Or maybe something your father's family did."

She blinked up at Jessup. "What?"

"In Gypsun tales, family curses are visited upon the children because of something their parents did. Not the other way around."

"So you think my father…?"

"No. I think somewhere, sometime, an ancestor of yours somehow acquired this Gift of the Dark, and it's been passed down. Tell me that's not already what you suspect."

Gryffine nodded. "You're right. That is what I suspect. But those stories are tales to frighten children into being good. They're not real. How can I do what I do? How could it possibly have been passed through my family? It makes one believe all those awful tales of the Infinite Lust and the Consort and the Beast."

Jessup gazed at her levelly by the uncertain light of the branch tapers in the dim sepulcher. "We need to go talk to Aeshe."

"Who is Aeshe?"

Jessup chewed his lip a moment. "She's a Fatereader. Some of the old stories are true, Gryffine. And I think yours is one of them. Though I admit… it's a very strange version of what I traditionally hear."

Gryffine frowned. "What have you heard?"

"The tale of the Boy and the Bones. It's the traditional story of Rollows. A young boy touches some bones and is cursed with the Kiss of Death, with which he kills his own mother. It's where the Rollows toast comes from."

"I've heard the story."

Jessup looked at her oddly. "You have?"

Gryffine nodded. "The evening we first met. I was with my mother at the Gypsun market that afternoon, and I heard an old raglady telling it to a group of youths at one of the bonfires."

"So you know how it goes."

She nodded again. "But I'm a woman. And my curse didn't start from touching some old bones."

He shrugged. "Other than that… don't you think the story describes your situation perfectly?"

Gryffine lifted an eyebrow.

"Come on." Jessup pinched out the incense and stood. "Let's have dinner in the Gypsun Quarter. I'll take you to Aeshe and then we can find Rennet and talk to him about your manse."

Gryffine took his proffered hand and stood, then made for the outer door of the sepulcher. "This way. I'll show you the backyard before we go."

They pushed through the heavy stone door and into the sunlight, flooding down on what was turning out to be a perfect spring afternoon. The air was moist and refreshing after the dry musk of the sepulcher, and Gryffine's mood lifted to the radiant sun and the bright-tempered man at her side. They shoved the stone door shut and traipsed the gravel walk through the verge to the back porch. She was already tripping up the steps with a much lighter heart when a small pull came at her hand from Jessup.

"Hold on a tic. What's that?"

"What?" Gryffine glanced over, then followed his gaze to a small fenced-off area with a wrought-iron railing that contained a fixture of the manse she had come to accept as one of its many oddities. Inside the railing, upon an extra side-swath of the stone back porch, sat an ancient wrought-iron coffin, its vellum gone and the bones inside long turned to dust under the protection of the gables and eaves. But as Gryffine glanced at it, she, too, noticed something about the coffin that made the hair of her neck stand on end.

Within the confines of the wrought-iron, right where a corpse's chest would once have been, grew a single, perfect yellow day-flower, nodding its sunburst head to the light spring breeze.

Gryffine blinked.

Jessup grinned at her. "Should I sneak through the bars of the railing and go touch it?"

But a rush of alarm went through Gryffine just then, and she hastily gripped Jessup's arm, drawing him back. "No! Leave it alone."

"It's just a day-flower. They probably grow there every spring."

Gryffine shook her head. "There have never been *any* flowers there. Mother tried every spring to grow some. She hated the coffin but was too superstitious to move it. She sprinkled lenou-seeds in the bone-dust, flush-horn seeds, pennybright. Everything she could think of. Nothing ever grew."

"Huh. Must have sprinkled day-flower seeds at some point and one finally took." But even Gryffine could tell that Jessup's teasing tone had gone to one of wary caution. "I'll speak to Rennet about getting that whole thing off the porch and putting it in the sepulcher where it belongs."

Gryffine swallowed and nodded. "That would be best, I think." She tore her eyes away from the nodding yellow flower and tugged him up the porch, trying to put it from her mind.

* * *

CHAPTER 5

The Gypsun Quarter was already lit with colorful lamps in the late afternoon, and as Jessup extended his hand and helped Gryffine down from the hansom-carriage they'd hailed, a chorus of laughter suddenly rolled through the air, followed by the striking of guitarres and bone-rattle drums. Gryffine glanced towards the raucousness as she stepped to the pavers in her high-cantled boots, to see a knot of musicians starting to play upon the front steps of an open-air bar across the street.

Her mouth quirked as she took Jessup's arm. "Sounds like Rollows."

He glanced over at the musicians, now attracting a crowd and some impromptu dancers. "Every day is Rollows here. Life is Death and Death is Life. We Gypsun don't know any difference."

They started walking down the paver-stone sidewalk angling towards a gardened patio on their side of the street, Jessup slightly in the lead. "Why is that?"

"Because we live for today, Gryffine," Jessup quipped brightly. "We don't worry about tomorrow. The passions that plague us today are gone tomorrow. And the blessings we have today won't last until tomorrow. Rollows, for most people, is the one night of the year they can indulge being exactly who they want to be, and they put off being themselves for the rest of the year, hoping for a better someday. But for the Gypsun… every night of the year is a night to be exactly who you want to be. A better someday never comes. We take the day we have, and make it the best day of our lives, right now. Here we are."

Gryffine was left pondering his suddenly insightful words, seeing a new side to Jessup that left her slightly stunned. She stepped up to the porch of a well-sequestered little shop buried deep behind a sprawling front garden of spring-flowering shrubbery in fat pots. Crouching within the embrace of the verge were a small collection of wrought-iron tables just for two, a number of which were already filled with couples sipping coffee and talking low. Bright umbrellas lifted from arching sconces set around the tables to keep off the spring rain, and above those was a trellis just budding with wisteria. Jessup led Gryffine in through the tiny stone doorway, ducking his tall frame a little to not bump his head, and

Gryffine found herself in a cozy coffee-bar, with stone walls and rib-vaulted ceilings much like her sepulcher at the manse.

A lively little woman in an eye-smiting multihued headscarf worked the coffee-presses behind the one-person bar, and served up pastries from a case. The bar was hung with lanterns in everycolor, causing the inside of the stone space to have a festival atmosphere, and odd paintings of nothing but colorful splotches and swirls hung at intervals between the cramped padded-leather booths. The overall effect was a colorful maelstrom safely tucked away inside a cozy cavern, a place for lovers to hide from the world and lose themselves in delights.

Gryffine couldn't help but smile. "This place is fantastic!"

Jessup grinned, tugging them into line to wait for a coffee behind a young, obviously Gypsun couple with burnished caramel skin and dark curls. "Just wait until you taste Aeshe's coffee."

Gryffine lifted her eyebrows at the tiny woman behind the bar, even smaller than Gryffine herself, with her fast, feisty hands and cheery smile. She was hardly older than Jessup, and exuded a warmth of good nature that was absolutely infectious. "That's Aeshe?"

Jessup nodded and smiled with obvious affection. "She's a little firecracker. What were you expecting, some old witch with a wart on her nose?"

Gryffine couldn't help but smile. "I suppose so. Most women I've heard telling tales and Fatereading down here were ragladies on the street."

"There's a difference between true Fatereaders and the drunken grammère you see at the fires." Jessup turned his laughing eyes on Gryffine. "Don't mention those pretenders to Aeshe. She'll spit in your coffee and tell you to get out. Being a Fatereader is a very serious business, not the petty showmanship you get for five pennies on Rollows."

They stepped to the bar, but as soon as the little woman behind it caught sight of them she suddenly gave a high-pitched squeal of delight and ducked under the bar-access with little arms wide and her plethora of colorful fringed scarves fluttering all about her person.

"JESSUP!" The little woman seized Jessup by the face with both teensy hands and pulled his head down to press his lips with a kiss, then rattled his face with a rather violent shaking of said hands. "Jessup!! Where have you been?!? The cards had some very *serious* things to say about you yesterday! Naughty boy! What *have* you been up to?"

Jessup laughed, infected by her charm as much as her other patrons seemed to be, and he flushed a deep rouge. "I've been... occupied,

Aeshe. Ah…" he cleared his throat. "Aeshe, I'd like you to meet Gryffine Toulunnet."

The little woman turned her liquid-bright black eyes upon Gryffine, and suddenly her little hands flew to her mouth with a startled, "Oh!"

Gryffine held out her hand. "Pleased to make your acquaintance, Aeshe. I've heard so much about you."

"Oh!" Aeshe said again, her myriad bracelets jangling as she trembled a little. Her eyes filled with tears suddenly, and she reached out to take Gryffine's hand with a slow, happy-sad smile. "This is *her*! I mean, *very* pleased to meet you, Gryffine. Oh, Jess! She's every bit as beautiful as you described! What eyes!" But one of her hands rose suddenly, and she gave a slight frown, reaching out towards Gryffine's lips. Gryffine saw her intent, prickles lifting the hair on her neck, and she flinched her face to the side before Aeshe could touch her lips.

"Oh…" Aeshe's hands went back to her mouth, her fingers feeling her own lips as if she felt something upon them. "Oh, dear…" She suddenly dodged past Gryffine and snatched a hefty copper pump-carafe off the counter and set it upon a table with a pile of cups and a sugar-bowl and empty woven basket. Then she snatched a sign from behind the bar and set it upon the counter.

Bar closed until further notice. Prices are upon the sign. Help yourself and leave a donation.

The Fatereader snatched Jessup by the hand and gave Gryffine a meaningful glance. "Both of you. Upstairs. Now."

Jessup glanced once at Gryffine, his eyes wide with unabashed surprise, and not a little fear, then back to Aeshe. "What are you doing, Aeshe? You're scaring the Light out of me!"

She put her feisty hands on her scarf-wound hips. "You want my help or no? That's why you've come, isn't it? You two need a reading, and you need it *right now*. And Jessup, you need to see the reading I did for you earlier."

His eyebrows lifted, but he nodded his assent. "Alright! Alright. Upstairs we go, then. Gryffine?"

"If it'll help."

Aeshe's dark eyes suddenly pierced her. "I don't know if I can help you… but I will try, so the Dark bless me." She nodded again, as if confirming to herself. "Yes. Upstairs."

Gryffine shared a look with Jessup, not comforted by the fact that he looked so shaken and was trying to hide it for Gryffine's sake. But up the stairs they went.

65

* * *

The staircase was a corkscrewing thing all of stone, curling up a turret to a second story of buttressed and arched stone just as cramped as the first story. But like the first story, this floor featured narrow little windows all done in stained-glass with images of saints and the hieroglyphics of the Immaculate Faith upon every surface. The second floor was entirely given over to residence, and the staircase ended in a cozy sitting area by a fireplace. There was a recessed alcove, like a prayer niche upon the southern side, lit by one tall stained glass panel, and in this alcove sat a stool, a wide wooden desk, two chairs, and a bookshelf. Potted plants and wooden-slatted or silk screens closed off the sitting area and the alcove from what Gryffine supposed was a bedroom area at the far end of the space.

"Sit." Aeshe wasted no time, immediately striding behind the desk in the alcove to plunk herself upon the stool with authority and indicate the two chairs to Gryffine and Jessup. Aeshe sat just to one side of the south-facing window, whose late-afternoon light spilled out over the desk and the array of odd items upon it. Aeshe sat out of the light, not letting it become obscured as the colors and patterns from the stained glass rested upon the objects. A tall, narrow bookshelf cluttered with items and books sat to one side, crowding the niche. Aeshe reached for it and took a white silk cloth out of a box, then swept the items upon the table to either side and laid out the cloth with authority in the colorful sunlight. Then, she turned to another box, pulled out a handful of tiny white and rose crystals, and simply dropped them to scatter upon the white cloth.

Then she sat there, looking at the crystals intently.

"What is it for?" Gryffine spoke hesitantly.

"Shush!" Aeshe gave her a fierce warning look, then went back to studying the crystals. She was at it a long time, before she finally sat back with a pleasant smile. "Same as yesterday. I'm balanced enough for a reading. Good. Jessup, gather them up and let them fall."

He did so with a grave diligence that surprised Gryffine, as if he was handling the most precious of contents, though none of the crystals were large enough to have been particularly expensive. They scattered from his hands and across the cloth, and again, Aeshe bent over them, peering and thoughtful.

"Balanced," she said at last, as if surprised that was the answer. "Huh. I've never seen your reading this balanced, Jessup. Except for this little patch right over here," she motioned her finger in a circle around a small cluster of crystals. "You're balanced." She looked up and grinned at Gryffine, her liquid-dark eyes pleased. "She's good for you. You're very happy, more than I've ever seen you. Good. Now Gryffine, your turn."

Gryffine scooped up the crystals and let them fall, a flutter of foreboding in her belly. But Aeshe bent over the table just the same, and slowly a smile blossomed over her face.

She looked up. "Very balanced. You've never been this balanced before." She winked. "Jessup is *very* good for you. Thought so. He's a very good man. Thank your saints, or whomever you pray to." She scooped up the crystals and put them back in the box, then folded up the white cloth and put that away. Next, she reached for a deck of much-worn Fatecards, and laid out a set that had been right at the very top. Seven cards she drew, placing them faceup upon the polished wood of the table, five in a cross and two paired to one side.

"So, Jessup," Aeshe began, with a slap to the table, "This is what I drew for you yesterday, and your Light reading says it's still true. At the center of your Holy Convergence," she indicated the cruciform, "is the Wanderer. We've drawn this before for you, so many times it's almost blasé." She glanced at Gryffine. "It indicates a lonely temperament, one who is constantly seeking but doesn't know what he seeks. But here," she indicated to the top card of the cruciform, "we see the Wanderer outmatched by Concordance. Something in his nature has changed, some discord has been soothed and all is now flowing like a calm river. We've never *ever* drawn Concordance for you, especially not as your Ruling Feature, Jess. Such a position indicates that today you are exactly where you want to be, and could not even imagine being anywhere else." She glanced at Gryffine with a smile.

"But here and here," Aeshe indicated the two cards to either side of the Wanderer, "we see Patience and Persistence. You're going to be challenged in this position of Concordance, and seeing two Trial cards in one drawing is very rare, especially in the Hold positions. But here," she indicated the bottom card, "we see Abundance. If you persist, you will reap incredible benefits and achieve a lasting Concordance. A *very* fortunate drawing. But now we come to the Infinite Soul cards, and here is where I see the mystery, and the warning I wanted to show you, Jessup." She glanced at Gryffine again, eyebrows knitting now.

"The Infinite Expression card holds Winter. Winter is a card of withholding, of something desired deeply but never indulged, never possessed. But it... goes deeper than that. Winter in the Infinite Expression position means... that if the current situation persists that gives you so much immediate pleasure and Concordance, it will... wither you. Wilt you, make you as barren as the boughs in wintertime."

She glanced nervously at Jessup, who was frowning deeply now, his elbows on the table and fingers interlaced at his lips. "And last, we come to the Infinite Essence position. And as you can see... it's the Death card. Death and Winter together in your Soul positions can be a very bad omen, Jess. But it can also mean something else. See the chalice that Death is holding? How it overflows into the pool and the pool seems to crawl up the rocks and connect to the waterfall that fills the chalice? Like a waterwheel? The emptying of Death is sometimes seen as a filling, a Rebirth, and when this card is paired with Winter it can sometimes signify the opposite pairing of cards, Life and Summer, which are very fortunate and abundant cards, indeed."

Aeshe paused for a moment, regarding Jessup's intense scowl, then sighed. "What I take from this reading, Jessup, is that you are in very serious danger. Something you are doing," and here she glanced at Gryffine, "threatens everything you are. It could damage you, hurt you severely, or possibly even... kill you. But your Holy Convergence is completely at odds with your Infinite Soul cards, and this I find most interesting. It seems to indicate that if you persist and persevere, you could have a very great abundance, which could turn the Soul Wheel for you, flipping Death into Life and Winter to Summer. I've never seen anything like it."

Aeshe sat back, folding her hands in her lap, gazing at Jessup for a long while as he frowned over the cards. Aeshe's liquid-dark eyes tracked to Gryffine and they exchanged a long, unreadable look, and then she regarded Jessup again. "Anything you'd like to ask?"

He looked up, but the frown was not gone. "Can I speak to Emlohaine?"

Gryffine saw Aeshe blanch, then blush. She looked down at her fingers, which were now fiddling with each other, and with the fringe of one colorful scarf. "You know it's not that simple, Jess."

"I wouldn't ask if it weren't important."

"I know." Her dark eyes flickered up. "Let me think about it. Let's do Gryffine's reading first."

Jessup nodded, then sat back with a sigh, long fingers drumming upon the wooden arm of his chair. Slowly, Aeshe reached out and gathered up his cards, then paused a moment and pulled a piece of paper and pressed charcoal from the bookshelf and notated something down. She shuffled Jessup's cards back into the deck, and fixed her eyes upon Gryffine.

"Ready?"

Gryffine nodded, and Aeshe closed her eyes. She shuffled a few more times by feel, then spread the entire deck across the table. Hovering one hand across the cards, she selected them one by one, placing those facedown in the formation. Then she swept up the rest and put them to the side. Aeshe opened her eyes and let out a breath. One by one, she flipped the cards, and began to study them. Her eyes flicked to Gryffine a number of times, and when she sat up at last, she was biting her upper lip and frowning. At last, she gave an irritated huff.

"Well. I can't make heads or tails of this mess. But you're here, so I'll try. At the center of your nature is Quarter. I don't see Quarter often in this position. It means, that on a deep, fundamental level, you are split. Something splits your true nature into pieces, prevents you from being whole. But your Ruling Feature," she indicated the top card, "is Endurance. Between you and Jessup, you've shown all three Trial cards today. But for him, Patience and Persistence are things he must do, while for you Endurance is what you *are*, what you can't help but do. Now comes your Holds. Here we see Winter again, but there, Summer. You are simultaneously denying yourself to the point of death, and also giving yourself incredible abundance right now. And beneath that," she indicated the bottom card, "in your Driving Feature, is the Wanderer. Some essential part of you has been lost, and you are lonely. It drives you to search for it mercilessly, though this is never in your conscious thoughts. And here, in your Infinite Soul, at the Infinite Expression position we see The Ruin. I've never drawn that for an Expression card before. It indicates some part of your soul is damaged, ruined, fallen to dust. And your Infinite Essence is the Lust card. Your soul hungers for that which has brought it to ruin, or will do so. Lusts for it. Mercilessly."

She glanced up at Gryffine, blinking rapidly. "What I take from this, is that some part of your soul is greatly damaged, and it has caused a terrible split, which you endure daily. But what you endure is simultaneously feeding you incredible gifts, and ruining you with incredible loss. And throughout it all, you're driven mercilessly, searching… perhaps for the piece that fits. The piece that will repair the Quarter and make you whole again."

Aeshe's fingers strayed to her lips again, and she blinked, her liquid-dark eyes fading to a faraway gaze, then shuddered and went very still. "What is wrong with your lips, Gryffine?" she whispered suddenly, her eyes staring past Gryffine off into nothing.

The hair on the back of Gryffine's neck stood on end.

Jessup sat up straight in his chair, then leaned forward over the table intently. "Is this Emlohaine?" He asked urgently.

"We are Emlohaine." Gryffine's body broke into gooseflesh at the chill that suddenly seemed to sweep the room, but Aeshe continued on in a voice that rattled with bones, staring at nothing, her dark eyes wide. "We see a great wind within her. A hungry, howling wind that devours. Someone has made of her a Sundered, and the soul yearns for completion. But the completion of Breath to Breath is not yours, Child of Light. The Sundered hungers for another. Doom. You hunger for Doom, Child of Light, and so does she. On the day of First Renewal will her Doom come, and you will see it, Child of Light, like no one has before. Hold her back from the Endless Moment and she will be free. Let her fall to it, and the Doom will go on. And on. And on. That is all."

A cold sweat broke upon Gryffine's body, and then chills. She watched as Aeshe shuddered back to herself, sweating and pale, and then stood abruptly from the table and dashed behind a set of screens. Gryffine winced as she heard Aeshe retch into a basin, and then again. She made to rise, but Jessup took her hand firmly and shook his head, his face very pale for his bronzed skin. He leaned upon one elbow, fingers stroking his lips, regarding Gryffine thoughtfully. At last, they heard Aeshe spit, then blow her nose, and she came back around the screen, wiping her lips with a colorful handkerchief.

"Well," Aeshe sat down shakily upon the stool once more, regarding the both of them wryly. "You heard him. Doom." She huffed with irritation, then blew her nose in the rag.

"What does it mean?" Gryffine ventured, fearing the worst.

"Everything is Doom to Emlohaine," Aeshe said sarcastically, then sighed. "Don't let his words frighten you. They are meant to warn, and sometimes his warnings are *very* stern. But that doesn't mean your situation," she glanced at the two of them, "is hopeless. Now," she folded her hands on the table, "tell me about this Dark Gift you have, Gryffine, that has to do with your lips and breath, and I'll see what I can do."

Gryffine's mouth fell open, astonished, and she blinked. And then found herself telling everything to this strange, amiable little woman with the colorful scarves.

* * *

Aeshe sat back against the wall of the niche, drumming her fingers upon the table. Her dark eyes shifted to Jessup, then back to Gryffine, then back to Jessup. "You take your life in your hands, Jess," she spoke softly, but not without sympathy. "I see that clearly now, as did the cards. And Emlohaine's warning, considering this, is severe indeed. He often speaks of doom, but this..." she shook her head, tired. "Forgive me, Gryffine, but this is a Gift that is Dark in the extreme."

Gryffine hitched a deep sigh. "I know. If I could... I would dissuade him." She glanced at Jessup, but he reached out and took her hand possessively, his dark eyes fierce.

"I won't let you hurt me, Gryffine. And I won't let this Doom befall you, whatever it is."

Aeshe nodded from across the table. "I don't think either of you have a choice, really. Emlohaine's Telling had a certain... well, *certainty*, about the whole thing. As if this is supposed to be the way it is, as difficult as the situation might be. And that Gryffine has yet to experience this Completion of Breath to Breath, whatever that is. But his warning was also clear, Jessup, that you may be the only person able to prevent Gryffine's doom. Provided," and here she eyed them both sternly, "that you two can keep each other safe until then."

"What is this Completion of Breath to Breath?" Gryffine asked tentatively, fearing the answer.

Aeshe gave an almost pitying smile. "Well... since your Gift has something to do with drawing someone's life out through their breath, Gryffine, I would think that's fairly obvious. At some point, you're going to draw someone so deeply, that you experience some kind of ultimate event. Good or bad..." she shook her head. "Or maybe the extremes of both, sundering you forever."

Gryffine nodded, and Jessup squeezed her hand. "So what is this day of First Renewal?"

Aeshe shrugged. "Honestly? I don't know. It doesn't correspond to any named days of any religion or spiritual calendar I know."

"How many have you studied?" Gryffine glanced at Aeshe's shelves full of arcane books and papers.

Aeshe crossed her arms. "Many. To tell you true, Gryffine, I've only ever heard of a few with Gifts as strong as yours. No one in my lifetime. And I've studied these kinds of things since I was very small."

"What of your own Gift?" Jessup ventured curiously.

Aeshe lifted an eyebrow and gave a wry smile. "Emlohaine? He's as much Gift as he is a wart on my ass."

"Is he a Gift of the Dark or Light?" Gryffine ventured.

Aeshe sighed as if irritated, though a vaguely pleased little smile graced the corners of her lips. "Sometimes a bit of one, sometimes a bit of the other. He has much perspective on mortal matters, but his Tellings come with a price, as you saw. If he stays much longer within me, I get very violently ill for days. He and I have a pact of sorts, that he won't speak through me for much more than a minute at a time."

"So it's demonic possession, then," Gryffine whispered softly.

Aeshe shot her a warning look. "*Some* might call it that. I call it a Gift, and so did all those who came before me. I've helped a number of people through Emlohaine's strange but accurate Tellings."

"So is my Gift from a demon, then?" Gryffine pressed, needing to know if her mother and Padrenne Henri Coulis had been right all along.

Aeshe shrugged, thoughtful. "I can't say. Emlohaine didn't have a sense of it, either. Just a strong sensation that you were split in two…" her liquid-dark gaze pierced Gryffine, "as if you're only half of a larger whole. And that the Breath is a way of drawing… what you lack."

Gryffine nodded soberly. It confirmed suspicions she had possessed for years but had never been able to share, nor even admit to herself. A vision surfaced in her mind, then, of impossibly blue eyes, clear like sapphires. Gryffine pushed the thought away, and stood with a sigh. "If you will excuse me, I must go for some air. This has been… a bit overwhelming."

Aeshe stood also. "We're done here. If I find out anything else regarding your Gift, or if Emlohaine has anything to say about it later, I will send word. Until then," she glanced at them both, her dark eyes settling upon Jessup, "be *very* careful. Please?"

"We will." Jessup reached out, and tiny Aeshe came into his arms for a fond embrace. "Thank you, Aeshe. I know what this cost you. It means much to me. If there is any way I can repay you…"

She pulled away with a bitter smile. "Just stay alive." Aeshe came to Gryffine then, and took her by the arms, kissing her once upon either cheek. "Go with the Blessing of the Light, Gryffine. I know Jessup's choice is not your fault. But… be careful with him. He's like family to me."

Gryffine nodded. "I will be as careful as I can."

Aeshe patted her cheek. "I know." She turned to Jessup. "Jess, will you collect any monies in the basket and put them behind the bar? I need a few hours rest before I go back out."

"Of course." He nodded, then turned and ushered Gryffine down the stairs, leaving the Fatereader behind upstairs. Jessup did as Aeshe had asked, plus tidying up the coffee-bar and table a bit and rinsing some dishes, and then they were back outside in the late-afternoon sunshine. He turned to Gryffine with a rueful smile.

"Well. That was a bit more than I had anticipated."

"It was accurate," Gryffine mused. "It confirmed much of what I already know or suspected."

"Really?" His eyebrows raised. "All that stuff about feeling incomplete?"

Gryffine nodded as they began to walk down the sun-drenched avenue, watching the bustle of the late afternoon, Gypsun men unloading produce-carts at neighboring cafes with shouts and good-natured curses for the dinner crowd. "Yes. I feel... torn... between myself almost all of the time. Like there is something that should be me that is not, and that I'm estranged, searching for it. She was right that I feel completion when I use my breath, my kiss. The moment it creates... is perfect. Whole. Undivided. And then the moment is gone, but I remember that feeling of being whole, the blessed eternity. And I long for it."

Jessup smiled rakishly, teasing. "Doesn't everyone feel that way during climax?"

Gryffine shrugged. "It's like that but... enduring. And infinitely more satiating. The few times I've almost kissed you, Jess... it was because I... I need it."

He chuckled. "Everyone needs a good, deep kissing."

"No." Gryffine stopped walking, halting Jessup with a hand to his arm. "That's not it. I *need* to be whole. And that is the *only* way I can find it. Everything else is just sweet release."

Jessup arched a dark eyebrow at her but said nothing, then took her arm casually and ambled on. Colorful lanterns were being lit garishly in the late afternoon, and tavernas had begun to flow with revelers, jeering and talking boisterously as they arrived for supper. Jessup led them along the street at a slow pace, and Gryffine noticed how his walk and manner had become decidedly more easy, with a subtle bravado at being upon the streets of the Gypsun Quarter. Twice, groups of revelers came towards them upon the raised paver sidewalk, and twice Jessup drew himself tall, pulling up his chest in a hearty swagger that squared his shoulders and filled his lean frame out. The revelers flowed around him, men giving him a wary eyeball and women a flirtatious, appreciative one. Once he was hailed from a doorway, and he hailed the shop proprietor back just as boisterously with a rakish grin. A duo of men approached with a glint in their eyes, and suddenly Jessup's stance was that of a fighting-dog, bristling with vicious energy even though he didn't remove his hands from his trouser-pockets.

The two men dropped their eyes and shrugged past with a nod.

Gryffine remarked upon it.

Jessup smiled ruefully. "Some know me down here, others don't. I don't spend much of my time deep in the Gypsun Quarter these days, not since grammère passed. Marnet's is just on the edge of it, you know, almost the Saints Commons, really. But I still remember how to walk like I belong here. You should know that if I get challenged, Gryffine, I'm not going to shrink from a fight. It hasn't happened in a while, but," Jessup glanced at her with a winning white smile, "any man on the arm of such a beautiful and obviously wealthy woman is going to draw a bit of attention here."

"I was never bothered in the Quarter when I was a girl," Gryffine remarked mildly.

"Children are never bothered here. We're a very family-oriented people. If you had gotten lost as a child, you could have asked even the most daring thief, and he would have gotten you safely home. Children are protected, be they ours or someone else's. But wealthy women who come to mingle with the lovely and dangerous Gypsun men," Jessup winked at her. "Well, they're fair game. Flirt, charm, pickpocket, trick, or simply shove, rob and run, anything goes here if you look like money."

Gryffine smiled up at him, charmed, fears dropping away like bees soothed by his honey. "And do I look like money?"

He laughed, bright and cheerful, dispelling that last of the afternoon's dire tidings. "Gryffine! You'd look like money stark naked. And you do." Jessup gave her such a smoldering gaze that Gryffine stepped in to nuzzle his nose. He pulled her gently but firmly away with a subtle shake of his head. "Not here. Not on the street. To be seen with a wealthy woman on my arm is one thing, but to show our affection on the street makes us a target. Especially since you aren't Gypsun. I don't fancy being beat up tonight."

Gryffine blinked and hastily drew back. "Oh!" Her eyes flicked around, suddenly noting the two men who were watching them intently from a nearby doorway. She glanced back at Jessup. "Would they really do that?"

He shrugged. "It's been known to happen. Falling for someone outside the Culture is still not done in some families, and more than frowned upon. My grammère thought all that was pish-posh, fortunately, and taught me better. If we turned off the main avenue onto a side-street those two over there would probably accost us. I can hold my own in a brawl, but if they have any friends… I don't want you hurt tonight."

Gryffine shuddered, thinking through a multitude of awful scenarios, most of which ended with her kissing someone with the intent to kill to save Jessup. "Is rape common here?"

Jessup shrugged. "Not generally. If a man is still up and fighting, it's usually slap his woman around a little to intimidate him into being still and until she's scared enough to give up her jewelry and pocketbook. But if he's out cold and it's dark enough…" Jessup gave her a warning look. "I hate to know this about my birthplace, but anything goes."

Jessup took a quick but surreptitious look back before angling them around the side of a building and onto a quieter street. His posture was tense for a minute or so, his eyes darting in the shadow-lengthened darkness to doorways and porches beneath the tall reaches of wash-lines strung from window to window. But at last he relaxed, seeing only a few amblers and old women out on the street heading home with their late-afternoon shopping. They walked on a moment, passing a lamplighter as they went, then Jessup turned and led Gryffine up a set of well-kept stone steps with a nice wrought-iron railing to ring the bell of a cozy older home with gay yellow paint and a red door.

The door was opened by a ruddy brick of a man with a shocking head of red curls, obviously not Gypsun. He wore a scowl upon throwing the door wide, as if he was about to yell, but when he recognized Jessup his face blossomed into a wide smile. "Jessup! Fancy seeing you here at this hour of the evening! And who is this *lovely* creature? Come in! Come in!"

They stepped into a brightly-decorated foyer, hung with the simple gay lamps of the Gypsun quarter and decorated in shisha-tiled mirrors from Darvhistan that scattered the light through luscious ferns in fat pots. It created a charming jungle atmosphere that glittered with light and color, and Gryffine felt instantly at home among such lighthearted opulence.

"Rennet!" Jessup embraced the man heartily, then gestured to Gryffine, introducing her. Rennet bowed smartly over her hand with a nod, clacking his bootheels together in a manner less Onvittaine and more Velkish, then gestured to the sitting parlor of the same jungle verve as the foyer.

"Do, have a seat! I've got cheese and a few delicacies out already. I was supposed to have a conference with the Dunnet family about their home over on forty-third and Blounne, but they've stood me up! I hope they have a *very* good reason. This is going to double my rate, waiting around like this!" Rennet huffed in a decidedly Velkish manner, and Gyrffine could hear a slight Velkish accent in his well-cultured Onvittaine.

Jessup sat in a red-upholstered overstuffed chair, and Gryffine sat also, around a table already set with trays of small pastry, cheese, savory cutlets of meat and an assortment of fruits. Jessup helped himself to a plate immediately. "The Dunnet house? I thought that was all settled to begin next month."

"Ah!" Rennet shook his head with a glower, picking up a pipe and settling it between his teeth and re-lighting it with a few puffs. "Those damnable Merrimountians! Rich and spoiled and still pissy with their Crowns. Can't make up their minds if they want to go to the expense of remodeling or selling the damn thing. We're paused, and you know how I hate being paused!! The younger Dunnets want to sell it, and grammère Renaulda wants it to stay in the family. You met her. They've been a pain."

Jessup chuckled, then glanced at Gryffine. "Renaulda Dunnet is one of those old women who can grip any man's nuts in a vise and give a good squeeze. I'm betting on dear old grammère to win out."

Gryffine gave a startled laugh at Jessup's language, but Rennet bulldozed over it with a wave of his pipe. "So am I! And I think she will, but the younger generation are putting up quite a stink. So. Jessup. What brings you to my doorstep? I told you I'd send word as soon as the Dunnets make up their mind." He arched one eyebrow curiously.

"Actually," Jessup grinned and glanced at Gryffine, "I'm here about a project of my own."

"Oh?" Rennet grinned widely. "Come into some money, lad? And does this project have anything to do with the lovely miss Gryffine?"

"Actually, it does," Gryffine interjected, feeling a strange pull to start the negotiations. She smoothed her beige highwaist-pants and crossed her legs at the knees. "I have a family manse on Rue Coullard, near Saint Sommes Park. I would like to have it remodeled."

Rennet sat forward with interest, his green eyes eager. "On Rue Coullard? One of the Mortuary Manses? With the sepulchers out back? Which one?"

"The three-story with red gables between sixty-third and sixty-fourth."

Rennet sat back, puffing his pipe, eyes still glowing with interest. "And what does it need?"

Jessup sat forward. "The structure is sound, Rennet, anyone can see that from a quick walk-around. The foundation is quite level and there are no gaps in the chimneys and the walls are square. The roofline has weathered nicely, it only needs a replacing of the shingles and an inspection of the supports at the eaves for rot. Mostly an interior-lift, and exterior freshening. No major renovations."

Rennet regarded them both. "A scuff and fluff project then. Alright. What's in it for me?"

Gryffine lifted her eyebrows. "Besides money?"

Jessup coughed, a grin lighting his face. "Rennet likes to leave his mark on his projects. It builds his reputation."

Gryffine nodded, then gazed about the parlor, noting the cheery, homey yet exotic feel of the colorful plant-filled room, and how much it reminded her of Jessup's bar. The ferns and trailing vines in their pots added mystery and intrigue, and all of it came together with a splash of debonair voudoo from the exotic tiled mirrors and strange odds and ends and statuettes half-hidden in the greenery.

"Like this." Gryffine decided at last. "I want my entire manse to look like this, but with more risk. Give me a combination of this and the festivity of Rollows in the Gypsun Quarter, and I will be well-pleased."

Rennet's bushy red eyebrows climbed his forehead, and even Jessup looked stunned. Rennet took the pipe from his mouth. "Like this? With more Rollows?" He looked Gryffine up and down, noting her demurre beige and cream clothing. "Forgive me, *madamme*... but are you quite sure?"

Gryffine nodded, suddenly certain. "Quite. Makes me a Rollows-manse, my dear Rennet, and I will be well pleased. I'm tired of being someone I'm not. Give me my life, and let me live. No more piety, no more death, no more sadness."

Rennet had a slightly confused look upon his face, but then he nodded. "Very well. Let us talk funding." And the night wore on from there, as Gryffine and Jessup discussed every aspect of the manse and its peculiars, and Rennet puzzled out a preliminary estimate of the possible expense.

***

CHAPTER 6

Morning dawned bright and cheery, with sunlight flooding through Gryffine's dirty windows and lighting its way across the dusty floorboards. She was up and out of Jessup's arms with a quick nuzzle, already excited about the day's events. Jessup grinned at her as she washed quickly in a basin and dressed in a long red skirt and corseted white shirt, and they made small talk about the coming day as Jessup washed also and donned his white shirt, pants, boots, and plain brown waistcoat sans cravatte with his shirtcollar undone. In less than an hour, they were both breakfasted from a light porridge Jessup had cooked, and gazing about the main drawing room at the eaves, chimney and various other features of the bleak room.

"Well." Jessup stood with his hands upon his hips, taking a full look around. Gryffine had finally given him a complete tour of the manse, and he had nodded at what he'd seen and taken a few careful measurements in the largest rooms. They had concluded in the main drawing room, and it was with this room that Jessup was particularly concerned.

"See there and there," he pointed to the arched ceilings and their ribbed wooden supports. "You've got a few beams rotting from rain-damage, and that plaster up there will have to come out. There's probably a gap in your shingling that hasn't been addressed in some years. Otherwise, you're in good shape. I didn't see any water damage in any other rooms, and this part was clearly an addition after the main house was built, as your father's family acquired wealth. That was often the way of these old manses, and they tend to leak at the junctures. But fortunate for you, the main house was built quite large, and only this room and the kitchen were added later. The room that you now use as the parlor was probably the original kitchen, before the family needed more space for parties and entertaining."

Gryffine nodded soberly. "And the rest of it? Décor? Paint? How much will that cost me?"

Jessup shook his head and smiled. "Not enough to worry about. My labor comes free, and I'll do most of it. Some of the exotic wooden plaquards and statuettes like Rennet has in his house will cost, but he imports them in quantity, so not that much. And any Gypsun items we can get quite reasonably if you allow me to haggle for them. The carpentry on your roof repair will be the expensive part. Rennet will have to calculate that out, depending on if he gets his regular man to do it, which he may not do if the Dunnets decide to move forward on their house. He may hire a Guild carpenter. They cost more, but they know these old manses, and their work is flawless."

Gryffine took his arm, gazing up at the water-sodden beams. "Couldn't you do it?"

Jessup shook his head. "I'm not a serious carpenter, and I don't know the proper load-bearing bracing for that kind of work. If you needed cupboards for the kitchen, I could do that much, but not this."

Just then, a ring came from the bell-pull, and Gryffine turned towards the hall. It was Rennet at the front door, and he swept off his debonair purple wool hat from his mussed red hair and clicked his heels as he bowed.

The Velkman straightened, eyes positively gleaming. "You have a *lovely* manse, my dear Gryffine! Such a treat this will be to work on! It is every bit as sound as Jessup said, and I am well pleased. Very little trouble we will have, and much reward! Yes!"

Gryffine motioned him inside, and Jessup guided Rennet through to the sitting parlor. "There is one major repair I've discovered, Renn. See, up there? How the beams have begun to sag and there are two large blotches of discoloration?"

Rennet sucked his teeth. "Yes, yes. Unfortunate. But better than I'd expected. These old manses are prone to their share of rot. Give me four days with a good carpenter and we can have all that fixed. Not to worry, boy." He turned in a circle, admiring the sitting-room in its dark-paneled entirety, his eyes noting every heavy piece of dark carven or wrought-iron furniture, then turned to Gryffine with pity in his eyes. "Was it always this bleak for you? This dark? Growing up?"

Gryffine nodded, then smiled. "Yes. But I am very eager for the change."

"Yes, yes." He gazed around again. "Looks like some of the poorer cathedrals along the Sentriat. Ghastly."

"My mother was very pious. She liked it this stark."

Rennet glanced over. "And you? I don't want to decorate your manse like Rollows if you have pious company over frequently."

Gryffine had to laugh at that, imagining Padrenne Henri Coulis' face if he walked into a Rollows-themed manse. She actually wanted to see it. "No! I assure you. I have long given up on piety. And propriety can go out the window, too, for all I care. Make it up like a bordello! Make it up like the Infinite Lust. Make it up like a jungle, I don't care, Rennet… just give me color and life!"

Rennet eyed her a moment, then grinned. "Very well. Take me through the entire manse and I'll see what else may need to be done, but I have a feeling this will be very straightforward. Shall we?"

Gryffine nodded, and then led the way, taking him through a tour of the lower level and then on up through the rest of the too-barren house.

* * *

The entire manse had been toured twice over, with the inclusion of the cellar, the passage to the sepulcher, and the sepulcher itself. Gryffine had even shown Rennet the hide-hole behind the bookcase and he had asked if there were any more like it. To her denial he had only made a skeptical scowl, and they'd moved on. They were finishing the tour with a brief circuit of the grounds, when Rennet stopped with sudden fascination upon the steps of the stone back porch, then walked to the railing surrounding the ancient wrought-iron coffin.

"Ah… you have one of these…"

Jessup and Gryffine stepped to the railing next to him. "We were hoping you could move it, Renn," Jessup murmured.

"Move it?" Rennet glanced at them both.

"To the sepulcher." Gryffine interjected. "My mother never liked it here on the porch. And neither do I."

"It would make a lovely sitting area for a day-table and a few chairs, I suppose." Rennet stroked his red-stubbled chin thoughtfully. "But you've already got flowers starting there, and the ironwork is devastatingly ornate. It's probably lovely in the summer. Why move it?"

Gryffine had noticed that the single yellow day-flower was still there, proudly alone and unwilted in the dust-pile of the ancient bones. "I'd rather see the space used for something else."

"Hmm." Rennet regarded it a moment, then vaulted himself over the railing in a surprisingly agile movement for such a plethoric man.

Alarm flooded Gryffine. "Don't touch it!" she yelled suddenly.

Rennet turned back with surprise arching his ruddy face. "Why not?"

Gryffine felt herself blush. "The flower… don't touch the flower."

Rennet glanced at the little yellow day-flower and then boomed a laugh that had him slapping at his knees. "Oh!" He chuckled and then grinned at Jessup. "Wouldn't have pegged her for the superstitious type! No, no! I don't have to touch the flower, just the cage." He strode forward, then bent, wrapping his meaty fists around portions of the wrought-iron casket and giving it a solid tug. The coffin made a groaning sound, but did not budge.

"Hmm..." Rennet gazed at the corners, getting on hands and knees. "Ah! They've had it bolted down. Strange. This is probably as old as the house. See how the original stone of the porch continues beneath it, Jessup. They planned this part of the porch, to place the coffin here. I've only seen this sort of thing at two other manses on this row, though to be sure I have not seen every house on this street. They called them *Ruine de Temps*, the Ruined of Time. I've seen it notated in the oldest deeds. Don't know the story, though, but for some reason, the folk buried in these were kept separate from the sepulchers, but closer to the house, as if those who buried them wished to look at them more often. But they left them out in the elements, and the two I've seen are in as poor shape as yours! Vellum long gone, bones turned to dust, iron of the cage rusting. It seems almost a punishment if you ask me, isolated out in the cold. But not to worry! These bolts are easily removed and the cage has a solid bottom of iron, it doesn't seem to be rusted through. We can lift the cage with a few steady hands and it's narrow enough to get in the sepulcher doors. Half an afternoon's work on a sunny day."

Gryffine nodded with relief, her surge of anxiety abating. "My thanks, Rennet. And none of the workers will disturb the flower?"

He laughed again, then vaulted back over the railing. "No, pretty ghost-watcher! I hire mostly Gypsun craftsmen. They're all as superstitious as you. Except Jessup here." He clapped Jessup upon the shoulder. "Very well! Let's go inside and talk cost."

***

The cost Rennet had quoted had not been as much as Gryffine anticipated, and she mentally calculated that if she put her university studies on hiatus for a few months to help with the work and asked Gabriel Henowe to trade some of her investments, that it could be done without undo financial hardship. Now that Marionne was gone and Gryffine was no longer paying for her hostelry and doctors and medications, her money was her own to use as she saw fit, and she couldn't imagine anything she'd rather spend it on. A fee was agreed upon over tea, half to be paid up-front and half upon completion of the work, and hands were shaken all around. Rennet left with a smile, and Gryffine closed the heavy front door, pleased.

Jessup took her in his arms and kissed her neck. "What next?" he asked. "Want to go back to Marnet's for a bite of supper?"

Gryffine took him by the hand, and led him back to the parlor. "Not yet," she said with a teasing smile. "I want to do something else first."

Jessup grinned, sensing her mood. "Celebrate?"

Gryffine pulled him down upon the brown velvet chaise-lounge in the drawing-room. "And work up an appetite…"

"Mmm," Jessup kissed her neck again, laying his body down and beginning to move against her. "I like the sound of that."

Gryffine sighed with delight. "I meant sweep the floors, you rake!"

"I'll sweep them with your shirt," he growled, "once I get it off of you!"

But they didn't get that far. Jessup's fingers stole up her red skirts and slid beneath her undergarment, and then Gryffine was sighing, riding his touch until she screamed into his shoulder.

***

Their rumpled bliss upon the chaise was interrupted by a ring of the bell.

Jessup sat up with a half-grin, smoothing his dark curls. "Probably Rennet back to take some measurements he forgot." Jessup leapt from the couch and hastily tucked his shirt and rebuttoned his waistcoat and trousers, then strode to the door as Gryffine straightened her red skirts and under-corset.

"Oh!" She heard Jessup's surprised voice from the door. "May I help you?"

"I'm here to see Madamme Gryffine. Is she in?"

Gryffine froze, one hand paused with a pin to her ebony locks. That fervent voice grated on her skin and made her instantly angry. Her face flushed, part of her responding with a foolish girl's fear that she and Jessup had been caught, then stilled in fury. And yet, Gryffine could not make herself go to the door. She was still frozen in place when Jessup led Padrenne Henri Coulis down the hall to the parlor. Henri's red-rimmed eyes showed the strain of age and too many late nights praying when he should have been sleeping. His tall frame was not just lean but gaunt, his black padrenne's day-suit hanging off his narrow shoulders. His eyes fixed upon her, grey and storming, and like usual, Gryffine could not tell if he was angry or simply tortured about the health of her soul.

"Ah. Gryffine." Her name clipped from Henri Coulis' dry lips like dropped bones.

"Padrenne." Gryffine's voice was icy. She couldn't have made it warmer if she tried.

Padrenne Henri glanced at Jessup with scorn, then back to Gryffine. Henri did not fidget, judgment in every line of his gaunt frame and hollowed eyesockets. "Living in Lust already? Your mother would be ashamed."

Gryffine's breath stilled in fury. She made her hand rise to her hair and casually insert the pin to the last wayward curl, making it absolutely obvious what she and Jessup had just been doing. "Marionne is dead. Why have you come, Henri?"

He opened his hands in a pleading gesture. "Why, to *pray* for you, of course. And to bless you and ask you to pray with me. Please. Gryffine. Think of everything your mother did for you. Come back to the Immaculate."

"No." Gryffine did not need to even think before answering.

"Your soul needs *cleansing*, Gryffine," Padrenne Henri Coulis continued fervently, a froth beginning to build at the corners of his parched lips. "You know it as well as I. Come to confession at the cathedral. Come pray with me. I have cleared everything for today. I will hold your hands and pray as long as we possibly can. I will do everything I can think of to undo this vile curse upon you."

Gryffine saw Jessup twitch, and then he was glowering at the gaunt Henri Coulis. "Do I need to show him out, Gryffine?"

Gryffine held Padrenne Henri's bruised and sunken eyes, and the gaunt masque of Death held hers with imploring and pity. "He was just leaving."

And then, Padrenne Henri sank to his bony knees right there in the parlor, his rose-beads coming to hand with a fervent fanaticism in his grey eyes. "Please. Don't make me do this, Gryffine!"

"Out. Now." Her voice was frigid, and Gryffine was cold with fury.

Henri began running through his beads, and his tremulous voice rose to the rafters. "And now comes the day of Great Absolution! And the Infinite Lust shall be in the woman, as she be of vile and deathly soul! And she shall writhe in torment, the Kiss of Death upon her lips! And with it she shall cast wide her nest of woe, devouring souls for the Pleasure of the Beast in the Great Forge! And she shall be the Infinite Consort of the Beast, the blue-eyed demon with his Breath of Iniquity!! And Ruin shall tempt them all, if she come not to Salvation from the moment of her Completion!! Come to salvation, child! It's not to late!

83

Come and be blessed in the waters, come and repent, and be absolved!!!"

Gryffine's breath had stopped in her throat. The words that had always poured from Padrenne Henri's fervent lips had merely sounded hateful and accusatory before, but now they had taken new meaning. And though none of the words had changed, suddenly Gryffine was sundered by them in a way she had never been before, and her legs abandoned her.

She sank to the chaise.

"Alright, you." Jessup had hauled Henri to his feet by both arms, not roughly but with finality. "Gryffine has had enough of your ranting for one day. I'm sure she'll come to Saint Sommes Cathedral if she's of a mind to. You don't have to come calling again."

And to Gryffine's dismay, Padrenne Henri turned and seized Jessup by the waistcoat, shaking him a little. "Beware!" He hissed. "The Infinite Lust is within her! Beware of your soul, young man! The Kiss of Death lies between her lips!"

"Out. Now." Jessup had taken Padrenne Henri firmly by the gaunt elbow and steered him resolutely towards the hall.

But before he could, Gryffine suddenly called. "Wait!"

Jessup turned, eyebrows knitting angrily.

Henri was expectant, his red-rimmed eyes blazing.

"What do you know about it, Padrenne?" Gryffine said at last. "What did you and my mother know about it?"

Henri Coulis took a breath, and smoothed down the fabric of his black coat. "Too little. And enough! Stories of stories passed down…but all ring of Immaculate Truth!"

Gryffine held his gaze. "You have one moment, Henri. Speak plainly. And then leave. What do you know about my curse?"

His breath hissed in, and his eyes widened in surprise. "The Kiss of Death! So it has happened already?"

Gryffine nodded slowly.

Padrenne Henri moaned, his eyes turning up in their hollow sockets, eyelids blinking rapidly. He would have sunk to the floor again had not Jessup grabbed him and steadied him. He came back from his near-swoon, his gaunt face full of woe. "And now has come the Time when the blue-eyed Beast cometh! His Breath will tempt Ruin! Do not follow him to Completion, do not Complete with him in the Whore's Dance! Do not follow the Beast… o Whore of Death, do not go thusly!"

Padrenne Henri Coulis was shivering now, shaking with a palsy so severe that Jessup had to step back and let him shiver on his own. But

Padrenne Henri kept his feet, and his piercing red-rimmed gaze never left Gryffine's.

"Is that all?" Gryffine's belly was clenched in cold knots.

Padrenne Henri moaned. "Is that not *enough*?!"

"Show him out, Jessup," Gryffine murmured, and turned her face away as Jessup took Henri by the arm again and showed him to the door.

* * *

Jessup had been kind after the Padrenne's visit. He tried to amuse Gryffine with wit. He tried to adore her with soothing words and tender embraces. He'd taken her to Marnet's and had them both served a fine dinner in the brightly-lit bar. But despite it all, Henri's words tumbled around and around Gryffine's skull for hours past the deepest part of the night, and still she was restless in Jessup's shabby but cozy bed above the bar.

Gryffine roused herself, throwing an errant blanket around her nakedness, and paced to the open balcony doors. She stood a while, breathing the night spring air, just starting to smell of warmed verge and budding flowers. A tinkle of laughter sounded down below, but Marnet's bar was relatively quiet this late, all but the most drunken revelers long abed. Gryffine leaned on the wrought-iron railing, not particularly caring who saw her half-clad here should they chance to look up.

She closed her eyes, trying to breathe slowly, trying to breathe away Padrenne Henri's vile poison of words. Always it had infested her. Always it had caused her to turn inwards, with loathing towards herself and this push-pull of longing to be free, and hating what her freedom did. Always this stern iron cage, closing her down every day of the year, into a façade of demureness she didn't feel. Like her manse, the reality of living this way was forcing itself into Gryffine's conscious mind, and like her manse, she hated every bit of it.

And she hated Henri's words, those words that scalded her, that shamed her to retreat into her stiff cage. Shamed her and caused her to shy away in fear from whatever she truly was, caused a girl of hope and levity to be pinned like a moth in an exhibit-box. Immobile. Afraid. Holding on so tightly to the lock each and every day as if it could keep her in, though the iron cage was wide open and beckoning her to step out of it.

Gryffine was shaking. She gazed down, noting how white her hands had gone on the iron railing of Jessup's balcony, gripping it tightly. She took a deep breath, letting it go deliberately, then sighed to lean back upon the wall of stone. It was cold and comforting where her bare shoulder touched the stone above the close-wrapped blanket, and Gryffine's head fell back with a sigh. A floret of newly-opened lilac hung near her from a potted bush on Jessup's balcony, and the sweet musk of it caught Gryffine's mind, sweeping it towards ease. Without thinking, she reached up, brushing the lilac with her lips slightly parted, inhaling one endless, perfect moment of scent and calm. It stretched and stretched, spinning out from the void of her mind, pleasant and without regrets. Gryffine sighed, letting her head fall back to the stone of the wall once more.

A low whistle sounded to her left from the open balcony doors.

Gryffine didn't open her eyes. "Did they die?"

But she already knew the answer.

Jessup slid close, wrapping one arm about her waist. She felt his other hand reach up, touching the sprig of flowers. "The entire branch is dead."

Gryffine sighed, then opened her eyes. The branch was indeed dead, the entire stalk from where it left the main trunk of the rangy bush and every single spray of flowers upon that stalk. It was a full fifth of the plant, and Gryffine's heart dipped in sorrow at what she'd done yet again.

Always from Life her curse made only Death.

But Jessup merely cradled her closer, and kissed her hair. "So that's what it does, huh?"

Gryffine nodded, and smiled wryly. "That's what it does."

"I'll have to prune it back. That bush was getting too rangy anyways."

"You can't prune out your heart once I've stopped it."

There was a long pause.

"No. That's true. But if you stop my heart with a kiss, Gryffine, I'll have what I want. An eternity of you. Forever."

She snuggled into his arms and sighed, letting her head drop back on Jessup's bare shoulder. "Don't even say such things."

He cuddled her closer, wrapping her tightly in the blanket against the late spring chill. "Someone needs to say it. It's time you talked frankly about what your Gift can and can't do, and all the ways you've been studiously killing yourself over time, not allowing yourself to live. My people's ways seem to inspire you, and I will nourish that as much as I can, but eventually you'll have to make a choice."

"And what choice is that?"

"Strangle yourself to death with your pain… or find those you might bless with your Gift."

"What?" Gryffine's eyes flickered open.

"You heard me."

"It's hardly a blessing, killing people."

"It could be." Jessup's voice was low and smooth, and he dipped his chin to kiss her bare shoulder. "Men and women die upon the street every day, Gryffine. From cold, from privation, from flux, and can't afford medicine. I know places where men and women go to lose themselves in the Faint, a far more powerful and destroying drug than opium could ever be. People who want to die. Who want to leave the world in one beautiful moment of peace. Elderly with no homes and no children to see them to their final blessings."

"You're asking me to kill people, Jessup!" Gryffine could not keep the scandal from her voice.

"I'm asking you to not *hide* who you are." He kissed her jaw gently. "For she is beautiful and tender and playful and kind. I've seen it. Saint Sommes herself could do no better, to call to her an angel of mercy such as you."

"I won't kill willfully." Gryffine hardened her heart against it, though a fantasy of woeful beauty spun on in her mind, tempted by his soothing and worrying words.

"That Padrenne who came today… he thought you were a *demonne*. But I disagree. My grammère always said that every curse has a blessing, Gryffine. I've been thinking about it all day. What would you do if I were robbed in the streets tonight, beaten within a breath of my life, back broken, bleeding out? Would you let me die in pain? Would you let me suffer? Or would you take me in your arms one last time, and give me that for which I desire most?"

Gryffine's breath had caught in her throat. "Do you desire it so?"

Jessup nuzzled her ear. "With my every sinew, Gryffine. Ever since I saw you, ever since I tasted your breath upon my tongue that first night… I have craved for you to devour me. It is all I can do to pull away when you're near to kissing me, and only because I know how very much it would slaughter you to have killed me so. But I cannot bear to see you live like you do."

Sadness gripped Gryffine's heart. "And how do I live?"

"Like a woman already dead. Except on Rollows."

It was too close to the truth for her to reply. Gryffine didn't resist when Jessup led her away from the balcony and back to bed, stoking the fire slightly higher to push back the spring chill. They didn't make love, merely lay with one another skin to skin, the closeness and warmth soothing some animal part of Gryffine long denied. Eventually she drifted into uneasy dreams, of walking empty streets by the light of the stars, kneeling in pools of blood by sleeping vagrants that desiccated into nothing but bones as she kissed and stole their breath.

A night wind wafted through the cozy room, and Gryffine shivered in her sleep.

***

CHAPTER 7

The next many weeks went by in a blur. Gryffine had returned to her manse with Jessup, who had secured short dinner shifts at the bar from Marnet in order to help Gryffine put the manse to rights before the real work begun. They scrubbed the austere house from attic to eaves and from cellar to scullery. No spider was left nestled in its high web, no birds nesting up under the eaves, and no slug to languish beneath last year's leaf fall. Gryffine felt constantly coated with dust, and she and Jessup looked like desert nomads of the Hotrene Wastes, hair swathed in dun-colored kerchiefs, mouths and noses protected the same way.

Days came and went. Rennet came to make inspection of the manse's furniture, and took the first load of sofas, chaises, and chairs away in his hansom-cart to be polished, stained, and upholstered as per Gryffine's desires. Furniture still in residence was shoved into piles and draped with sheets to keep it some semblance of clean. Rugs were hauled up to the second floor balconies and beaten, in a tireless display of strength by Jessup, whom Gryffine would often take breaks to admire as his muscles and lean bulk worked at the whupping. Floors were scrubbed, over and over, sluicing through thick layers of ancient grime, and Gryffine discovered how to fashion kneepads from kitchen pot-mitts.

After a full week of this, everything shone to Jessup's initial satisfaction, and then he announced brightly that the real work could begin. And tedious it was. There were days of sponging and pulling strip after strip of ancient dark wallpaper from the two upper stories. More than a week of carefully sanding dark paint or ancient varnish from panels of wainscoting, which left Gryffine sneezing hopelessly despite her nose-cover. And night after night of scrubbing and treating the grout between the tiles in the bathrooms and kitchen, the ones that Rennet had decided would stay, of course. And those which he said must go they set to pulling out with iron pry-bars. That particular afternoon Gryffine had thoroughly enjoyed, the irresponsible hedonism of breaking tiles she had hated for years lifting her heart like Rollows drums. She and Jessup had made their particular brand of love lustily that night, and stayed up far too late into the evening laughing by her parlor fireplace and devouring bottle after bottle of wine.

It was a blessing, for life to finally be so simple. Every day Gryffine would work at Jessup's side, and they would trade stories to pass the tedium of the hours or simply work in a comfortable silence. Gryffine learned of Jessup's mother's death, taken by a flux when he was only eight, and of his grammère's stern yet uncompromising adoration. Jessup learned of Gryffine's history at Padrenne Henri's cathedral, her baptism in the Immaculate faith, how she had accepted it as rote, especially as long as her father had been alive. Gryffine learned of Jessup's introduction to Gypsun Fatereading when his grammère had first taken him to see Aeshe's now-dead mentor, Mère Borozhnia, just after his own mother passed. Jessup learned of Gryffine's happy life in the country, back when they'd owned horses and joined in the hamlet's annual fox-hunt. And through it all they worked, and then broke for supping and wine, and sometimes simply drank wine all throughout their days.

And the long nights were their own, undisturbed and happy.

Provided they observed a few simple rituals.

And all through the blossoming of early summer, the manse began to transform, and with it went Gryffine's dark spirits and her hatred of the place. With every scrubbing-out, she felt she was cleansing her soul. With every dousing of water upon the floor, she sluiced out her woeful heart. With every cartload of drab and dark furniture taken away and brought back striped and patterned in bold color, Gryffine felt her world lighten into gaiety. And with every pruning of the yard, she felt her misery cut away.

There came a day when much of the manse had been attended-to, and Gryffine decided that though it wasn't quite finished, it was time for a fête. Summer was hot and humid, the flash-bugs swirling their merry dances out over the freshly-pruned garden in the early evening. Gryffine, Jessup, and Rennet lounged in newly-cleaned garden chairs upon the recently-installed flagstone patio between the back porch and sepulcher. The patio was designed like a combination of Marnet's bar and Aeshe's coffee-shop, surrounded by a wealth of greenery in fat ceramic pots and strung above with Gypsun lanterns to light the night like the little flash-bugs with their whirring wings.

Gryffine gazed around the patio, her heart light and her mind merry. Her mother had never had parties at the city manse, and it had been shuttered before Gryffine had come to live here, and for many long years before she was even born. But now, the manse's first party in living memory was in full swing as the summer night capered on, and Gryffine found she was thankful for those she called friends.

Dotorre Krystof Fausten had come to his invitation for their impromptu garden-party, and brought merry conversation, plus a selection of fine wines and cheeses. Aeshe had temporarily closed her coffee-shop and lounged in the grass off the patio, sans shoes, her colorful scarves aflutter in the occasional summer-night breeze. Gryffine had invited a few colleagues from the university she had been pleasantly cordial with, and to her surprise they had all come. Her university mentor had also come, a calm yet powerful gray-maned woman by the name of Justine deLis, who was getting along fabulously with Dotorre Fausten. Jessup had invited a number of friends and extended family, mostly merry-eyed Gypsun rogues who kept flirting ostentatiously with Gryffine and Aeshe and the university girls. The university ladies were all giggles and polite conversation, but Gryffine found herself admiring the breezy way Aeshe prattled right along to the wit of the Gypsun men, but somehow managed to cordially and inoffensively dismiss every surreptitious or blatant offer of trysts.

Talk turned to laughter as the evening deepened, and boisterous Rennet commissioned the lighting of the new patio-brazier with a drunken toast and much puffing of his pipe. Wine flowed round, then coffee, courtesy of Aeshe, then more wine and small bites Marnet had spent the day slaving over. His famous beignets were a particular delight, which everyone soon found paired excellently with an orangine chutney Dotorre Fausten had provided, and a musty cheese from Madamme deLis. Tasting gave way to songs as a friend of Jessup's named Pierre produced his guitarre from the manse and began to tune and strum. Which gave way to other delicacies passed from hand to hand by a small pipe, which Gryffine refused with a sudden wariness, remembering her mother's habits.

"Not going to have some?" Freder, one of Jessup's more boisterous and incorrigible Gypsun colleagues grinned from where he'd fought off Pierre to sit next to Gryffine. Freder took a long puff from the pipe and held it awhile, lips smiling, his dark, teasing eyes mellowing by the moment. At last he breathed out, then offered the pipe back with a nod and a suggestive raise of his eyebrows.

"What have you got to lose?"

Gryffine thought about his words, and gazed around the gay party, feeling at home in her manse for the very first time. The yard flowed with song and laughter, low talk and the sounds of merriment. Jessup was true to his nature, moving seamlessly from group to group, enlivening the night by his very presence. Friends mingled with acquaintances and others Gryffine had just met. The summer was perfect, the night was perfect, and the manse was well on its way to becoming perfect.

Death had become Life.

"What have I got to lose?" Gryffine took the pipe from Freder's hand with a smile, and closed her eyes, touching her lips to the wooden stem and pulling in a long draw.

"Good girl..." she heard Freder mumble, but Gryffine was already lost to the night. The moment rolled on and on. Her mind expanded, rolled out through the party, through the yard, through the manse itself and out to the street, rippling away towards the park and beyond. The smoke lingered in her mouth, heightening the sensation of her perfect moment, and it was as if some web of darkness suddenly slipped away. Light stole in beneath her drowsing eyelids, a crystalline light that shattered her darkness and illuminated the perfection of her endless moment.

It stretched and stretched, breathing her in as she breathed the smoke.

And stretched.

"Oops! I think the coal went out."

Gryffine felt the pipe taken from her hand, the sensation of it faraway and small. She heard a vague tapping, like someone trying to dislodge the substance in the bowl, then the fleeting acridity of a phosphor match.

"Strange. That was a fresh press. I'll have to get another one. Hold on a tic."

Freder disappeared from her side, but Gryffine didn't need to open her eyes to feel him go. She could feel the people around the party, their endless surging of energy, their beings like crystals with endless facets, the ceaseless inhalation and exhalation of their breaths, curling about the patio and creating its own tides. The night breathed all around Gryffine, and Gryffine breathed with it, riding those strange tides in something akin to ecstasy.

She felt a presence draw near, one she could nearly taste.

"Jessup," she whispered, a smile curling her lips.

His hand settled over her unbound hair, then stroked beneath it, to linger upon her neck. "I didn't figure you for an Allouenne girl."

"Allouenne?" Gryffine breathed.

She felt Jessup shudder at her sigh, and knew he could feel the tide of her own breath and dark gifts. Then Jessup chuckled in an amused sort of way. "Allouenne. The musk-bud. That's what Freder just gave you."

"I can breathe the night, Jessup…"

His chuckle beside her was knowing, and slightly amused. "Can you?"

A sudden certainty flooded through Gryffine. "I need to go breathe something, Jessup."

She felt him startle. "What do you mean?" His words were wary.

"Someone dying…" Her whisper was quiet enough that none nearby could have heard.

His fingers trailed lightly over her neck. "The Hospital of Saint Sommes is not far," he murmured at last. "I'm sure there is someone receiving their Final Passage as we speak."

"Would that be heresy, to do what I do within sight of a Saint? Padrenne Henri would think so…" Gryffine thought of the Padrenne, of his fevered, raw eyes and his parchment-thin lips, ever-concerned for her very soul. He would curse her as a demonne for wanting to draw the breath of the dying, for doing it. But some part of Gryffine knew there was a blessing in this curse, that Jessup was right, even though she feared it.

That from Life came Death, which led back to Life again.

Gryffine pushed Padrenne Henri from her mind, focusing instead upon the image of Saint Sommes, her white marble statue in the park with her upturned wrists and her doves and her rapturous bliss at her understating of the Immaculate. That was what Gryffine wanted her curse to be. Rapture, endless bliss, a perfect moment gifted to her and to someone else, someone who needed a sweet release.

Someone who needed the Immaculate Bliss of Death.

As if reading her mind, Jessup murmured, "Saint Sommes was a bastion of mercy, they say. She brought the peace of the Immaculate to the dying and the wounded, from sickness and in battle. Aeshe's told me a little about her. Maybe the Padrenne doesn't understand you, Gryffine, but Saint Sommes would, I think."

Gryffine paused, breathing in the slow undulations of the night around her. And then she stood, taking Jessup by the hand, eyes still closed. "Take me to the hospital."

***

They had abandoned the party, and Gryffine cared not. Rennet or the dotorre or one of the others would have the sense to clean up or remain until she and Jessup returned. The night was alive all around Gryffine as she walked without sight along the quiet cobbles and beneath the gaslit lamps of Rue Coullard in the deep night. Oceans of breath stirred around her, fragrances lit her mind with color, the air itself was like a soft cloth that could be handled, caressed, and woven with her fingertips. Jessup's arm was steady about her waist, and Gryffine did not open her eyes until they breathed the calming herbal scents of the hospital and stepped up its stone entry-stairs. There were no guards at the wrought-iron gates before the sprawling hospital compound on Rue Coullard, no interruption to the solemn beauty of the night.

The high stone vaulted ceilings of Saint Sommes Hospital echoed with the night, their plinths and columns carven with flowers and vines and the shadow-shrouded faces of faunus peering out from the stone here and there. A fresh summer breeze cooled its open-air hallways from courtyards of flowers and herbs that Gryffine could smell, drowsing deep in night, and retrofitted gaslamp sconces turned low gave a gentle, comforting glow. Gryffine could hear the sweet chuckle of a fountain as she and Jessup entered the lofty, grand foyer and passed a quiet admittance station, where a lean dotorre in a white coat with night-ruffled russet hair was speaking low with a nurse. He glanced curiously at Gryffine and Jessup, noting them, but Gryffine moved forwards with certainty, and he went back to his conversation with the pretty blonde nurse, unperturbed.

Gryffine could feel the patients as she moved forward into the arched outdoor corridors of the hospital quadrangle. Her breath curled out from her lips, seeking, tasting each person one by one. She could taste cinname upon the lips of that one, and henbane upon the breath of another. Bitter tinctures to revive the blood, and sweet tinctures to revive the heart. Sour tinctures to replete a woman who had just given birth, and the thick sweetness of breastmilk to the newborn babe.

But there was one who tasted fetid, rankling of disease uncured. And there was another whose breath was too sweet, the sugar-thirst disease a plague that would soon kill in stealth.

And there was one more, who tasted of dust. Bones so old they had desiccated and crumbled into nothing, and the dust lingered upon this one's breath. Gryffine altered her course, moving silently through a vaulted stone corridor and up a short flight of stone steps, searching with her breath. The death upon the breath of bones beckoned. There was no one to watch Death's door, and Gryffine and Jessup flowed silently into the room like specters and closed the stout door softly behind themselves. Gryffine sat upon the edge of the dying woman's bed, and Jessup took a vigil behind her, standing with his hands upon her shoulders for comfort. A slight nervousness rippled through Gryffine, gazing down now upon the thin-boned woman whose brittle hair was white as new snow. Her breathing was rattling and unsteady, coming in rapid bursts and then dying away again. Gryffine took her hand, feeling the bare knobs of bones and the papery fragility of her chill, dusky skin.

The woman's eyes cracked open. And widened as her breath paused. "Saint Sommes?" She whispered in a broken, failing voice.

"No," Gryffine murmured, "But I can help you. I can give you... mercy, if you wish it."

The old woman breathed once, considering her, then her rheumy eyes twinkled a little. "So it's time, then. I wondered if someone... would come."

Gryffine nodded, her hand smoothing kindly over the old woman's, a fierce love rising in her heart and pushing her nervousness back. "It's time. Would you like me to release you? There will be no pain. I promise it." And suddenly, Gryffine knew that whatever change had come over her tonight, that her words were true. No longer would her breath bring a tortured death of writhing and agony after that moment of bliss. No longer would anyone suffer at her lips, at her Gift. No longer would there be any pain.

Not if she used it for which it was intended.

To release the dying back to the Immaculate.

From Life to Death, and back to the Life of the infinite.

The old woman nodded, her kind eyes smiling. "Give me release, my Saint Sommes. I am ready."

Gryffine nodded, gazing over the old woman's dying beauty one last time. She felt her entire heart swell with a vibrating joy, and then leaned forward, curling her fingers behind the woman's thin neck, and pressed her lips lightly upon the old woman's. Gryffine's kiss spiraled inward, diving deep to the source of the woman's breath, the source of her life, and gathering it all up for one final release.

The old woman arched a little and her lips curled in a faint smile beneath Gryffine's. And Gryffine sighed into ecstasy, the universe blossoming out before her in one endless, enduring breath. Time stopped. Space stopped. Her very being stopped, replaced by an awareness of all that was and all that is and everything that could ever be, whole and complete and perfect. Her mind strayed, expanding outward and inward simultaneously upon that perfect, immutable breath.

Hours might have passed. Days.

But when her lips finally parted from the woman's now-silent smile, it had only been moments.

***

"I'm fine, really…!"

Gryffine laughed to Jessup's third query concerning her mysterious silence, her heart light as clouds moving upon the endless breath of the summer night. She and Jessup had strolled arm-in-arm back from the hospital along Rue Coullard, and the night continued to surge all around Gryffine, breathing in and out in slow tides. She had been aware of her breath's effects before, but this sensation of knowing to whom it went and how far and how beautifully it meshed with the flow of the world was intoxicating, and it had taken her thoughts away with it for a time.

"Are you *sure*?" Jessup finally bore a hint of his amused smile as they neared the manse, but it flickered, tinged with wariness.

"You were the one who suggested it, Jessup. I know you are uneasy about my deed tonight, but you yourself encouraged it."

"I know." Jessup ruffled a hand through his black curls. "But to have a mental understanding of the peace you can bring is one thing, but to see death happen… I guess that's quite another. Shocked me a bit, I think." Jessup grinned, covering his wariness.

But Gryffine herself felt only elation, and a deep answer to a call that had paralyzed her entire life. Her limbs buzzed with excitement, her mind spun down the avenues of possibility, and beneath it all was a deep sense of satisfaction.

"I took a life tonight, Jess, and it was beautiful," Gryffine murmured as they neared her manse, sounds of the fête still full in the yard. "It was *beautiful*. Not horrible, not terrifying, and not a curse, but a blessing. The endlessness of that perfect moment… it spins on within me, a gossamer thread of spider's silk that connects to infinity…" Gryffine gripped Jessup closer by the arm, and he laughed uncertainly.

"I think you're a little buzzed from the smoke, Gryffine."

"I was at first, but now… Jessup!" Gyrffine sighed, hanging lightly upon his arm, breathing in the night. "If only you could feel what I feel! The smoke… it merely opened up something that has lived inside me all along, but I wasn't ready to face it, not until tonight. Until the manse's completion, until our celebrations, until I let down my barriers and let life come flooding back in. And how it floods me! If you could only feel it…"

Gryffine whirled, her elation overcoming her, and pressed in close against Jessup's chest as they reached the wrought-iron gate of her manse. An overabundance of sensation gripped her suddenly, and before Gryffine knew it she was lifting up to press a kiss upon Jessup's lips.

"Gryffine! Slow down!" Jessup's voice rang with shock and dismay as he jerked away, gripping Gryffine's waist and pushing her back a step.

Gryffine blinked, confused, feeling like he had just thrust her underwater from the sun of a bright, cloudless day. A moment passed between them, Jessup with a wary shock, and Gryffine with a flare of anger that she'd never felt before, that Jessup would reject her so and cause this imperfect jolting moment. But then she blinked, realizing that she had just violated every careful agreement they had ever made, both spoken and unspoken. Suddenly ashamed at what she had almost done upon the heady crest of her elation, Gryffine felt herself blush furiously, and she raised her hands to her lips.

"Oh, Jess!" she whispered, "I'm so sorry...I didn't... I shouldn't have...!"

He shook his head with a measured outbreath through pursed lips, pulling her into an embrace with a kiss to the top of her head. "It's alright. I should have seen it... it's my fault. I wasn't being careful. Musk-bud breaks down inhibitions... *Merde.*"

"No," Gryffine murmured into his chest, still reeling from what she'd nearly done. "I was careless. Oh, gods, Jess! It's just this *feeling*... it sweeps me away."

"Don't get so swept away that it lifts you from my arms." Jessup's voice held a chuckle as he held her close, but Gryffine heard the worry beneath it.

"I'll be careful. I swear it. I won't do this often... maybe I shouldn't do it hardly at all. But I feel like I *need* to do it for some reason. Maybe we should have a... a plan for it."

Jessup looked down at her. "You mean, maybe you should be alone after something like this? After taking a life?"

Gryffine nodded, her urge to kiss him mastered enough that she could look up. "Something like that. This elation... just now. It was almost too much to control, especially with you so near. All I can think about is kissing you. I can *feel* you Jess... your breath..."

Jessup chuckled, carefully nuzzling her ear instead of her nose, but his chuckle was dark with need. "You too, huh? That breath of yours is quite the item. It's like I feel you moving all around me, all the time. I don't even need to look when you enter a room, Gryffine. I *feel* you. Every damn time..." He shivered a little, and Gryffine heard him give his carefully-measured breath. "Let's get back to the party. They'll wonder why we've been gone so long."

Gryffine nodded, and they entered the gate, then rounded the corner of the manse to the backyard to find that indeed, everyone was still there. The party was only becoming more boisterous, with tambourines somehow added to the variety, and Freder juggling a set of small green spheres as Aeshe danced barefoot to the tambourines, fringed scarves awhirl. Jessup and Gryffine were greeted by hearty cheers and shouts, and drinks pressed into their hands, something that was not wine but a split mixture of red and green in tiny glasses from Marnet's bar. Gryffine glanced at Marnet, and he smirked and twirled his mustachios, then stood to raise a toast.

"To Jessup and Gryffine! Long years and heated nights!"

A chorus of cheers and ribald taunts went up among the assembled Gypsun, and the rest lifted their glasses with infectious good cheer. Gryffine downed her beverage, and fire spread through her belly, making her spirits soar and pushing back her worry for another time.

***

The fête had continued nearly until dawn, and Gryffine had opened her manse to the drunken revelers to overnight. Some had gone home, like the fastidious Dotorre Krystof Fausten with a few quiet words to Gryffine, his blue eyes smiling with tired, drunken delight behind his wire-rimmed spectacles. Others she had not thought to be boisterous, like Justine deLis, had stayed until the end, quietly sipping her beverage and holding court among the younger men, tapping her foot to the tambourines and smiling contentedly. She had hailed a hansom cab near dawn, and was now gone.

Gryffine gazed around her now-brightened and Gypsun-styled formal parlor, then located Freder, who had fallen asleep on a red-and-gold striped chaise, cradling Pierre's guitarre. Gryffine tossed a bright purple throw-blanket over him and the guitarre with a smile, and he snuggled it up to his whiskered chin with a drunken murmur of nonsense. Others she had provided rooms for upstairs in the redecorated and brightly-patterned manse, and some of her university colleagues and Aeshe were double-bunked in the guest beds. Like her and Jessup, the boisterous Rennet had reveled through the night and was still up, padding about the yellow and white kitchen quietly and making coffee to take back out to the patio. Gryffine nodded as he trundled by, a red blanket wrapped around his shoulders, and he smiled and winked, then was gone through the kitchen door to the back porch.

Steady hands slid around her waist as Gryffine admired the clean brightness of her new kitchen, and she leaned back into Jessup with a smile of contentment. "Is Rennet going to sleep at all?"

She felt Jessup shake his head behind her, and could almost feel his infectious grin. "He's like that, sometimes. He gets inspired and then he doesn't sleep. He'll probably pad all over this house until breakfast and then have a hundred more ideas to talk about over eggs and coffee. You ready for bed?"

Gryffine glanced out at the lightening sky through the now-immaculate kitchen windows with their gay cream trim. "I don't think we'll get much sleep."

"It's enough. Come on."

Gryffine allowed herself to be led up soft red runner-carpet of the gloss-polished stairs, and trundled into her own red and purple lantern-lit canopy bed after only pausing to lock her door and shuck her corset and boots. She and Jessup cuddled together beneath the cream duvet, still fully dressed, sinking into the peace of the reds and yellows and purples now flooding the cream-light room, and all felt safe and serene. The house was renewed, full of life and complete as it had never been before, and Gryffine felt complete in her own way. She burrowed into Jessup's arms with a satisfied smile, and by the soothing surge of his breathing could tell he was already fast asleep.

***

CHAPTER 8

Breakfast had been more like lunch, and was attended by Freder, Pierre, Rennet, Aeshe, and a few young ladies from the university who had bunked upstairs. Talk had been subdued but warm, and they had taken the meal out to the back patio once more to enjoy the cicada-thick summer stillness of the early afternoon. All the others were gone now, save for Rennet, who was standing in the middle of Gryffine's yet-undecorated family parlor at the rear of the manse next to the kitchen and gazing up at the rotting beams and sodden plaster that had not yet been attended to.

"Well, almost every other room is finished save for this," Rennet mused, tousling his wayward red curls, "and moving that cage off your pack porch. We can't proceed forward here until I secure carpenters, but my usual man has been tied up in projects! The Carpentry Guild is offering me another fellow by the name of Luc Tournet. I've met him and he seems to know what he's doing. I've viewed three instances of his work, and all were meticulous and *very* fine, including a beam and roofline repair similar to yours, though hand-carving is his real talent. What a fine set of hand-carved cabinets I saw of his, all flourishing with gargoyles and dragons and the like! But he's a dastardly quiet fellow. Can't get five words out of him in a row! I suppose he'll do, though. His work *is* very fine, in many ways better than my usual man. With your permission, Madamme Gryffine, I would like to move forward with those repairs this very afternoon. This fellow Luc is free for a week just now, which I hear is *quite* rare, and the sooner we start, the sooner we can finish!"

Gryffine nodded. "I am eager for the manse to be complete, Rennet, and if you say this fellow is trustworthy, then I believe you. I shall be here to meet him this afternoon. Jessup?"

He shook his head. "Marnet is cruel sometimes. I have to be at the bar, but I'll be free after the dinner crowd. I'll come back then."

Rennet nodded. "I'll see if I can be back by noon for Misseur Tournet's arrival, Gryffine, but if I can't then simply ask to see his Carpentry Guild badge, and he'll show it to you. He's a tall fellow, lean, blonde hair and very light blue eyes. Nordes stock, I think, but he speaks like an Onvittaine native from Julis. When you can get him to speak. Mostly he just nods and peers at things and then gets right to work. Don't let that fluster you. I would have thought him simple except that when he does speak, he uses beautifully complex language, just like his carvings."

Rennet shrugged, then stepped forward to kiss Gryffine upon either cheek, which she only mimed back, kissing air. "In any case, I will stop by this evening to check on how the work is progressing and see what he may need. Expect him to show today with ropes, harness, and perhaps some scaffolding to do the preliminary inspections."

"Thank you, Rennet, for all your hard work." Gryffine clasped his hand, then turned to Jessup and nuzzled his nose.

"See you tonight?" Jessup kissed her cheek carefully, then smiled.

Gryffine nodded. "Tonight."

Rennet and Jessup showed themselves out, and Gryffine turned to the kitchen, cleaning up after the morning meal and pondering going back to bed.

***

A pull of the bell roused Gryffine from a thoroughly deep sleep. She blinked twice, disoriented and trying to surface from dreams she suddenly did not remember. Her mind raced furiously, trying to remember what day it was, what time it was, and who could possibly be at the door. At last, her thoughts shuffled into place and she launched off the bed and towards the window. She glanced over the sill and looked down, seeing a tall, slender gentleman in carpenter's attire with a rope slung over his shoulder and tousled white-blonde hair standing at her door.

"A moment!" Gryffine called down from her window, then dashed to the mirror for a quick inspection. She straightened her sleep-rumpled white shirt and tan slacks, and the corset beneath that she'd accidentally slept in, and tried to smooth her mess of black curls into something tame with a few extra pins. She patted her cheeks and splashed water on her face from the basin, and hastily rubbed dry with a handtowel. Gryffine sped barefoot down the stairs to the front door of the manse and threw it wide.

And stepped back from the door as a shiver raced over her entire body.

"Oh!" Both hands flew to her mouth.

101

The man standing before her was tall and lean, with a brush of white-blonde hair and skin so pale it was almost alabaster. He was smooth-shaven with a nice jaw and good bones, and his rough carpenter's clothes were plain but neat. All of this Gryffine registered in a moment, but it was his eyes that held her. At once pale and rich, the color of his eyes caught the daylight. They shone like a cloudless sky from underwater, perfect and clear like sapphires. It was the color of drowning in a lake as pristine as ice, and suddenly Gryffine was breathless under his steady gaze.

They stared at each other a very long while.

"Luc Tournet?" Gryffine murmured at last, fingers still at her lips.

He did not blink, and he did not smile, but it was as if a current between them intensified suddenly. Gryffine both saw and felt him give a small shudder. "Gryffine Toulunnet." He cocked his head slightly, appraising her. "I was hired by Rennet Blounne through the Carpenter's Guild. I believe I am expected?"

"Oh! Yes, come in, please…"

Gryffine stepped back from the doorframe, allowing Luc Tournet to pass, but as he entered the foyer and came abreast of her by the ebony bench, the current between them intensified again. He halted, gazing down curiously with his perfect sapphire eyes, and it was as if he would say something, when his shoulders gave a slight twitch. He drew one breath and let it out slowly, measured, and Gryffine felt that breath curl all around her, undeniable and inescapable like eddies in a rip tide. It pulled at her, that single breath, calling her to wade in, to be sluiced, and to drown. Gryffine stumbled backwards a step, feeling dizzy, and put a hand out upon the wall to steady herself, wondering if she had drunk too much the night before.

"Which room, Madamme?"

Gryffine blinked, realizing she'd been staring at Misseur Tournet, and gestured weakly to her left. "The family-parlor. Just down the hall. Last room to your right across from the kitchen."

He nodded, sapphire eyes lingering a moment longer, then turned and walked casually to the back of the manse and into the parlor. Gryffine waited a moment in the bright entry-hall, trying to get her body under control. The sense of drowning in his breath only lessened a little as he moved on, but did not cease altogether, and Gryffine shivered as she attempted to pull herself together enough to be a proper hostess. But by the time she had reached the parlor, Luc Tournet was already gazing upwards, his perfect eyes narrowed upon the damaged beams. He produced a heavy hook from a utility satchel at his wide leather belt, and lifted a harness from among the ropes at his shoulder, which he stepped into and buckled about himself. In one long throw, he sent the grappling hook to the ceiling and had it up and over a stout, healthy beam near the damaged ones, catching it as it fell. He removed the hook and threaded the rope through a pulley, then had himself fastened in and winched up to the damaged beams in no time.

"What do you see?" Gryffine called, as much for some way to distract herself as to provide conversation.

Luc Tournet stared down at her with those uncanny blue eyes for a very long moment, and said nothing. But at last, his eyes snapped away from Gryffine's like a cable breaking, and he went back to his work, maneuvering along the healthy beam to get a good look at the ceiling and reaching up to prod at it. Gryffine started to fidget, wondering if she'd said or done something to make the man uncomfortable or angry, trying to remind herself that Rennet had said his strange, intense quietude was simply the man's way. But even from where she stood, Gryffine could feel his presence, Luc Tournet's breath sighing and curling around her even though he was focused upon his work and nothing else, high above. Damaged plaster rained down in chunks to patter the hardwood floor, and dusted his pale skin all the more white. Gryffine stepped out of its way, and a few bits of rotten wood came after it as he dug strong fingers into a beam. She heard, and also felt him grunt as if in confirmation, and then he was on his way down, unbuckling from the rigging but leaving the rope, pulley, and winch in place.

His pale blue eyes flicked to the plaster upon the floor. Gryffine saw his eyelashes were almost as white as his hair. "Apologies for the mess, madamme."

Gryffine shook her head quickly. "Not to worry! I have yet to sweep today."

They stood in awkward silence for a long moment, his oceanic eyes fixed upon her, his quiet, almost studiously rhythmic breathing sighing around her, lulling Gryffine like wave after wave of a vast ocean. She found that she had begun to sway to it, to match her own breathing to it, and that as they breathed together, standing almost close as they were, that it seemed to weave into his, pulling tighter like a corded rope, and then tighter again with each breath.

Gryffine found with idle surprise that she was leaning in towards the man now, as if they were actually being pulled towards each other by their intermingling breath, on the verge of falling a step closer. She leaned backwards a little, trying to counteract the pull but found that doing so only intensified it like stretching already-tight cord.

Gryffine cleared her throat awkwardly.

"Would you like tea? Lunch? Will you stay?" She cursed herself for that last question, flushing scarlet.

But a flicker of a bemused smile crossed his face, and the otherworldly Luc Tournet murmured softly, "Lunch would be fine. And tea." His pale blue eyes roved over Gryffine's face, taking her in. She felt those eyes upon her like a touch, like his breath followed where his eyes went, smoothing over her skin with a rippling caress. She felt his eyes fix upon her lips, his breath curling up to find hers.

"And I will stay. To work…" Luc Tournet murmured, and that murmur was utter devastation to Gryffine. The pull of his breath around her was strong as a river in full spring flood, something unleashed by speaking that had been previously held back. His words curled in eddies and tugged at her skin, her hands, and her spine, urging her closer. Tingling had taken Gryffine from head to toes, and she shivered, violently.

"Are you cold?" He whispered the question, blue eyes steady upon Gryffine and searching, the caress of his breath making her shudder again.

"No," Gryffine murmured, transfixed, lingering upon his breath. "No… it's not that…"

He cocked his head slightly as his lips dropped open in a silent surprise, blue eyes regarding her carefully, hiding something deep and baring his soul all at once.

"Can you feel me?" Luc Tournet asked at last. "Can you feel this? Do you know what it is?" He parted his lips and sighed, his breath rushing forth and wrapping Gryffine from head to heels, diving up her body and hunting her lips. Gryffine broke out in shivers and stumbled from the force of it, terrifying and ecstatic, that languid breath towing her to the center of deep currents, seeking to drown her.

"Yes," Gryffine whispered, less like a whisper and more like a moan.

She didn't know what she expected, but it wasn't what happened next. Luc Tournet stepped back a pace, and then a pace more, denying her, denying the strong pulling of the connection between them, his perfect sapphire eyes full of woe as much as they suddenly flared with desire.

"You can't touch me," he murmured, imploring her with beautiful blue eyes, "You can't be near me. Please… leave me be."

Gryffine felt herself drawn forward by that invisible cord as he stepped back. "But why…"

"*Enough!*" His quiet voice cracked harsh as a whip in the silent parlor, emphatic. "I will do work on your manse, but that is all. You may leave food upon the table, but please abandon me to my work, now. *Please…*"

Gryffine blinked, his harsh tones rattling her as if she'd been physically slapped, such a coarse contrast to his earlier manner. But the moment he'd ceased speaking, his face suddenly contorted into a woe so palpable that it rolled over Gryffine's skin and doused her heart in ice. Gryffine staggered back, gripping an overstuffed chair for support, her other hand to her chest, the cord between them having frayed and lashed her from the dismissal in his breath.

"Yes… forgive me…" she stammered, her eyes dropping in shame, "I should never have… I don't know what I'm saying…"

Turning suddenly, she fled into the relative safety of the kitchen and slammed the through-door shut, bolting it. Gryffine leaned back against it, breathing hard and resisting the pull she still felt from the other side of the stout oak door. She reached up, trying to fix the pins in her hair but getting them hopelessly tangled from her shaking. She ripped them all out instead, letting her curls fall, brushing them over one shoulder.

Gryffine stepped to the icebox, and went methodically about the business of fixing bread, cheese, a few cuts of cured sausage and a selection of summer berries for the man with the drowning blue eyes and pulling breath. She made a sweet mint tea, set it all upon a tray and then pushed her way through the kitchen door and set the tray quickly upon a side-table in the parlor. Her eyes tracked upwards, drawn there by his pull. Luc Tournet was back in the rafters, taking measurements. He paused in his work, as if feeling the pull between them the same as she, gazing down upon her for what seemed like an eternity, his perfect sapphire eyes ablaze.

Lust was in them, infinite desire. And woe, endless woe.

And a careful, studious and iron-bound precision. The only possible way to hold it all in, to keep from going mad.

And Gryffine knew all about those things.

* * *

Gryffine had gone upstairs after that, and locked herself in her bright bedroom. It hadn't helped. She'd paced, she'd twiddled with her fingers, she'd tried doing some sewing repairs and stuck herself hopelessly with her needle until she bled and cursed. She'd gone to the window to sit and reflect. She'd risen from the window to grab a book of poetry from the shelf. She'd flipped through the poetry only to settle upon a poem about obsession, and had hastily put it away. And she'd gone back to pacing, her heart deepening further and further into misery.

The front door slammed.

Gryffine hurried to the window, gazing down to see Luc Tournet standing upon her stone porch. He paused and looked up, as if he could feel her watching. Gryffine gasped to be seen, to be found by him, resisting the urge to hide behind the windowsill. Luc Tournet watched her with his fascinating, needful blue eyes. A moment passed, an eternity of moments. The curls of his breath found their way up the side of the house to her window, and then Gryffine felt them touching her skin like fingers, smoothing, caressing, easing beneath her clothing, touching her intimately. Breath like kisses pressed at her neck, breath like the smoothing of fingers touched her breasts. Breath like a tongue licked between her legs, slow and certain, diving deep inside with a driving need. Gryffine moaned and swayed where she stood, one hand gripping the windowsill hard. Luc Tournet stumbled down below, his own hand flying to the doorframe to steady himself. His white-eyelashed eyes flashed wide and he blinked a few times, as if coming awake from a deep reverie, then gave Gryffine a final pained, devastated, and deeply needful gaze from his merciless blue eyes.

And then he turned, and was gone.

***

"Well, Gryffine, I don't know what to tell you."

Rennet was pacing across her unfinished parlor floor, gazing up at the rafters and shaking his head. "That carpenter Luc Tournet has suddenly decided he isn't the right man for the job. He gave me all his initial measurements and assessments, which were *quite* thorough, I must say, and then simply asked to be dismissed. He didn't even ask for *pay* for his time today! Of course, I'll send it along to the Carpentry Guild to be given him, but I say! Such an unpredictable fellow!"

Rennet scrubbed a hand through his thoroughly-tousled red mane. "But there's nothing to be done about it! Fortunately for you, I contacted my regular man Vincent, and he's agreed to help, but he can't begin for another two weeks. So… we are paused my dear, so very sorry!" Rennet stepped forward, patting Gryffine's hand as if that were a comfort. "But we have *plenty* to discuss in the way of décor for this room in the meantime, and I'm sure you and Jessup could use a bit of relaxation, considering all you've done in the past few months. Yes, yes."

Gryffine nodded, hardly hearing Rennet at all. It was late already, and Jessup was still not home, and she was longing to be wrapped in his arms, longing for him to take her upstairs and wash all this day's strange tidings away in heady delights and sweet comforts. But he was still not here, and Rennet lingered, sipping orangine liqueur and prattling on about fabrics and urns.

"... but of course we'll have to move that cage off the back porch."

"What?" Gryffine startled out of her reverie.

"The iron coffin. Gryffine? Are you well?" Rennet held the back of his hand to her forehead. "Are you feverish? But you feel quite cool, my dear..."

"No, no... I'm just thinking. What did you say about the porch?"

"I have secured a crew to take that thing off your porch tomorrow, dear, and put it in the sepulcher where it belongs. There is ample space for it. And my boys will be bringing large flower-urns for that area. Tomorrow. Perhaps you should sleep? We all got very little from that *fabulous* party last night!"

Gryffine smiled wanly, steering Rennet surreptitiously towards the door. "Yes, it was quite the time. But I believe I am tired, Rennet. When will you be back tomorrow?"

"By nine." He downed the rest of his orangine liqueur from its crystal glass and set it down upon a hall half-round table, then patted Gryffine's cheek affectionately. "Get some rest, girl. We need you chipper tomorrow to tell us where you want those pots placed so we don't have to move them twice! They are heavy as elephanti!"

Gryffine smiled, and this time it was genuine, though her thoughts were still occupied a world away. "Yes, Rennet. See you in the morning."

"Goodnight." Rennet let himself out, and soon it was just Gryffine inside her refurbished manse. She paced down the brightly-lit hall, remembering those drowning blue eyes and the way Luc had caused her to tremble. She paced to the unfinished family-parlor, gazing up at the rotting rafters, hoping to see him gazing down. She paced upstairs to her window, remembering how his very breath had curled up to greet her, tugging at her flesh, diving deep within her.

But worst of all, urging her to come down, and to kiss him.

To kiss him until eternity persisted and she was drowned.

To kiss him until the moment stretched, perfect, infinite, and utterly complete.

Gryffine shook her head, trying to banish such thoughts, trying to banish the feel of that breath from her skin. She tried to think of Jessup, his dark-golden skin, his laughing black eyes and bright white teeth. But then it would all change, alabaster skin replacing brown, pale hair replacing dark, perfect sapphire eyes replacing black. And then the woe was swallowing her, drowning her, breathing her until Gryffine thought she had no breath of her own left.

With an anguished cry, Gryffine strode from her room and down the stairs, opening the front door and slamming it closed behind her, abandoning herself to the night.

***

She knew where her feet were taking her, of course. From the manse, Gryffine had walked the few short blocks to Saint Sommes Hospital, and was now mounting the steps to the compound and moving down the stone-arched, gaslit halls. Sisters and nurses were still going about their rounds in the night, and the russet-haired, lean dotorre Gryffine had seen before, but they only gave such a well-dressed lady a cursory glance, assuming she was going to visit some relative or another.

Gryffine knew where the dying man was the moment she entered the vaulted foyer. Her feet took her unerringly down the right open-air corridor to the proper room, to the one who already tasted like desiccated bones when she breathed. She was startled to see a young man in the linen-draped bed, barely in his twenties, and yet shockingly pale and wan. There was nothing left to him but bones stretched over skin, though he had been handsome, once, and some of that still lingered. The dying man's eyes were bright and fevered when Gryffine lingered at the open doorframe, but his voice was robust, a deep baritone.

He chuckled. "More blood, nurse? I haven't any left to give. Go visit Alfre down the hall. I'm sure he'll oblige." He turned his face away, and Gryffine saw that it was the only movement really left to him.

She sidled silently to the bed, and the dying man turned his face back, gazing at her curiously from where he was propped up by thick white pillows, his mind and green eyes yet-sharp. "You're not a nurse, are you?" He looked her over appreciatively. "Or a sister."

Gryffine sank to the bed beside him. "No, I'm not."

"So what are you?" he snorted chidingly, green eyes flashing in anger. "An angel of death to ease my sweet passage? They've given me enough morpha for that, dear one. Just a few more strong drips, and I'm gone. Unless the cancer eats the rest of me before they hurry with the medicine." He shifted restlessly, just a motion, but Gryffine could see what it cost him, how he winced even to do that much and a fine sheen of sweat glistened his forehead over his ashen complexion.

"I can take it all away," Gryffine murmured, feeling a strange calm sweep over her, just as it had with the old woman. "The pain."

The young man lifted one blonde eyebrow sarcastically. "What wonder drug are *you* peddling? I'll take it. Give me a full ounce, give me six! Just kill me, please, and tell my family I went in my sleep. They'd like that. Not pissing and shitting myself in a bed because I can't hold my bowels any longer." He lifted his voice in a mocking soprano, bitter with rage. "What a disgrace of a deTullaine!"

Gryffine reached out, and took his hand solemnly, feeling the bones of death just as she had with the old woman, though his hands had once been firm and strong and were hardly lined with age at all. "I sell no medicines. I have merely come to give you myself, to ease your passage."

He lifted an eyebrow, a mocking sort of flirtation. "And I'd take you, if I could do anything about the taking anymore. But *that* hasn't worked in a long while. I'm just waiting to die, pretty girl. Best you go away and let me wait."

Gryffine leaned forward, feeling her breath beginning to mingle with his, her gift reaching out, seeking to give him that one endless, beautiful moment. "You don't have to wait any longer. I've come to release you."

Her lips were inches from his now, and a strange light of comprehension suddenly dawned in the young man's green eyes, his mocking face now sober and attentive. "What is this…?"

Gryffine leaned closer, her lips seeking his. "Your death," she murmured. "If you want it."

"My *death*?" He lifted his chin the slightest amount, lips tasting of ashes hovering over Gryffine's. "So what… you kiss me, and I *die*? Just like that? Just like that Gypsun Rollows-tale?"

Gryffine nodded, gazing into his clear green eyes. "Just like that Gypsun tale."

The dying man blinked, considering it, taking a moment to face it. And then his clear green eyes sharpened upon her, honing with a bitter anger and a thousand regrets. "You'd better mean it. You'd better not leave me alive afterwards. Kiss me deep, sweetheart, and if you can kill me with those pretty lips, do it. I don't want to live like this anymore. Kiss me… and make it hard."

His passion and bitterness stole Gryffine's own breath for a moment, and she was returned to Jessup's words about killing mercifully. And

109

thoughts of Jessup turned to guilt, and then turned to sorrow for the dying young man before her.

He sighed, watching her face change. "You're not ready to do this, are you? To kiss a *dying* man." He gave a harsh, wrathful snort. "Figures."

"What is your name?" Gryffine murmured.

He blinked at the change in conversation, then smiled. "Justin. You?"

"Gryffine."

He lifted his chin again, lips whispering over hers. "Well… now that we've just met…kiss me, pretty Gryffine. Take my breath upon your ripe lips and let me die."

And then the restraint in Gryffine broke, and she wanted to kiss this beautiful dying man with every ounce of her being, to unbind the passion Luc Tournet had summoned in her soul. She rushed to his lips, kissing him with a furious passion that unleashed every sorrow and torment of her life, and he kissed her back with everything that was left to him. And when the endless moment finally sighed away, he fell back with green eyes now dull, and triumph upon his face.

* * *

CHAPTER 9

Gryffine sat in the darkness with her back up against a broad oak in Saint Sommes Park, sobbing. The red-blossoming regalia-bushes to either side hid her misery, and she let go, wracking breaths heaving from her soul as she cried, hands over her weeping eyes and elbows upon her bent knees. She sobbed for Justin, the young man she had just killed, and she sobbed for Jessup and his frustrations and worry that he never voiced and never could voice. She sobbed for her mother long ago, cooped up in a bleak manse and going mad for her worry over her cursed daughter. She sobbed for herself, and the happiness she had so recently found that had tumbled like a house of cards from the pull of fascinatingly blue eyes and devastating breath. And she sobbed for those blue eyes, and the pain and yearning within them.

A rustle sounded in the first of autumn's unraked leaves around the spreading oak, and Gryffine's sobs choked to instant silence, her body suddenly tense and alert. Part of her wanted to challenge the intruder, but part of her knew it was best to lay silent, hiding. The Saints Commons and the park were not the most rowdy part of the city, but it had its crueler patrons, especially at night from the Gypsun Quarter upon the other side. Gryffine shrunk down into the niche between the bushes, her back to the tall oak, hiding herself in its dark shadows. But then she felt a curl of breath, misting over the dew-moistened grass and twining up her ankles, touching her skin like moth-wings, tentative and silent.

"Are you all right, Madamme Toulunnet?"

Her heart leapt to her throat, and Gryffine choked. She saw his shadow move around the side of the bushes, and then he crouched before her. His blue eyes were only vague glints in the deep shadows, but as Luc Tournet knelt, Gryffine could feel his breath surging all around her.

She shivered, but not from cold.

And yet, a jacket was produced, and draped carefully around her shoulders. "You're shivering. Allow me to escort you home."

"How did you find me?"

Silence answered her query for a very long moment. "I've been in the park most of the evening. I think I was hoping you'd happen by."

"Why did you leave?" Her voice sounded plaintive and raw, and Gryffine regretted the moment she spoke.

But Luc Tournet only gave a soft chuckle. "Forgive me. I was frightened earlier this afternoon. I'm not used to someone... startling me so."

He reached out, offering a hand to help her stand. More than anything, Gryffine longed to touch it, but instead she hesitated. "I thought I wasn't supposed to touch you?"

Luc Tournet gave a long exhalation, carefully controlled so that the curls of it barely touched Gryffine. "It's all right. You startled me this afternoon, but I've had all evening to adjust. Please. Let's get you home."

Gryffine took Luc's hand, and a surge of energy caught her breath as he helped her rise. A jolt had taken him also, shuddering him from head to heels, and his breath caught but his movements did not falter. They rose through shadows to moonlight, and at last she could see Luc's eyes, shining like opalescent silver. His breath curled around her, surging up Gryffine's spine, easing into her mind through the base of her skull. Gryffine rested back upon the trunk of the massive oak, trying to catch her own breath and failing.

Luc Tournet gazed at her, transfixed for a moment, then stepped forward, coming close so their breath mingled, one hand still holding hers, but the other up around her waist as if they were dancing. So carefully he held himself away, only breathing Gryffine in by the light of the moon, eyes closed with rapture upon his face. At last, they opened, and Gryffine felt herself pulled under, deep into his currents.

"You feel me, as I feel you..." Luc Tournet murmured. "This. Our breath."

"Yes. I do." Gryffine knew exactly what he meant.

Luc's fingers strayed to her chest, lingering over her heart, touching the skin beneath the open collar of her cream silk shirt gently. His work-calloused touch riveted Gryffine, and his breath followed his touch, curling through his own fingers and caressing her skin with deep desire.

"I almost broke, this afternoon," Luc whispered, his lips so very near and yet not. "I almost gathered you into my arms, to kiss you and take you as mine in one, utterly perfect moment... when you came to the door... and I felt your breath... pulling me, *needing* me..." he sighed, a shiver racing over his tall, lean frame. "I knew... I knew I had found you..."

"If I kiss you, you'll die," Gryffine whispered.

Luc gave the saddest laugh she had ever heard. "Yes. And if I kiss you, *you'll* die. And if we kiss each other…what a jolly pair are we?"

Gryffine had no answer. But as she stood there, she felt a sense of rightness, like some part of herself long-lost but yearned for was suddenly near. And though she was far from complete, she felt herself settle deeply into the mystery that breathed around them and curled between them both, their joined breath curling out, tasting each other as if they were truly locked with lips and tongue and heart. And as Luc's fingers trailed over Gryffine's skin, and his breath followed, the bliss of the moment rolled on and on, a sweet yearning between them that no other pleasure could possibly match.

* * *

At last, it was Luc who broke the moment, pulling Gryffine gently away from the oak by the hand, guiding her to the gravel path beneath the nearly-full summer moon. They strolled in silence, not heading back to the manse, though Gryffine was certain Jessup now waited for her at this very late hour. It was a vague ache in her heart, to be out walking hand-in-hand beneath the moonlight with this strange creature when Jessup was there, creating a cozy and trustworthy warmth in their restored home. But another part of Gryffine felt complete from the breath curling all around her, from the strange man walking by her side, and from the occasional glance of his perfect sapphire eyes.

"So…" Luc's tone was polite but with an undercurrent of extreme interest. "Do you know what we are? The breath… what it is?"

Gryffine actually laughed. "No! I thought you might. I thought perhaps you were the answer to all my questions."

Luc gave a rueful half-smile in the moonlight, just a brief twitch of the lips. "Hardly. I have so many questions of my own… and never any answers."

They strolled for a time along the crushed-gravel path, meandering from gaslight to gaslight like moths without destination, until Luc Tournet spoke again, his voice low and confidential. "So how old were you? When it… happened."

Gryffine glanced over, feeling strangely at ease trusting Luc with the most intimate things. "I was thirteen. I killed my father."

"I killed my mother. I was three." Luc's voice was nearly expressionless, polite and calm. He gazed upwards, admiring the moon, its pale light bathing him in night's solace and making his alabaster skin luminous.

"Three years old... just like the Boy and the Bones..." Gryffine's anguished whisper died out to the moonlight, but she felt Luc shiver, and he had to halt a moment, eyes slipping closed.

"Don't do that." Luc Tournet murmured, keeping his eyes shut and shoulders immaculately square. He swallowed and let out a carefully-measured breath. "Don't whisper like that. Not with such passion. I can't stand it. Just keep your voice neutral, like we are having a pleasant chat, and keep your breath loose and easy. That's the only way..."

Gryffine startled, realizing at last just how much her breath affected this man, then took up a more neutral, carefully casual tone. "You can feel my emotions?"

"As you can feel mine. Through the breath. And it *devastates* me." As if to demonstrate, Luc's whisper was suddenly rolling around Gryffine like waves, pulling her from the shallows and out to the depths, ripping her from safety and into a vast ocean of bliss and passion where all she could do was drown in his kiss. She was lost in it, she was drowning, she was not herself as her body opened wide to breathe him in, to surrender to that vast, needful pull.

Gryffine's knees buckled, and she caught herself upon Luc's arm.

"I see your point," Gryffine stammered after a moment, after she had mastered herself.

Luc opened his eyes, and the anguish in their blue depths was dire. "It's not so bad when you're further away. But close like this," his presence intensified as he took a deep breath, and Gryffine felt its sudden, unstoppable pull. She tightened her grip upon Luc's arm to keep from collapsing completely to its demand.

"You see..." Luc murmured, his voice carefully-controlled once more.

Gryffine nodded, controlling her own breath carefully, trying not to let her passion master her, trying to not let it affect Luc Tournet. "I do. Have you ever met anyone else like us?"

"Like us?" Luc glanced at her sidelong, and the small, relieved smile wisped over his face again. "I thought I was the only one in the world cursed with this until I met you. Just today." He turned to face her then, twining his long, calloused carpenter's fingers in hers. "I thought I was *alone*. All alone, Gryffine."

"So did I."

The silence stretched between them, thick and fluid, their mingled breath controlled now but surging between them both anyways, ebbing and flowing, lifting and settling, gathering and receding. Gryffine closed her eyes, breathing slowly, feeling Luc's breath like a thousand touches of silk, wrapping her, moving her, loving her in the darkness beneath the moon.

"I should take you home." Luc murmured.

Gryffine nodded, eyes still closed. "Perhaps that would be best."

Another moment stretched, her fingers lightly twined in his, suddenly so perfect.

"May I see you again?" Luc's tone was careful, neutral, but Gryffine could feel the desire that thrummed through him upon his breath. It wound his breath closer, seeking deeper places than skin.

And Gryffine wanted it, badly.

"Perhaps that's not a good idea," Gryffine breathed, and suddenly Luc shuddered.

"Not when you say it like that." He shivered again, and Gryffine felt how Luc's body pulled closer to hers, felt that implacable cord thicken and pull them closer. "Maybe I really *should* take you home."

"Have you ever indulged it, Luc?" Gryffine opened her eyes, needing to know.

"What?" His eyes had also been closed, but now they snapped open, deeply concerned. "It would kill you, Gryffine. Or it would kill me. We can't *possibly* indulge this."

"No, but have you... indulged with anyone else?"

Luc's sapphire eyes were sad. "Once. I killed her. It nearly drove me mad. Carpentry... was the only way I could take my mind off what I'd done. I've never tried again. Focus is my only option now. My only restraint."

"But what if you could... help people?" Gryffine pressed.

"*Help* people?" Luc gazed at her oddly, "you mean by killing them? What sort of person would willfully kill another?"

"I have," Gryffine murmured. "When they were dying and in pain. When they asked for it."

"*Asked* for it?" He gave another odd glance, his judgment on the subject plain. "Who would ever ask for such a thing?"

"Some do." Gryffine fidgeted suddenly, feeling like she had done wrong to give those blissful deaths, feeling judged and condemned by Luc's sapphire eyes in the moonlight.

Luc stared a moment, and Gryffine could feel his incredulousness and his horror in his breath where it sharpened upon her like needles. "Would they have asked had you not been there?" Luc murmured at last. "Regular people feel our breath too, Gryffine. They feel it enough, though they don't know quite what they feel, not like you and I do.

Those people you killed in supposed mercy, would they have asked to die, would they have asked you to kill them with your breath, with that beautiful pull of yours, had you not been there?"

Gryffine blinked, a sudden deep worry tarnishing her bliss and writhing in her guts, twisting deep and making her feel miserable. "I don't know…"

Luc stepped closer, and Gryffine could feel his presence, undeniable. And suddenly, the needles of his judgment turned to desire, deep and sensual. His breath caressed along Gryffine's skin, his breath dove through her lips and wrapped her close like an embrace, and Gryffine swooned.

"The number of women, and men," Luc murmured as he caught her about the waist, using the full passion of his breath now, "who have asked to *be* with me, to kiss me, is far too many, Gryffine. When they step near us, they ask to die and they know it not. They *feel* this, what you feel now. Desire. Need. Passion. *Helplessness* before it's pull. They seek their very deaths, all to kiss us just once, heedless of anything else. I know that. You should. How many people meet you and suddenly want to touch you? To kiss your cheek or your hand? Brighten when you are near? I'd wager many. It's not looks, Gryffine, though you are a lovely woman. It's *this*. Whatever we have. This curse has a draw that anyone can feel. And they do. Dangerously."

Gryffine was helpless in Luc's arms, her body surrendering with languor and desperation for his kiss. But her mind churned, thinking back to all the bright young men she'd met who suddenly asked for her presence, for an evening walk, who pressed too close and had boldly snuck in for a kiss. She'd not duped herself into thinking it was mere masculine roguishness, or that she was beautiful enough to warrant rash behavior from men. The truth was, Gryffine had tempted it, used her breath when she wanted to, like the night she'd met Jessup, like Luc was doing to her now. And there were too many, far too many who had felt her breath's pull and wanted it.

Gryffine's heart sank even as her body ached in Luc's arms, and then her belly clenched in woe, thinking about those lives she'd taken at the hospital. Wondering, if they would have chosen to live had she not been there, another day, another week, another month. She could see the rapture again in their eyes as they felt her breath curl around them, the old woman and the young man.

And Gryffine wondered, suddenly, if she had done them a terrible wrong.

Luc saw her realize it, and slowly nodded, and he carefully drew his breath away, releasing Gryffine from its relentless pull, and also from his arms at the same time, though he shuddered to deny it.

"And now the draw of our breath pulls the both of us the same way, but more so. Seeking our deaths. Come." Luc Tournet offered his arm again, his breath and his passion carefully locked inside once more, strengthened by a lifetime's worth of denial. "Let's get you home."

* * *

Jessup was beside himself by the time Gryffine alighted upon the porch stairs. As if he'd been waiting, listening intently for her very footstep, Jessup was suddenly at the door, flinging it wide and gathering her into his arms with a crushing embrace. Luc had left her beyond the edge of the wrought-iron fence, after Gryffine had mentioned it might be best. He hadn't queried her, and hadn't let himself betray any emotion at their leave-taking, which had been almost stiff and sudden after such an intimate night. And now Gryffine felt guilt as Jessup embraced her, his warm goodness flowing from every pore to envelop her like fresh-baked bread.

"Gryffine! Gods of the Dark, where have you been?! When I got here tonight, the manse was lit like you were home, but I looked everywhere! I called, I even went down to the sepulcher, but you were gone! I thought of all the worst things... I was about to run for Marnet to form a search... Gods... are you alright?" Jessup pressed her face tenderly between his hands. "You've been crying! What's happened?"

Gryffine smiled, her heart leaping to his concern like a well-trained hound. Jessup's warmth and normalcy flowed through her, and Gryffine wrapped her arms about his lean-muscled frame, laying her head upon his chest. "I'm fine. I was just a little upset. I went out for a long walk in the park."

"So late," Jessup turned, guiding her inside and shutting the heavy door of the manse behind them. "The park is dangerous this late."

"Not really. I hid behind an oak tree."

Once they were in the warmth and bright gaslight of the hall, Jessup eyed her more studiously, his dark eyes keen and his long-fingered hands gentle as they smoothed over her shoulders. "Did something happen?"

Gryffine smiled weakly. "The man Rennet hired to do the carpentry assessed the situation and decided it was beyond him. He's declined. Rennet has to wait two weeks for his other man to take the contract for the parlor. I was upset, that's all."

Guilt gnawed its way through Gryffine's belly as Jessup kissed her temple. "Are you hungry? I brought a few things from the bar." He led her to the kitchen, where a cheery spread of crusty bread, herbed butter and cheese, homemade beef stew and a lovely fresh salad of summer greens sat upon the table. Gryffine found she was actually hungry for Marnet's savories, and tucked in once she was seated. She ate with relish, partly because the food was good, and partly to avoid eye contact with Jessup.

Jessup ate along with her, seemingly mollified by her explanation, though he was still eyeing her curiously. "So tell me about this man who turned down our contract today. Rennet says the fellow is vastly odd."

Gryffine nearly choked, and it was all she could do to not let her eyes flinch up guiltily. "He seemed like he knew what he was doing, and took his time about the inspection and the measurements. But he had a taciturn demeanor, and I heard from Rennet later that he'd not take the work. He's left all his inspections and measurements with Rennet, though, so that part is done at least."

"Huh." Jessup poured a cup of coffee from the small press upon the table, then raised his dark eyebrows. Gryffine declined with a small shake of her head. Only Jessup seemed unaffected by coffee near midnight, and could fall asleep immediately afterwards no matter how much he drank. Jessup sat back with his cup to hand, sipping his black coffee, his dark eyes thoughtful. "Rennet seemed to think he could do the job. Rennet's almost never wrong."

Gryffine shrugged, breaking off a piece of crusty bread. "Maybe he doesn't have experience with this type of manse."

"Maybe." Jessup knit his brows, then sighed. "Well, there's nothing for it. We'll have to wait. What do you want to do for two weeks?"

"Rennet's sending men tomorrow to move the cage from the back porch. And place the urns."

"Oh! That's right!" Jessup grinned suddenly. "I talked Freder and Aeshe's cousin Gui into helping. Between the four of us, we can get that damnable thing moved. It's lovely in a strange way, but better to get it off the porch and in where it belongs."

"Jessup?"

"Hmm?" He sat up, his dark eyes attentive, coffee to hand. "Yes?"

"Why do you think the coffin's there? And should we actually move it?"

Jessup's dark eyebrows knit, and he sipped. "You know, I was thinking about that myself." He grinned, flashing his very white teeth. "It's not everyday one has a Gypsun tale right in the yard. That little day-flower hasn't wilted a bit. They're usually gone by highsummer. But that one's been a hearty little thing. Maybe it's waiting for someone to touch it and get cursed." Jessup waggled his dark eyebrows at Gryffine and grinned over his coffeecup.

Gryffine laughed at his infectious good humor despite her own dour mood. "Be serious! What if it has some significance, or it's an omen of some kind?"

Jessup shrugged and sipped his coffee, then stuck a finger in the herbed butter and sucked it thoughtfully. "I suppose. I've never really been one for superstition, but since I met you... anything goes, I guess. You want me to invite Aeshe over tomorrow when we unbolt the thing? See if she or Emlohaine sense anything?"

Gryffine shook her head, taking up a forkful of greens. "That's not necessary. I'd hate to keep her from her shop."

Jessup grinned and took up another fingerful of butter, his favorite foodstuff. "Aeshe lives for this kind of thing. Solving Gypsun mysteries and otherworldy conundrums. Channeling Emlohaine is difficult for her, but she loves what she does anyway."

"You never told me about Emlohaine, about what she can do."

Jessup shrugged, and his face took on a serious cast as he had another fingerful of butter. "Aeshe is an odd one. We met back when we were children. My grammère and her mentor were friends. Two grumpy old Fatereaders, watching lives spin out in the cards and never living it themselves. But grammère was never a public practitioner."

"Did Aeshe's mentor have a channeling gift?"

"Oh, no." Jessup shook his head. "Aeshe's unique. My people have stories about that kind of thing, but apparently it's not been seen in centuries. At least, not around here."

"What *is* Emlohaine, exactly?" Gryffine leaned over the table on her elbows, intrigued, her supper forgotten and her troubles with Luc Tournet pushed to the back of her mind now with this vastly interesting conversation.

Jessup grinned, mysterious. "You want the full story, or the proper one?"

Gryffine lifted an eyebrow. "The full story."

Jessup grinned wider. "Don't tell Aeshe I'm telling you all this, she would actually kill me. Probably. Do you know why she turned down all the nice young men at our party?" Jessup grinned wider, then sipped his coffee.

Gryffine blinked, starting to see the pattern. "Because of Emlohaine."

Jessup nodded with a congratulatory salute of his coffeecup.

"They're lovers. Emlohaine has a number of physical effects upon Aeshe. When he channels through her to speak to someone else, it causes severe nausea and headaches, and sometimes a palsy, which lays her up for days. But when it's just the two of them conversing internally..." Jessup shrugged, still grinning, except now his grin was salacious. "She's described the sensations to me. It's nothing short of scandalous."

"So is he a demon, then?" Gryffine pressed, wondering about her and Luc's gifts, wondering if some kind of demon within the two of them could cause such physical effects, like Aeshe's Emlohaine.

Jessup shrugged noncommittally. "Maybe. It's a force we don't understand, certainly. Her own mentor didn't understand it. For Aeshe, it has benefits and drawbacks both. It keeps her from taking a normal man, that's for sure."

"Would Emlohaine be jealous?"

"Would? Is. Very. He doesn't punish her for taking a lover, but from how she tells it, he sulks. He won't come when she tries to call him. He has perspective, but can be quite childish, or so it seems." Jessup shrugged. "But Aeshe seems perfectly content with it. It's as if he... completes her. She says she wants for nothing when he is near, speaking only to her. As ludicrous as it sounds... when she tells it, it's almost romantic."

Jessup reached a hand out across the table, and Gryffine slid her fingers closer so they could touch. It was soothing to touch him, like a balm for the tumult of her day, and a part of Gryffine sighed in relief, feeling Jessup's sturdy hand ready to accept her, no matter what.

"Jessup?"

"Yes?"

"I haven't been entirely truthful about today."

He nodded his head slowly, his dark eyes keen and curious about her withholding, but not angry. "I figured. I rarely see you so taciturn, and such a minor thing as a construction delay was a pretty weak excuse for red-rimmed eyes and a puffy face."

Gryffine enjoyed holding Jessup's hand across the table, the trust that was in it, and hoped she wasn't about to shatter everything they had together. "I took another life today."

Jessup nodded but said nothing, merely stroked his thumb over her fingers, allowing her to continue.

"He was a young man. Dying of a cancer of some kind. He was angry, bitter that his life was so short, that there was nothing left to him but misery and pain. Angry that his family thought it a disgrace. He thought he was beyond loving."

Jessup nodded again, saying nothing but simply hearing her out. "I kissed him, Jess. I gave him release. But when I kiss... Jessup... I feel *love* for them. It's a pure love, something infinitely beautiful, and merciful. Like I see every facet of what lies beneath the skin and the bones, and I love them. Everything they are. The light, the energy, the hopes and fears, the dreams and failures. It's beautiful."

Jessup took a deep breath, then sighed. "Do you want me to be jealous?"

Gryffine shrugged. "I don't know. Are you?"

His smile was wry. "A bit. I can't kiss you and they can. I can't make love to you or fulfill you in that way, and they can. I think any reasonable man would be jealous. It's a satisfaction we can never have together, and that rankles." Jessups leaned forward, taking her hand between both of his, pressing them together, sturdy, strong. "Gryffine. I love you. I know you know that, but ... I really do. All my life, I feel like I've been waiting for something, for someone. And then you came. And now... even though it's not easy or simple... I'm willing to try. No matter what."

"No matter what?" Hope rose in Gryffine's heart, but her confessions were not yet complete.

Jessup nodded. "No matter what. I'm not such a callous cur as to deny you your pleasure. If you feel that love when you kiss them, the dying ones...then you should."

"Even if that love might be something false generated by my breath?"

Jessup paused, frowning. "What do you mean?"

"I mean... what if my breath has some physical effect on them?" Gryffine murmured, voicing all the concerns aroused by Luc Tournet tonight, and by his judgment. "What if my breath pulls them... to *want* their death. Like you. When you want me to come near, to kiss you and die in one moment of utter bliss. What if my very presence causes people to *want* to die, who otherwise might wish to live, were I not around? What if... those people I killed... might have wanted another day?"

Jessup was still frowning, and his frown had deepened, his dark eyes concerned. "One, two days, what does it matter, Gryffine? They were dying and they knew it and they wished release. So what if it was a day or three early? And besides, I don't think the love I bear for you is generated by your *breath*, Gryffine. Your breath has a pull, that's undeniable, certainly... but my love is my own. I love you for who you are. Not because you make me shiver." Jessup grinned a little, then, his white smile debonair. "But that's nice, too."

Gryffine's heart was broken open wide by his honesty. "You truly love me?"

Jessup grinned wider, his dark eyes bright and merry. "I said I did, didn't I? We Gypsun know the best kind of love when it comes. It's in all the tales, you see." But his fingers were kind and they didn't tease, smoothing over Gryffine's hands and pressing them close. It bolstered her courage, and she sidled nearer to the topic she truly wished to discuss. And Jessup was so comforting, his hands so warm, his white smile so bright in his caramel skin and his dark eyes so loving, that Gryffine bared her utter vulnerability.

And spoke the truth, the one she truly feared. "I met a man today."

Jessup sobered at her tone, and his smile faded. "Not the dying one?"

Gryffine shook her head, quailing inside but needing to tell him. "No. A different man. One who shares my gift. The breath, the death, the curse… all of it… he's just like me."

Jessup took a long, slow breath and let it out just as slowly through carefully pursed lips. His dark eyes had closed from loving to unreadable. "And?"

Gryffine's mouth was dry. "It's hard to explain."

Jessup gave her a sober look, and it was daunting. "You have to give me more than that, Gryffine. Was that why you were at the park so long?"

Gryffine nodded, her heart gripping her chest with fear.

Jessup took a long breath again, then nodded. "I knew there was something different about you. Who is he?" Jessup gave her a glance like a hawk, dark eyes glimmering with ferocity but not violent. "Should I be jealous?"

Gryffine swallowed. Her breath could barely leave her lips. "I don't know."

Jessup pulled his hands away, and Gryffine felt them go with a lurch in her heart, the world chill all around her as Jessup retracted his love and his comfort. Jessup sat back, rubbing his palms over his face and stubble, scrubbing a hand through his dark curls.

"*Morte lucentie.*" His eyes were dark, indeed. "Is this what Aeshe warned you about?"

Gryffine blinked back tears. "Maybe."

"Your Completion? The one that will Ruin you? And us?" His words were sharp and angry, hurt.

Gryffine's tears fell. "Maybe," she whispered to the tabletop, unable to meet Jessup's eyes anymore. A long silence stretched at the table as tears continued to stream down Gryffine's cheeks. She couldn't stop them, and the longer the silence grew between her and Jessup, the more her heart twisted, vile and bitter that she had met Luc Tournet at all. Gryffine's heart clenched, and a sob escaped her lips, and then she covered her mouth with her hand and cried all the harder for her silence, trying to stop the breath and her anguish from touching the silent Jessup. But at last, Jessup heaved a great sigh, then stood, walking behind Gryffine's chair and leaning over to wrap his arms about her shoulders and nuzzle her cheek.

"Hey... we can weather this... Don't cry like that...*lucentie listo*, Gryffine. Don't cry like that. Gods, it breaks my heart..."

She stood suddenly, and she was wrapped in Jessup's arms, safe and warm once again. Gryffine let her sobs go, shuddering out every misery to his calm comfort, sobbing out the schism and pain and doubt so uproariously burning within her at the tumultuous day. Jessup walked her slowly upstairs to her bedroom, and sat her down upon the cushions at the hearth as he kindled a fire, more for comfort than to heat the room in the balmy summer night.

Gryffine burrowed into his shoulder, and he smoothed her ebony locks.

"Want to tell me about it?" Jessup murmured, drawing her close and leaning his cheek on her temple.

Gryffine shook her head. "Not really, but I must. I feel *awful*, Jessup! Like I'm ruining everything we have, everything I value, everything I want! Everything we've built in the past few months, everything I've ever wanted. But he *knows*, Jessup. He *knows* what it's like, what I am, the terror, the heartache, the woe and the denial. He knows me, inside and out... And it's frightening. And I crave it. It satisfies something... deep within me."

Jessup brushed a lock of ebony hair carefully away from her face. "Like part of you that was separated... made whole."

Gryffine swallowed, she, too, remembering Aeshe's words, then hugged Jessup closer. "What am I going to do? It's like being drowned, Jessup. And I keep going under and under, over and over, and the only breath I can take will be the breath that he takes from me. And then I'll *die*. I'm craving my own undoing, Jess..."

Jessup was silent a long moment, just holding Gryffine close and stroking her curls. And then at last, he sighed, and chuckled sadly, then kissed the top of her head. "Now you know how it feels to be me." Silence stretched between them, but then Jessup petted her hair again, and rubbed her neck.

"Do you love me, Gryffine?"

Gryffine clutched Jessup closer, feeling her love for this kind, patient, affectionate, and joyous man surge through her very soul. "Yes. With *everything* I am! I love you and I want you with all my heart. I've never wanted something so beautiful as you are to me. When we're together... I feel safe. And home. For the first time in my life, Jessup, I *feel* like I'm home."

Gryffine felt Jessup nod, and a soft sigh escaped his lips. "Then we can figure this out."

If she could have, Gryffine would have kissed him for those words.

* * *

Jessup was cuddling her, naked in the bed. The fire had burned down, and a cool breeze had finally come in through the open window, moving a fresh night air through the room at last. Gryffine was exhausted, her nose to Jessup's ribs and her body half-draped over his as his arm snugged her close, his long fingers tracing idle patterns up and down her spine.

"So, he's got some magic breath that pulls you just like I get pulled to you?"

Gryffine smiled a little to hear Jessup using humor to make light of the situation, knowing that they would be alright now, come what may, the danger of losing their happy life together passed. "It's not magic breath. It's just what we are, how our breath feels to others, like a wind, or water, wrapping around you and pulling at you."

Jessup nodded, tracing his fingers over her ribs now. "Well, that's accurate. That's what I feel around you. So you feel him the same way?"

Gryffine nodded. "Yes, but he also feels me that way. Just like you do."

"Interesting."

Gryffine rose to her elbows to look at him. "How can you be so calm about all this?"

Jessup grinned, then traced his hand down to palm her bare buttock. "Because *I'm* in your bed, and he is not. Is he?"

Gryffine smiled, and Jessup grinned wider, and at last she laughed. "No."

"Do you want him to be?"

"We'd kill each other!"

"So there." Jessup nodded decisively. "Unless you're suicidal, we've got that going for us."

Gryffine raised her eyebrows. "Don't make fun!"

"I'm not." Jessup's hand traced over her back again. "Don't mistake me, I'm jealous as the Beast in the Inferno, Gryffine. But I'm *trying* to figure this out. Gifts are strange things, and just because you have one that affects you physically doesn't mean that's exactly what you want. *Tell* me what you want."

Gryffine rubbed her nakedness over her beloved man, nuzzling close. "This. You. Us. Security, a home, a community of friends I can call family. A place to bring them all, to fill my heart with light and laughter and music. To have Rollows and the joys of Life every day of the year. Right here. Right now. With you."

Jessup nuzzled her nose. "Good. Those are all things I want also. Sex is good, Gryffine, but it's not everything. We're not defined by our animal pleasures. And you're not defined by your Gift."

"Am I not?" The thought had never really occurred to her before, and Gryffine found herself suddenly confused, pondering the possibility that she was not her curse.

"No," Jessup confirmed. "If you were... you'd be in *his* arms right now, instead of mine."

Gryffine cocked her head, mulling that over. It was true, a part of her still wanted Luc and his powerful draw, but the fortress of home she had with Jessup had turned back those mighty waters, until they beat futilely upon the stone, a distant rumble in the night. She sighed, laying back down upon Jessup's lean length. "You're right."

"I know I am."

She slapped his stomach lightly, and he chuckled. "Let's get some sleep. We've got to move that cage in the morning, and damned if I'm going to do that on zero hours of sleep two nights in a row."

Jessup yawned, and Gryffine caught that yawn just after. She snuggled down, and he pulled the cream duvet up over them both. Gryffine still felt Luc Tournet, a thread of connection far off in the night, but Jessup was near and warm and their home was beautiful by the fire's light. Gryffine gazed around her once-dark room, noting all the rich reds, yellows, and purples, her walls and wainscoting now painted a buttery white to smooth it all together. Greenery sat in pots about the room, softening the natural iron and hardwoods. Lanterns in red and white and purple were strung high above, fashioned into a chandelier, and Gryffine smiled.

"It looks like Rollows in here."

Jessup blinked up. "It does. We should have masques."

"Mine is still behind the bookcase."

"Your silk lace masque? From all those years ago? Mmm." Jessup smiled with eyes closed now, already halfway to sleep. "Get it out tomorrow. I want you to put it on… so I can do dirty things to you..."

Gryffine nuzzled his chest. "I would do anything to keep you." But she realized that Jessup had dropped off to sleep already, his breathing deep and slow, a twitch passing through his long lean body in preparation for dreams. Smiling, Gryffine breathed him in, tasting his warm hearth scent. And brushed gently into sleep, his sweetness upon her lips.

***

CHAPTER 10

Gryffine and Jessup were already breakfasted and dressed by the time the bell-pull rang. In Rennet's distinctive manner, the bell was rung not once but thrice in quick succession, as if the Velkman couldn't be bothered to wait for anything. Gryffine listened from the kitchen where she was finishing the last of the dishes as Jessup strode down the hallway and opened the door, and soon the merry sounds of Rennet's booming baritone were cascading down the hall, followed by the more raucous tones of Jessup's comrade Freder. Gryffine hastily piled the rest of the dishes in the soapy water to soak, then dried her hands with a towel and shucked her apron to the counter. She primped her pins and curls as she stepped out of the kitchen, and soon was in the bustling hall, getting scooped up in a bear hug by tall, enthusiastic Freder.

Freder squished her bones until Gryffine peeped in protest like a bird, then he shook her about some for good measure while growling in her neck like a bear until Gryffine giggled at his completely uncouth manner. "Gryffin! Magical beauty! We mighty heroes have come to save your porch from that wretched lump of iron at last!"

Freder let her go with a belly laugh, and Gryffine had to straighten her curls again as she turned to greet the much more polite Gui, cousin to Aeshe. He extended a hand like a gentleman, flushing scarlet at Freder's impropriety. "Gryffine. Good to see you again. Fantastic party the other night."

Gryffine took his hand, and he stepped forward quickly to give her cheek a kiss in the Gypsun manner, then flushed scarlet again and hastily let her go, glancing sidelong at Jessup. But Jessup was already in conversation with Rennet, and had seemingly missed all the antics of his comrades, though his half-turned posture told Gryffine otherwise. Jessup was alert this morning, careful in his own way and monitoring men's interactions with Gryffine. And Jessup reached out after Gui's greeting to place a possessive hand at Gryffine's back, though his conversation with Rennet didn't miss a beat.

"So!" Rennet turned to Gryffine. "Let's see this iron monster. We've already picked up the flower urns, they're waiting in the furniture cab

127

out front. The horses have everything they need to wait the morning until this is all done. Freder has the bolt-cutter," Freder hefted a huge contraption of iron from where it leaned against the hall wainscoting, then grinned as Rennet continued, "and I have the know-how." He gestured down the hall as if he owned the manse. "Let's go!"

The little party tromped down the hall past the front room, the drawing-room, and sitting-parlor, and then through the kitchen, and out the back door to the porch, led by Rennet. The wrought-iron fence around the coffin had a gate that had recently been cleaned along with the rest of the fence, and the ancient padlock to it all had already been snipped off. Rennet entered first, followed by Jessup and then Freder and Gui, and Rennet once again took to his knees upon the stone of the porch, inspecting each bolt, then stood and brushed himself off.

"Well," Rennet turned to Freder, "They're not rusted. Damn thing's hale as hale can be. You'll have a time of it, my boy. Get to it. This corner first," he pointed to a spot beneath the eaves. "They're looser."

Well-muscled Freder set to, stripping of his tan waistcoat and white shirt first with a blithe grin and a waggle of his eyebrows at Gryffine. Then he wedged the flat end of the bolt cutter beneath the first bolt, and levered his entire body weight down upon it so the pincers gripped. The whole thing groaned, and then there was a grinding scream as metal bit metal, and suddenly the bolt-cutter chomped through. Freder staggered, cussed and grinned, then went to the next one. In a few minutes he had all the bolts cut, and the iron cage of the coffin wrenched sideways with the last one. Freder caught himself from falling once again, but stood staring down at his feet on the far side of the coffin, the bolt-cutter hanging from one idle hand.

"Hey! You should see this!" Freder called, motioning with his unencumbered hand.

Everyone shuffled around the far side of the massive wrought-iron beast, and Gryffine followed, blinking in surprise at the sliver of dark emptiness exposed now beneath the edge of the dislodged coffin.

"Well!" Rennet was distinctly pleased, his plethoric face beaming. "You don't see many of these! Even these old Mortuary Manses don't generally have such secrets! Everyone take this side and push on three, but mind the hole! No broken ankles! One, two, three!"

They all heaved, even Gryffine applying her weight to the edges of the wrought-iron behemoth, and with a series of groans the coffin slid over the newly-cleaned porch stones towards the railing. Daylight flooded down into a dark hole beneath, thick with dust that had wormed its way beneath the iron-floored coffin after all these years. A puff of disturbed dust rose through the humid summer air, and Gryffine raised a hand to cover her mouth and nose before it thinned away on the light morning breeze.

The hole in the porch-stones beneath was not large, nor was it terribly deep, but in the bottom of it sat ancient bones in a tattered shroud, surrounded by bits of this and that which might once have been precious to the one entombed within. Fascinated, Gryffine sank to her knees on the porch-stones, reaching in to run a finger over the tarnished metal of what looked like a round silver locket resting upon the corpse's dry breastbone. It sang to her, this locket, and as Gryffine touched it, she suddenly had the sensation of a light wind sigh over her entire body, not unlike an ocean breeze at high summer tides. But none of the dust upon the bones stirred further, and Gryffine drew her hand away, perplexed at their discovery and by what she'd just felt.

She wondered if Luc Tournet were nearby.

"Well!" Rennet's tones were properly respectable, and utterly impressed. "That's surely a surprise. I wonder why this poor fellow was down here, rather than in his own coffin."

"She hid him," Gryffine murmured, before she knew she was even going to speak. But know it she did, with a certainty that wracked her bones. Gryffine suddenly felt terrible for the wretched man in the hole, for a man she somehow knew he had been. Just as she knew that the grit in the coffin above had once been a woman. A strange dizziness came over Gryffine, as if she twirled with her arms extended upon a high mountain, and to hide it, Gryffine leaned in again, her fingers stroking over the tarnished silver locket upon the man's breastbone.

"They were lovers. Him, and her..."

Gryffine nodded at the wrought-iron coffin, but her eyes remained in the hole, roving over the scattered possessions entombed with the shrouded man, with more and more certainty flooding her as her dizziness and disorientation increased. She saw something that had once been a leather-bound book, and knew it was a journal. She saw a tattered box, and knew that within were two strings of pearls, one bound into a choker with a teardrop pearl in the center, the other a short bracelet. A sapphire gold ring graced one of the man's desiccated fingers, and she knew it had been a gift from his lover in the wrought-iron cage above. Tatters of an embroidered pillow lay beneath his head, and the remnants of the shroud had been lovingly embroidered also, and Gryffine knew it was done by his lover's careful fingers. Other things there were, mementos of their secret relationship, a blue-glazed ceramic bowl, a hand-wrought wooden pipe with fanciful carvings, a sachet long moth-eaten and devoid of scent, but which had once been lavender they had picked together.

Carefully, Gryffine reached in and unclasped the silver-etched locket to open it. Within were two enameled engravings, one of a stunningly handsome man, pale as the luminous moon, sapphire eyes perfect and serene. And the other was of a woman with dark ringlets and pink cheeks, her pale green eyes level and cool.

"She looks like you."

Rennet was at Gryffine's elbow, sitting upon his knees and leaning over, peering in. "Hmm. He looks like that carpenter fellow who abandoned us yesterday! The Luc Tournet. Fascinating. Well, Madamme Gryffine! This *is* a new development. Perhaps something for the Julis historical society? We could have everything gently catalogued, and this fellows' own coffin made so he can go in the sepulcher with the rest. You think they were lovers? Fascinating. Buried on the porch, right on top of each other, and his grave a secret! Perhaps there's room for two coffins side-by-side down there somewhere…"

Gryffine left the locket open, but sat back upon her heels. The dizziness had decreased, but she still felt strange, as if the wind had taken her mind far away, and she sat now in limbo, part of her with her fellows upon the porch, and part beyond time.

"No…" Gryffine spoke slowly, and it was with great effort that she'd spoken at all. "They should have been buried together in the first place. Two halves of a whole." She reached out again, brushing her fingers over the dead man's grinning, desiccated lips, her certainty growing and growing, devouring her. "Put him in the coffin with her remains. All of it. Then put it all in the sepulcher."

Gryffine rose, gazing down upon the open tomb from a terrible height, feeling sick to her stomach. Something crowded her mind, something dire, something that pressed forward, wanting to come through. Gryffine's breath sped as that feeling pressed, like hands compressing her skull and ribcage now, strong and insistent. Gryffine put a hand to her head and the other to her chest, but the pressure continued, squeezing her, burrowing into her, and yet somehow also expanding from the inside out. She felt sick. She felt she was going to be sick, bile rising to her throat from that infernal pressure, from feeling it twist its way into her.

Her head lanced suddenly, and her world tilted dangerously. Gryffine turned away from the tomb, from his bones, reeling and disoriented, not wanting to watch his death, yet again.

One stab.

But her brother had always known how best to kill a man.

One deep lunge had been all it took during their duel.

One deep lunge to the belly.

And then Marisseaux had been bleeding out beneath her hands upon the grass, and Duriant threw down his sword in disgust and turned away. Marisseaux had never been a fighter, not even when they were children. But he fought against her that day, imploring her with his final breath and those perfect sapphire eyes to not kiss him, to not end his life in mercy.

To not take her own in despair.

And so he had died. And all she'd kissed was a cooling corpse, her perfect moment of mutual bliss, planned between the two of them since they were children, stolen away forever. Her heart hardened, her fingers clenched, and the fury rose again. Gryffine bent, picking up her brother's shed sword from the grass, still slick with blood. Her brother Duriant heard her, turned as she lunged, his dark eyes full of surprise. And then filled with pain as she struck home, piercing him right through the heart.

Alea had always been a faster swordswoman than her brother Duriant, though he was the stronger.

"Gryffine! Dark's love, girl!"

Some part of her mind vaguely registered Rennet.

Gryffine's knees buckled and she collapsed to the bloody grass, but the grass was porch-stone, and the dark-haired man fallen before her was strange, collapsed upon the porch and gasping, holding his chest in shock and still very much alive, his dark eyes wide with surprise and alarm.

Gryffine gazed at the sword in her hand, and found it was a heavy iron bolt-cutter.

She dropped it.

And then both hands went to cover her face, and Alea was sobbing, sobbing, sobbing.

* * *

Alea accepted the mug full of hot beverage, but there was no solace in it for her, and she did not drink. A blanket had been thrown over her shoulders, and she knew she was still in the garden, laying back in a yard-chaise. Her feet were up on a stool and bare, and dark-eyed Duriant sat before her, rubbing one foot gently, deep and slow, his eyes full of concern and darting to the redheaded fellow now and then. Alea's gaze swung from him, out over the garden, seeing the height of its summer bloom. That was strange. It was autumn, wasn't it? The leaves had already turned, hadn't they? The oaks towering over the meadow had been golden and brown, the leaves half-fallen, and Oblenite had been upon its First Day. Hadn't it? Alea gazed out towards the meadow and frowned. When had houses been built so close to the farmstead? She gazed up at the gables of the house, frowning that it was painted white and yellow and red.

She recalled it a deep green and a tawny brown.

"Who painted the house so bright?" Alea murmured, and absently sipped her beverage. She choked on it, screwing up her face at the sharp bitterness, unlike any tea she'd ever tasted. It was a tonic for her dizziness, she supposed, and forced herself to have another sip.

"We did, girl. Don't you recall?"

A kindly man with a portly middle and shocking red hair clasped one of her hands. He looked like the Velkish trappers that came through occasionally, overnighting at the hospitality of their farmstead in exchange for pelts of ermine and river-fox. Alea blinked and frowned again, some part of her aware of who the redheaded Velkman was, though she was certain they'd never met.

"Do we know one another? Have I hit my head?"

The man rifled his tousled red curls, and glanced at her brother Duriant, sitting to one side, still rubbing her feet. Though Duriant was caramel like an almonne in the sun, unlike his usual care to not let his white skin become terribly sunburnt. But his dark eyes held a deep confusion, and unfathomable sadness, and it surprised Alea to see Duriant so full of woe when he was normally so merry.

And then Alea remembered stabbing him.

A certain righteous anger filled her, recalling why she'd done it.

Duriant had stabbed Marisseaux.

But Duriant must have recovered from her lunge?

"Don't look so miserable, Duriant." Alea couldn't keep the bitter anger from her voice, and she kicked Duriant's long-fingered hands from her foot. It was right that he know how she felt, all her pain at Marisseaux's death. "You should have died from that wound I gave you."

Duriant's soft lips dropped open as he gaped at her, wounded by her words.

But Alea frowned, then. Something was wrong with her memory. She had a vision of Duriant's limp and bloodless body being brought in late that night, stumbled upon by their huntsman Gurie. Long after Alea had dragged Marisseaux's dead body to the stream to clean it, and had bundled it carefully in linen and hid it in their secret place, deep in the woods by the oak. But here Duriant was, alive and well, though he kept rubbing his chest as if it pained him still from his sword-wound, and frowning at her with his confused and alarmed dark eyes.

"Gryffine?" Duriant spoke slowly. "What are you talking about? And who is Duriant?"

Alea shook her head, and her anger was mixed with a strange woe now, some part of her certain that Duriant was dead, that she had killed him, but another part utterly confounded to see him alive before her. And suddenly, words were flooding from Alea in a rush, emotions tumbling without heed.

"I never should have lunged at you in anger, brother, I know... But oh! You cannot fathom my distress when you stabbed Marisseaux! He was your friend and mine! Since we were *children*, Duriant! I loved him, and he loved me, and we were destined to be together. It was *my choice*. Not yours! It was *my choice* when I wanted to die! And I wanted to die by his lips, and his alone. Our curse was not yours. You should have left us alone to be married and die in peace, as we chose...!"

Alea gazed down at her hands, her emotions tumbling inside of her, her confusion so very strong. She still recalled Duriant, pale in death upon the kitchen table. She glanced up, seeing alarm in his dark almonne eyes now, and back down at the warm china cup in her hands. She focused her reeling mind by noting the red of the china's glaze. It was very fine, probably traded for from Chenou. No red they made around here would fire so very fine in the kiln.

Alea frowned again.

I don't know how to work pottery, a small voice in her mind protested.

But Alea had always known how to work pottery. Lady Sanie had been very fine at the wheel, and had taught her well. Alea had made every single tile that graced the kitchen and the lower hall washroom. She sighed, then met Duriant's dark eyes just as squarely as she always had, as if they dueled even now.

"Well? Have you nothing to say for yourself, brother?"

Duriant blinked, confusion and dire sadness warring upon his features. "I'm not your brother, Gryffine. You don't *have* a brother."

Some part of that rang true, and it alarmed Alea. Her head felt as if it possessed two minds, and for a brief moment they raged together, pressing into each other, one mind identifying this man as *brother*, the other as *lover*. Alea laughed uncertainly, and the uncertainty suddenly extended into her own flesh. She gazed down at her hands, spying a plain silver band with an etched oakleaf.

"What…? I've never worn a ring on my third left finger."

"I gave that to you." Duriant's dark eyes were solemn, urging Alea to come back.

But his name is Jessup! And I am Gryffine!

And suddenly, she doubted deeply.

"Duriant," Alea whispered fearfully, reaching out for him, "send for Dotorre Fausten. Something's very wrong with me."

Her brother clasped her hands, pressing them earnestly. "Immediately."

And he leaned forward, pressing her temple with the tender kiss of not a brother, but a lover. Alea shrank back, her throat working soundlessly. A stranger, a lover, stared back at her through her brother's eyes, and his caramel skin she saw now that she was close, wasn't tanned at all.

It was simply his coloring.

Duriant hastily took his leave at a run from the yard, circling the farmstead and out of sight. Alea glanced around the yard as he went, utterly confused. Everything was wrong. The bougainvillea were gone, the ones she had so loved to smell. The open fields and scattered forest were all houses with cramped little yards and streets, as far as she could see from the porch. The house was painted wrong. The porch and the yard were wrong.

And Alea realized with a shock that her own body felt wrong. It didn't fit, suddenly, like she had been stuffed inside it thoughtlessly like too much fluff for a childrens' velveteen rabbit. Alea moaned, then clutched her own throat, realizing that even the sound of her voice was wrong. But something about the moan had caused the two men near her to shiver sharply, and she realized with a shock that the only part of her that remained was the part she hated most.

Her hands drifted up, fingers trembling as they touched her lips.

And her Dark-cursed breath.

***

Alea had been taken upstairs to her own room, but it was bright, the walls white, color adorning every surface. She sat at the dressing-table before the mirror, staring at her reflection. She lifted a hand, and touched cheeks that were too sharp, like she'd fasted or been ill. Her forehead was slightly high, her petite nose utterly foreign, and her green eyes were pale like cymbellite rather than stormy like a gale. Her ebony curls were loose and far more easily tamed, and their texture was soft rather than coarse. Her collarbones were more sharp, her neck slightly thinner.

She looked down at her body, noting that she was more petite than she'd been, like a fey of the woods. Like someone who had never held a sword in her life, nor run her hands for hours upon hours on the potting-wheel. She gazed at her fingers. Those were thinner, too, muscles from dueling and working the bellows of the kiln absent.

The thought was absurd, but some part of her knew it for truth. Some part of Alea knew that she had grown old and died, a spinster upon her farmstead porch in her rocker, rocking and gazing at the wrought-iron cage in which she waited to be placed, close to her lover Marisseaux forevermore. Some part of her had felt her very last breath come and go, and had not been startled by leaving her gnarled old body. Some part of her had wiled away her solitary days making vases and urns and tiles by herself down in the basement, and had taken a sledgehammer to her kiln and wheel the day she'd realized her fingers could no longer work the clay.

Alea looked at her hands again. They had grown gnarled and unsteady with a palsy, Alea recalled. She hadn't been able to hold them still at the end, and hadn't been able to feed herself anymore. So she'd sat on the porch and starved, waiting to die.

Her thoughts were interrupted by a kindly-looking older gentleman in a smart tan waistcoat and jacket, who pulled a chair over and sat, taking his wire-rimmed spectacles off to polish them. Part of Alea's mind thought *dotorre*, and was soothed by his presence.

The dotorre placed his spectacles back upon his nose and threaded the wires behind his ears, peering at her with keen blue eyes. "Well, then. Can you tell me who you are?"

Alea nodded, then paused, unsure, and felt herself flush. "I... I can tell you who I feel I am, dotorre. But... I doubt myself. I think."

He nodded calmly as if everything she'd said was commonplace. "You recall I am a dotorre. That's good. Do you know my name?"

Alea thought for a moment, then nodded. "Fausten. Krystof Fausten. I called for you. You helped my mother." Her brow wrinkled, suddenly confused once more. "But our family dotorre was Gregor Dautain. He delivered me and my brother Duriant..." Alea put her face in her hands, confused and embarrassed.

The gentle dotorre reached out and pulled them down, clasping them warmly instead like a grandfather might do. "How do you feel?"

"Confused," Alea answered honestly.

"Confused is good," the dotorre smiled gently. "Confused we can work with."

Alea smiled weakly, comforted. "You're really a very good dotorre, aren't you?"

He patted her hand. "Some say so. Do you, child?"

"Yes." Some part of Alea felt certain it was so, felt that she knew him.

"Good. That's very good. Now, can you recall who you are? Anything about yourself?"

Alea sighed. "My name is Alea Toulunne. I live in this manse, this is my room." She gazed around, wondering at all the bright gaiety of the upholsteries and the lanterns comprising the chandelier above, the saturated reds and purples and yellows colors she'd never had in her lifetime. "But this room is really very lovely now. If I'd had colors like this available, and fabrics so very fine, I might have decorated this way." Her fingers strayed out, touching the red and purple striped upholstery of the chair upon which she sat.

"Alea. Can you recall who decorated your room this way?"

She smiled, answering quickly. "Of course! It was me and Jessup."

A small sound of relief sounded from the doorway, and Alea looked up, seeing Duriant leaning his tall sinewed length in the doorframe.

"Focus on me, now," The dotorre urged gently. "Can you locate this Jessup in the room?"

Alea lifted her hand to point at the man in the doorway, and was again tremendously confused. Tears began to prick her eyes. "I... he's... but he's not..."

"There, now, be easy," the dotorre patted her hand. "Can you name the man in the doorway?"

Those dark brown, almost black eyes were so known, and yet not. His ringlets were longer than Duriant had ever worn them, and pulled back in a short tail. His cheekbones were higher, his nose and chin sharper, his skin darker, and Duriant had always worn a clean face where this man wore stubble. His clothes were genteel but somehow wrong, even though the fabrics were very fine but in a somber black and white that Duriant, in all his gaiety, would never have worn.

Alea blinked. "His name is Duriant... but..."

"Yes?"

"Some part of me wants to call him Jessup."

"And?" the dotorre prodded gently. "Who is Duriant?"

"My brother. Older by two years."

"And Jessup?"

"My...lover." Alea flushed, thinking about her brother in an entirely uncouth fashion. She could suddenly feel herself in his arms, feel their surging together upon blankets by the fire in a shabby little room, feel his kisses and his deep touch and her own longing for so much more. She caught his eyes, and saw that for her brother, passion surged for her. Alea let out a breath, wondering, and felt it curl around him, certain of its destination.

The man that was her brother and yet was not shuddered in the doorway, closing his eyes briefly in ecstasy.

"Alea? Come back to me," the dotorre urged. She focused upon him again. "Now. How can this man in the doorway be both Duriant, and also Jessup?"

Alea flushed and looked down at her hands, clasped in her lap. "I don't know. But he is."

"And you? Is your name Alea? Only Alea?"

She shook her head, drowning in confusion. "Some part of me wants to call myself Gryffine. The part of me that considers...him," she nodded to the doorway, "a lover. Not a brother."

"So Gryffine considers Jessup a lover?"

She nodded.

"And Alea considers Duriant a brother?"

She nodded again.

"What else can you tell me? Do you remember what happened earlier?"

Alea nodded, then paused. Her gaze swung fearfully to Duriant. "I recalled the time I tried to kill you, brother. I was so horribly angry, as if it was all happening again. But it's such a relief to see you alive," Alea licked her lips, "I can't tell you how many nights I dreamed I had killed you. Dreamed of when huntsman Gurie brought you in, white and cold, and how mother had screamed. There were flowers for the wedding reception all through the house... I dreamed we used them for your funeral instead. But I kept some," she choked now, recalling the vividness of the dream like a true memory, "to bury with Marisseaux." Tears began to fall down her cheeks. "Marisseaux was so beautiful... why did you have to kill him, Duriant?!"

"Easy, now," the kind dotorre patted her hand. "Can you tell me *exactly* what happened earlier today, Alea?"

"I..." Alea looked down at her hands. "I think I lunged at my brother. Maybe I hurt him? He made me so angry... that he killed Marisseaux. I think I lunged at Duriant again. I don't know what came over me the first time, but it must have happened again. Oh, I'm so confused...!"

"That's all right. Yes, you did lunge at your brother, but fortunately he is fine."

"But dotorre..." Alea struggled with her vivid nightmare, some part of her knowing they were memories in truth, of Duriant pale and dead. "I remember killing him! I think it's a dream, because he's there, standing in the doorway... but it's so vivid! The death, the funeral... everything."

"Oh? And what if this man standing in the doorway is not Duriant, but Jessup?"

Alea's world spun like a badly-thrown top. She gripped the dressing-table with one hand. "What?"

The dotorre nodded over his shoulder. "What if his name is *Jessup?*"

"Is it?" Alea's voice was weak.

The dotorre nodded again.

"Is it?" Alea glanced at her brother, pleading for the truth.

But the man nodded, and in that single movement she realized it was not her brother at all, merely a man who looked like him, so very closely that they almost could have been twinned brothers.

"My name is Jessup, Gryffine."

Another tear leaked down Alea's cheeks. "Then I *did* kill Duriant, didn't I? The funeral... it all happened, didn't it? And Marisseaux..." her voice broke in a sob, "he's down under the cage I had made for myself, isn't he? With my locket... and the pearls he gave me for our wedding, and the sapphire ring I gave him. And I... and I..." she choked again. "The shroud I embroidered for him... to match our wedding pillow..."

"You put Marisseaux down there in the porch, Alea?" the dotorre spoke gently. "Why?"

"I couldn't order a proper *vesilleunt* for him!" Alea moaned, reliving her nightmare over and over in her mind. "No one knew he'd died! And no one but Duriant and I knew why. Their duel was a secret, over a secret. Only Marisseaux and I knew what we were. He'd killed his mother, you see, and I'd accidentally killed my father when we were both so very young, but we knew what we'd done. I told Duriant about myself, but when Marisseaux came apprenticing with Lady Sanie's husband, he was a carpenter, you see, and they'd taken in Maris as an orphan, and I went to the Sanie farmstead to learn pottery for my trade, I found out what he was. My brother Duriant was the only person in the world that I told. We shared everything."

138

"How did Marisseaux die?" the dotorre pressed gently.

Alea swallowed. "Duriant killed him. In a secret duel the dawn of Maris and I's wedding day. Duriant was going to tell the men of the town all about Maris, about how Maris would kill me if we wed. Marisseaux was proud and had no birthline, no family to stand in support of him if such a tale was loosed. He would have been strung up or burned, or lashed to death as a demon. He had no reason to not duel Duriant, to protect himself, to protect us, and his own honor. But I didn't want them to duel. I urged Marisseaux to run away with me… to leave, go somewhere far away where we could live in secret… but he was proud."

"Maris was proud?"

Alea nodded, then gave a wry laugh. "Die at dawn upon a sword, or kill my brother and die hanging if anyone found out. Or kill my brother and hide his body, and die with me at the wedding later… such choices we had, then."

"Then?"

Alea lifted a hand to her temple, feeling a pressure there, like another mind inside her own. "Something tells me it was long ago, dotorre. Like I should be an old spinster now… I remember all those lonely years after mother died. I remember I never married, never courted. I taught pottery after Lady Sanie passed, and walked the fields and woods. I put it in my will to pass the farmstead and grounds to my nearest living relative when I…" she glanced up fearfully. "I think I died, dotorre! I remember dying. And this body I wear… it feels all wrong."

The dotorre nodded sagely and patted her hand. "And what if I told you this body you wear *is* all wrong, Alea?"

She pressed her lips together, but did not cry. "I would believe you. It doesn't fit me. Some things are wrong, just very slightly. My nose, my hair, my cheeks, even my eyes."

"But not everything?"

"Not my lips, nor what they can do."

A small sound of pain escaped the lips of the man leaning in the doorframe.

The dotorre ignored it. "And what if I told you, that like Jessup over there, this body you wear has a different name?"

Fear gripped her, but Alea was strong. She licked her lips. "I would believe you."

He nodded. "Do you know what this body is named?"

And Alea realized she did.

"Gryffine. Gryffine Toulunnet."

A slow sigh issued from the man at the door.

* * *

Hours had come and gone. The man who was not her brother, Jessup, had disappeared for a while and come back with a cabbage soup thick with sausage and onions, and they had eaten in her room as the good dotorre asked her question after question about her life. Alea came to realize that her name was actually Gryffine, and that the woman she'd been had died long ago, though to her it still felt absurd. They'd taken her down to see the cage, and the dust of ancient bones within it. She'd knelt upon the porch and gazed into Marisseaux's dead and desiccated face, and realized the truth of all that had happened. She'd touched the shroud she'd made for him, and her bowl, and her costly wedding gift. She'd lifted the pearls from their tattered velvet and placed them around her own neck and wrist, as they should have been on her wedding day, and as she had worn them for so many years before her own *vesilleunt* had been made.

Lastly, Alea had unclasped her oval locket from around Marisseaux's dead bones and returned it to her own neck, slipping the tarnished silver down between her breasts. He'd not need it anymore, and if she was to live in this body, she decided that she would. She'd allowed the dotorre and the man Jessup to move Maris' bones from the hole she'd had made when the stone porch was built. They'd put Maris' bones in her own *vesilleunt*, and she'd lovingly placed the rest of their memoria herself, and the men had promised to move the bones to the sepulcher proper tomorrow, down next to her mother and father and Duriant.

And now the good dotorre was tired and taking his leave, asking her if she'd feel safe staying with Jessup in her house. Alea had nodded and said she did, and strangely felt it was true. The dotorre had left instructions to find him at the hospital if she needed and promised to return upon the morrow, then had left her alone and taken Jessup downstairs for a few quiet words. The front door opened, and Alea watched the dotorre leave, then let himself out the wrought-iron gate, a gate Alea didn't recall, but that the other woman inside her did. She sighed, dropping her chin to her hands at the windowsill, remembering a night when she'd sat here and the world had rippled with color and sound, a festival to be remembered.

Rollows.

"Gryffine?"

She turned, regarding the man in the doorway, so like her brother and yet not.

"May I come in?"

Alea nodded, gesturing to a gaily-striped chair near the window.

The man entered and sat, and they regarded each other by the thin glow of the gaslamps for some time. He was handsome, she decided, in a way that women had often spoken of her brother, but Alea herself had never noticed. He had the same genteel manners, though something of his spark showed a sweet liveliness that wasn't as easily enraged as Duriant.

"You're really not my brother, are you?"

He shook his head, then smiled wryly. "We're lovers. I'm," he hesitated slightly, "not your kin."

Alea nodded, feeling and remembering something of the man Jessup. Her cheeks flamed. He leaned forward, running the backs of his fingers over one cheek. "You do remember me, don't you?"

Alea pulled away, feeling his touch flame her ardor. "Please, don't. I hardly know you."

He sat back, letting his hand drop, and then it went to his chin and lips, and his dark eyes shone as if he might cry.

"Don't do that," Alea whispered, reaching out for his other hand, somehow terrified that she had hurt him. He held her hand loosely, but when she squeezed his hand, his fingers tightened.

"I will fight for you," he murmured, his dark almonne eyes deep with dedication. "Whatever it takes."

"We are lovers… in this life?"

He nodded.

"And do I… do I still…" Alea's free hand went to her lips, and her heart plummeted as Jessup nodded. "I do… don't I?"

"You do."

"How do we…?"

He sat forward, taking her other hand also. "We work around it."

Remembrances came back then, of his touch, of their interactions, of how they had to be so careful when everything in her that was this other woman wanted to abandon herself to this Jessup entire. Shame filled Alea. "How you must hate me. Always aching for that which we can never have."

He reached out, dark eyes passionate, stroking the back of her neck. "We have more of it than you think."

Alea turned her face away, but did not pull from his soothing touch at her neck. It was sweet and generous, and though he was not her brother, it somehow reminded her of Duriant. Before he'd found out about her betrothal to Marisseaux. Before his unstoppable rage. "You love this woman, this Gryffine?"

"I love you."

Alea looked back, stunned.

"I love you." This beautiful man's dark eyes were utterly earnest, and they implored her for everything he wanted. "Gryffine. Alea. Whoever you are. I love *you*, and I always will."

Alea smiled wryly. "You sound so like Duriant."

He paused, gazing at her, his dark eyes careful and slightly sad. "We could see him, if you like."

"The sepulcher," Alea breathed.

The man before her shuddered, and Alea recalled she had to constrain her breath around him. "He's probably still down there."

Alea nodded, then stood with certainty. "Yes. I need to see... that Duriant's gone."

Jessup stood and offered her his arm in a polite, almost genteel fashion. Alea took it, and he escorted her like a high lady from her bedroom.

***

She'd known Duriant's coffin the moment she saw it down in the dim, dust-choked sepulcher. It was in the same place as it had always been, in a recessed alcove along the far right wall next to father's. Mother's was yet upon the other side, though the dim recesses and niches of the low-vaulted stone sepulcher were far more filled than Alea remembered. Alea reached out, stroking the iron filigree of Duriant's coffin in its niche of stone, noting the doves mother had insisted upon having twined into the vine-baskets of foliage, seeing how the ancient vellum had rotted away to nothing, the bones within utterly dust and unrecognizable as her beloved brother.

"Mother was always saying how he was such a peacemaker, even as a little boy. That's how I like to remember him, lively and bright with laughter. If only she knew his temper, his rage... and why he died. But Duriant didn't like anyone to see him rage. He only let it out around me, when we were alone."

"Was he cruel to you?" The man Jessup asked with mild curiosity.

Alea shook her head, and smiled a little in remembrance. "No. Duriant was the best brother a girl could hope for. Kind, trustworthy, challenging. I felt safe with him, always. And even when he raged, it was never directed at me. He only needed an outlet, someone to witness what dwelled within. But he'd become enraged at Marisseaux and I's engagement, how we'd brazenly announced it to the entire township, invited them to our wedding at the new Cathedral of Saint Sommes. But why shouldn't I have? I wanted to die with my beloved in my arms, and I wanted my community to witness before Our Immaculate. It was to be *our* wedding… in the only way Marisseaux and I ever could have been wedded. One single moment of bliss, our perfect union. And it was all stripped away."

"Marisseaux refused to kiss you, at the end?" Jessup had stepped up behind her now, and she didn't flinch as he wound his comforting arms around her waist.

Alea nodded, still stroking Duriant's coffin, then sighed. "Maris wanted me to live. To remember him. He didn't want me to die with his blood upon our lips. Not the both of us. Not like that. Ours was supposed to have been a joyful union, forever."

"You could have kissed him."

She shook her head, and sighed. "It doesn't work like that. Both partners have to be willing. If I kiss someone who is not willing to kiss me back… I tried to kiss him. I put my lips upon his, but he held himself away from me. He wouldn't be kissed, nor kiss me back. And so I was left with nothing but the feel of his blooded lips upon mine and the taste of sour iron upon my tongue."

Jessup let the memory linger a long moment, then asked, "So it won't work if someone is not willing to kiss you?"

Alea snorted wryly. "Who is never willing to kiss me? You've felt my breath. I saw you shudder in the doorway. Even the good dotorre couldn't resist it entirely. His embrace when he left was far too familiar."

"He's known you since you were a little girl, Gryffine."

"Still. I can taste the licentiousness in it. In anyone. You hold yourself back so carefully right now, Jessup, but I can still taste it upon you. I can smell it in the air around you. I breathe you in and all I smell is need and desire. You hold me to comfort me, it's true, but you also hold me to feel me."

"Would I be any kind of man if I didn't?" His lips were near her ear, and Alea found herself leaning her head back against his collarbones. He slid his hands over her touch-starved skin, her body youthful and willowy once more, and she let him.

"You're my lover, aren't you, in this lifetime?" Alea sighed as Jessup's hand slid up, carefully unbuttoning her shirt, sliding in beneath her corset to cradle her breast. "My brother's long dead."

"Your brother is long dead. I'm your lover, Jessup. And you're my lover, Gryffine."

"Gryffine." The name tasted strange in her mouth, as if it didn't quite fit. A girl who hid her passions. A woman who tarried long hours at a university studying something to pass the long hours of her caged life. A deep longing for Rollows and the heat and color of the Gypsun, the pulse of life in her ears. "I am Gryffine."

"You are Gryffine."

He laid his soft lips upon her neck, and kissed her there. Pleasure flooded Alea, a pleasure she'd never had the joy of in life. Something she'd always wanted, to be kissed this way by a man who loved her, and as he kissed her, it broke her other set of memories wide open. Gryffine came flooding back with a fury, pushing Alea away, to the corners of her memory that were now unlocked but not dominant.

It was Gryffine who turned in Jessup's arms, not Alea, and reached up to hold him around the neck. "Kiss me, Jessup. Take me upstairs… take me to our room and kiss these memories away. Back to wherever they come from."

"Gryffine!" Jessup scooped her into his arms, nuzzling her nose and brushing his lips deftly over hers without kissing, and without a word, bundled her back out the door towards the sepulcher tunnel and up the cellar stairs.

* * *

CHAPTER 11

Gryffine turned over in Jessup's arms, dozing, not quite awake and not quite asleep. The fire had burned low, and a chill of burgeoning autumn tinged the summer breeze wafting in through the open window. The breeze curled around her bare shoulders above the blankets, and she tugged them up to her neck, shivering. It tousled her ebony locks, and curled around her ears. Gryffine sighed, enjoying the way the breeze played along her skin, and slid down her neck, curling along her jaw like kisses. The breeze lipped along her skin, and she sighed, her own lips parting in near-sleep. The night air slid between her lips, teasing her tongue and searching down her throat.

Gryffine blinked awake.

The fire had burned low, and the windows were open.

Jessup stirred but made no sound as Gryffine deftly untangled herself from his arms. She padded naked to the window, listening carefully to the silence of the night. Standing at the sill, she looked down to the front porch.

He was there, standing stock-still in the moonlight, gazing up.

Gryffine's lips parted in astonishment, and she felt Alea surge within her body, violently, desperately. Luc Tournet breathed out as their eyes met, and his breath stole up to Gryffine's window, wrapping her in soft touches. His breath searched for her lips, and found them. He breathed in, and Gryffine's breath went with it, mingling out upon his, flowing down the side of the manse like a trailing vine, creeping up his body until it found his own lips, diving in. She felt their souls lock. Pulled by the lips and the tongue and the throat, Gryffine closed her eyes and kissed him from a distance, like Alea had done all those many years ago with Marisseaux. It rocked her forward, and she gripped the sill. Luc fell forward down below, one hand bracing himself upon the frame of the door.

They kissed a long time, tempting each other.

Almost complete, but not quite.

Not until we're married. Our perfect moment of unity.

The thought was Alea's.

Gryffine knew it for what it was now, this cursed woman and all the memories that lived inside her. And she knew also, that Marisseaux had not died upon that field, upon that bloody grass. He was there, waiting for her down below, and Gryffine felt the part of her that was Alea surging forward again, desperate to complete their long-ago vows.

"In a cathedral," she murmured.

Luc looked up, his sapphire eyes lonely and pleading. She saw him mouth a single word. *Forever.* His breath slid along her lips, and sighed down her throat, straight to her heart.

Gryffine felt his promise bury itself there, as it had so long ago, as it had for Alea.

"Forever," she murmured back, and her promise went out upon her own breath, stealing down the building and in through Luc's lips, straight to his own heart. Their souls locked again. Gryffine moaned, and she saw Luc stagger, and with a last pained look, he turned and fled her porch.

***

"I saw you at the window last night."

Gryffine froze, her coffeecup halfway to her mouth, the part of her that was Alea flaring in warning. "Oh?"

"Don't play with me." Jessup's words had a low growl of warning, of anger and danger, something they'd never held before. Gryffine glanced up, meeting his angry dark eyes. "He was here, wasn't he?" Jessup almost snarled it, his dark eyes livid.

Gryffine set her cup down, taking the moment to flash through her options, trying to suppress the emotions of Alea, who was surging with alarm, urging her to run. Gryffine focused, taking measured breaths, trying to siphon through Alea's thoughts back to her own. She debated lying to Jessup, but that was terrible, and made her feel wretched.

"He was here," she managed at last.

"And you stood there for him. Naked." Jessup's dark eyes were ferocious.

"How much did you see?" Gryffine hedged, her heart plummeting.

"Enough." His voice was cutting, harsh, and his eyes flashed fire.

Gryffine closed her eyes, and pushed her half-finished plate away. "I don't think I'm hungry anymore."

"Not for food, at least." Gryffine opened her eyes at Jessup's tone, and met his gaze squarely, forcing herself to witness. His livid anger was wretched, and his misery was even worse. "Is that what you two *do* together? Breathe each other in and *swoon*? Does his breath feel to you like it does to me? Does he *touch* you, with his breath?"

Gryffine swallowed, but the poison of the truth was upon her lips, and she could ot deny it. "Yes."

"How many times?" Rage was simmering through his muscles now, causing him to tremble, his hands flexing into fists at the breakfast table, something Gryffine had never seen from Jessup Rohalle.

"Leave it be, Jessup."

"How many times!?" He growled.

Gryffine's gut twisted, but she found that some part of her, the part that was Alea with Alea's memories, wanted this fight. Alea wanted to fight the man who looked like her brother, wanted to lash him with her tongue and spear him through the heart once again for every way Duriant had killed her love with Marisseaux.

"*Enough* times!" Alea shouted through Gryffine. "Enough to know what he means to me!"

Jessup paled, then flushed darkly. "And what is that?" He snarled.

Alea glared out at him, pushing the despairing Gryffine back into the recesses of her own mind. "None of your concern."

"It *is* my concern," Jessup insisted, livid. "I *love* you. Pursuing him is going to kill you, and we both know that."

Alea snorted. "You love me for yourself. Selfish."

"So what if I do?!" Jessup rose from his seat and pounded the rough kitchen table with one fist in a sudden violent display, making her jump. "I love you for *us*! I'm good for you, and you know it! But this?! This *man*! He'll take your kiss and your breath and your soul, and then you'll be gone! And I'll have to stay…" his voice cracked suddenly, desperation in his dark eyes, "*here*. All alone."

"You'll have mother." Alea's words and her mistake were out of Gryffine's mouth before she could put them back. Their mother was long dead, and besides, this man was not Duriant.

"Mother's not the issue!" He snarled, dark eyes flashing murder.

Alea rocked back in shock, and Gryffine went utterly still. "*What* did you say?"

Jessup flushed scarlet, and looked down, not meeting her eyes.

Gryffine felt Alea push forward again, shocked. "*Duriant?*"

Jessup stared off at the iron stove for a while and sank back down to his chair. He raised a hand to cover his mouth and his dark eyes tried to flicker back, but he held them away as if with a will. Then they tried to flicker back, and they came to meet Alea's squarely, and the life behind them was utterly Duriant, livid with rage.

"Sister."

Gryffine's world reeled, and she braced herself against the table where she sat, and Alea was ill within her. "How long…?"

The man before her looked down as if he wrestled internally, and suddenly his dark eyes were Jessup again, pained and miserable. "Since we opened the hole," he croaked. "Since you touched that locket. He's been weaving in and out. I thought I was going mad, until I heard everything you spoke to Dotorre Fausten. I've been trying to push Duriant back… but…he's strong…"

Gryffine felt her stomach churn, and wasn't sure if it was Alea's reaction or her own. She was going to be sick. She reached down to clutch her belly, her corset far too tight where she sat at the kitchen table, her breathing wretched and constricted, her head faint.

"And last night? When we…"

Jessup looked away, watching the stove carefully, not meeting Gryffine's gaze, despair in his every movement, in the lines etched around his beautiful eyes. "He was there. Since the sepulcher. He enjoyed it… all of it."

Gryffine pushed up from the table so abruptly that the heavy wood shuddered over the floor-tiles. "I need some air."

Jessup rose from his seat, his dark eyes concerned. "I'll come with you."

"No! No… I just… need to be alone."

He wouldn't meet her gaze. "I can call Marnet. He'll make a basket for you…"

Gryffine turned away, one hand over her stomach. "No… thank you."

She didn't look back as she walked carefully down the long hall, Alea's memories sliding in and out. Duriant, so solicitous at night, helping her brush her hair. Duriant, helping her pick outfits for the day, his careful appraising eye roving over her figure. Duriant, when they were adolescents, rubbing her shoulders. The time he'd tried to kiss her lips during a childish game and she'd pulled away in alarm, and the truth about their father's death had come pouring from Alea's mouth in fear. How he'd listened, how he'd stroked her hair and soothed her, how his fingers had traced her back and her limbs, calming her from her panic. How they had cuddled together in the midsummer fields, watching butterflies as he held her close and kissed her forehead.

With Duriant, Alea had always felt so safe.

But the lies were suddenly all too plain.

And his rage was here now, too, devastating and vicious.

Gryffine stumbled, reaching out for the coat rack to find her summer hat, and tying the velvet strips loosely beneath her pinned curls. Her hand brushed the pearls at her throat, and the fine silver of the tarnished locket-chain. She heard Jessup or perhaps Duriant call her name, pleading, but it fell on deaf ears. Gryffine opened the door and stumbled out to the porch, hurrying down the stone steps, whipped onwards by Alea's horror and her fear.

Her feet hit the path and kept walking, out the wrought-iron front gate. They turned down Rue Coullard towards the park, and carried her on, oblivious to the bustle of the summer day. Gryffine entered the park and kept walking, not seeing the people around her, only Alea's memories of these lands as woods and fields and hunting grounds. She turned from the path and stumbled through a short patch of grass, until she came to a mighty oak. Gryffine sank to her knees, one hand upon the bark. The oak was ancient, its spreading leaves and limbs towering over its neighbors, the kind of matriarch-tree that lived hundreds of years.

The very tree that had been hers and Marisseaux's.

Gryffine leaned forward, setting her forehead to the bark, and lost all thought as she broke into lurching sobs, misery coming to claim her entire.

And she wasn't sure, if it was hers or Alea's.

***

She didn't know where her feet were taking her until she was there. The Gypsun Quarter bustled this afternoon, but people took one look at Gryffine's tear-stained face and turned away. But Aeshe's coffee shop was a haven of quiet solace under the late-summer sun, its vines in full bloom and the colorful umbrellas opened wide to drown the place in shade. Gryffine found a wrought-iron table and sat, staring at nothing, empty and drained. The pattering low talk of lovers surrounded her, and they droned on, not a balm to her soul, but an ease nonetheless.

She felt a presence at her elbow.

"Oh, dear," Aeshe breathed. "Would you like to come upstairs, Gryffine? What has happened?"

"I'd just like to sit here, if you don't mind." Gryffine's voice sounded more than hollow to her own ears.

It sounded positively vacuous.

"I'll fetch some coffee and a few bites." Aeshe was off quickly, but soon returned, a fresh, steaming cup of porcelain set into Gryffine's hands like a mother might do, and a plate of pastries nudged close to her elbow. Gryffine ignored the delicacies, still not hungry, but she did sip the coffee, and the smooth aroma soon set to easing her mind, though the part of her that was Alea detested the bitterness.

Gryffine pushed Alea and her woe back, but it did nothing for her own horror. "Thank you," she murmured to Aeshe.

"Of course." But Aeshe did not leave, simply sat and sipped her own cup in companionable silence, until it was obvious that Gryffine was not going to touch the pastries. Aeshe reached forward, colorful shawl fringe spilling over the table as she selected a peach truant. "So? Emlohaine wants to know what happened."

Gryffine sipped her coffee, her heart roiling in despair. "Everything's ruined. What else does he want to know?"

Aeshe peered at her, then lifted her eyebrows. "Gods of the Dark…You have two souls inside of you, merged into one somehow."

Gryffine looked up. "What do you know about it?"

Aeshe shrugged, her liquid-dark eyes wary. "Emlohaine and I share a similar, if uncertain kind of truce. He says you've met your Doom at last."

Gryffine despaired, cradling her cup, sour bile tainting her mouth. "Can doom taste sweet? And love bitter?" Tears were close behind her eyes, though she'd thought herself cried out after the oak tree in the park.

Aeshe laughed sourly. "Doesn't it always? Does yours?" Gryffine nodded, and Aeshe chuckled again. "So does mine. And gives me blistering headaches, damn him. So. What happened?"

And suddenly Gryffine felt she wanted to tell. And there was no one better to confess such strangeness to than to the strange little Fatereader with her odd understanding of otherworlds. "You know the iron coffin on my porch? We moved it yesterday. There were bones beneath. When we opened it… it unleashed something within me. A personality, a woman, memories. She took control for a while, but now I can simply feel her, in the background. Watching, listening, feeling. Like she's a part of me… and has been ever since I was young…but silent until now. Now she's awake and watching. And she pushes forwards sometimes."

"Like I said, two souls merged into one," Aeshe nodded. "A precarious balance between the two. Does this mystery woman have a name?"

"Alea. But it's not just me that this is happening to."

"No?" Aeshe's eyes widened.

"Jessup's got one, too," Gryffine despaired. "My brother. *Her* brother. Duriant."

One hand flew to Aeshe's lips, and she inhaled quickly. "Oh! That's what I saw... oh, dear...!"

"We made love last night," Gryffine stumbled on, her words a fast roll of despair. "He didn't tell me Duriant was with him...was... *directing* him! I don't know how much of what we did... was Jessup... or...! Oh, gods!" Gryffine turned her face away, her horror rising as Alea's own blush of shame and vile disgust flared over her cheeks.

"Oh. Oh *dear*." Aeshe's liquid-dark eyes were wide. She blinked, then sipped her coffee, staring into an unfathomable distance beyond the cloister of greenery in their pots on the veranda. "Emlohaine says that's very complicated. The Savior and the Killer are one. Gryffine... it's not safe for you to stay with Jess... if this man Duriant is truly unleashed within him."

Gryffine nodded, blinking back tears. "I know. He got violent and rageful this morning, in a way Jess never has. Can I stay here?"

Aeshe nodded quickly, then reached out to take her hand. "As long as you like. I have another pallet upstairs." She cocked her head suddenly, as if listening for something, then hissed. "Emlohaine says hiding you here will do no good. He'll find you."

"Jessup?"

"No, the other one."

"Duriant?"

"No, the other one! Your Doom." Aeshe almost shouted it, so adamant was she. Other patrons turned to look at their shady corner, then returned to their own talk.

"No. Gryffine. *Listen* to me," The Fatereader continued, spreading her befringed hands over the table. "Your Doom is not the man, but the creature *inside* the man, and inside you. *Listen.* I couldn't say all this around Jess, because it's private for you, but Emlohaine told me more than I shared. He speaks with me constantly, Gryffine, and that's something Jessup doesn't know. The thing that drives your Doom, and theirs, is the lust within. Not lust for sex or seduction, not something so base as that. But Infinite Lust... literally... a lust for *infinity*. An infinity of moments. Each one perfect and pristine. But that is not our Gift in the flesh, Gryffine. Our *imperfection* is the very thing that allows us to be human, to live with joys and regrets and woes and relief. Life is brief, fleeting. Only the infinity after death is the one that continues forever. Your Lust is literally for Death itself. For the Infinite Life after Death. And this Lust will not stop, reborn generation after generation, Lusting for perfection itself, which it can never attain. Not with a simple kiss, Gryffine. Alea's perfect moment will never come, no matter how hard you and your Infinite Partner try. And then you'll both be born again. And again. And again, sowing misery lifetime after lifetime in pursuit of perfection of that one moment. Don't do this, Gryffine! Don't go to him, this man who is part of your Doom. Emlohaine has warned you."

"But what can I *do*?" Gryffine's voice cracked and she threw up her hands. "He *calls* me. He *breathes* me, Aeshe, and I breathe him! Have you ever felt something like that in all your life?"

Aeshe gave her a flat stare that made Gryffine's blood run cold. "I have tasted more ecstasy in a moment than you will have in your entire lifetime. I have felt my blood sipped and my bones shuddered. I have had passion that ripped through all my channels and tore through my throat, only to start again and again, for hours. I have tasted the pure energy of the Dark and drank it like wine. I have wrapped myself in the essence of the Light like quilts of wings. Do not presume to tell me what I have and have not felt, Gryffine. There is a reason I take no mortal lovers."

Gryffine found she was gaping, and shut her mouth.

"Now." Aeshe smoothed her hands over the table again as if smoothing fine silk. "Do you wish to condemn Alea and Duriant and Marisseaux to eternal suffering once again, and annihilate yourself and Jessup in the process?"

"How do you know Marisseaux's name?" Gryffine whispered, shocked.

Aeshe nodded absently. "Emlohaine knows much. So do you?"

Gryffine shook her head. "No. I want us to all be able to live. I want this curse broken. Forever."

"Then you must do as I say. As *Emlohaine* says." Aeshe's liquid-dark eyes were grim.

Gryffine nodded again, desperate. "Anything. What must I do?"

* * *

Gryffine had heard Aeshe out, and it was all she could do to come shakily to her feet and politely refuse Aeshe's offer of refuge and a bed. A part of her that was Alea had run cold, horrified at Aeshe's words, and the part of her that was Gryffine felt sick and dead inside. Aeshe had called it merciful, just like what Gryffine did at the hospital.

But Gryffine wasn't so sure.

As she stood, Aeshe put a hand out to Gryffine's collarbones, and Gryffine stopped. Aeshe muttered something quickly, and Gryffine realized she was saying an incantation over the strand of pearls that she was wearing about her neck.

"Now the locket," Aeshe insisted

Gryffine didn't ask how Aeshe knew about it, simply drew it out of her shirt. Aeshe repeated her mutterings, while touching the silver etching, then did the same at the pearl bracelet. Her eyes flicked up. "One for each of you, when it is time. Emlohaine has blessed them. They will... hold you back. Hopefully. And the masques. You mustn't forget *why* Rollows appeals to you. Trust me. Trust us."

Gryffine was cold inside. "What is Emlohaine, Aeshe? A Beast? Or an Angelus?"

Aeshe twiddled with some of her fringe, her liquid-dark eyes uncertain. "Truly? I do not know. Sometimes I think he is one... sometimes the other. But he *knows* things, Gryffine. I suffer so that others may live better. It has always been thus. His blessings to others are not double-edged. That, at least, I do know."

"But they're double-edged to you."

Aeshe smiled secretively, and a part of it was sad. "I take my coffee bitter, not sweet."

"Will he punish you... for speaking to me this way?" Gryffine ventured.

"Mm... Emlohaine only punishes me... when there is a need."

The Fatereader's vagueness left much unanswered, and Gryffine donned her hat, preparing to leave. But Aeshe's tiny hand shot out, gripping her wrist in a sudden flutter of colorful scarves. "Don't take them off, the blessed items. Not until the very last moment when you are ready to place them where they must go. The triple-bind upon them holds you until then... and you'll need every inch of it."

Gryffine nodded once. "Thank you, I suppose."

"I don't have to say you're welcome. I wouldn't wish this upon anyone. Least of all someone as good as you."

Gryffine swallowed, and tears pricked her eyes. "You think I'm good?"

Aeshe smiled. "I *know* you are. And Emlohaine knows it, too. Rest. Try to get some sleep tonight. I know you won't stay here, not after what I've said, but you can't go home to Jessup. Not yet. Not with Duriant unleashed inside of him. Do you have someplace else?"

Gryffine thought a moment, then nodded. "I do."

"Remember, Gryffine. Rollows. Sunrise on Rollows."

Gryffine nodded again, and turned her back on the little Fatereader. "I could not possibly forget."

***

CHAPTER 12

Gryffine sat in her ample room, her hands finally idle, gazing out the window to the backyard and watching the curling oak leaves fall. It was two weeks yet until Rollows. The height of summer had whittled by, almost a month gone since she had left Jessup that awful day for the Fatereader's and not returned home to her manse. It had been inconvenient, living with Dotorre Fausten, but he had been kind, never prying into why Gryffine had so-suddenly abandoned her home and her relationship, nor why she did not resume her university studies. And he'd been kind and yet firm in turning Jessup away from the door, over and over.

And Luc Tournet.

Gryffine had made all the proper preparations for two weeks from now, all according to Emlohaine's words. Her costume was prepared, her porcelain half-masque had been made, and she'd made one for Jessup and also one for Luc Tournet. They lay out with her dress before her upon the bed, and Gryffine admired the scarlet and black lines of the Rollows-masques, refined with decorations of silver or of gold. Lust was in every line of her black silk dress, scandalously cut and yet somehow still demurre with its absence of decorations. Lust was in the arching brows and adornments and clever, undulating lines of each and every masque.

Lust to bring out the Lust in them all.

Gryffine felt Luc's breath, then, curling up the window as it so often did of late. It tickled along her skin, licking her here and there, searching for her lips. Gryffine leaned back against the red velvet of her rocking chair, succumbing to it, though the sensation was faint. She'd purposefully chosen a rear-garden room in the good dotorre's manse, overlooking the yard down below with its locked gate. Luc was by the front corner of the house, she knew, where he'd come often of late, standing beneath a willow tree to kiss her, though his kisses had to creep around the side of the manse to the back and finally up to the third floor where Gryffine's room was. So their sensations of each other were wan in the moonlit night, but not completely gone.

Gryffine kissed him for a long while, tasting Luc's lips made of breath, feeling him reach deep into her throat and down into her heart. Her hand crept up to the oval silver locket, gripping it and praying for Emlohaine's blessing, and the sensation lessened.

She could breathe again, think again, barely.

"Later, my love," she whispered to Luc through the night. "Rollows. Find me upon Rollows..."

But the sensation of his kiss surged then, desperate, and Gryffine's hand fell away from the etched silver locket with a moan, straying to her breasts upon that insistent tide. She lost herself in sensation, resonating with his desperate abandon, writhing and drowning in the bliss of Luc's breath. Gryffine unbound her shirt and her corset with hasty fingers, touching herself as he kissed her, as his breath licked along her skin and dove deeper, between her thighs. Sliding one hand up under her skirts, as needful of Luc's touch as he was of hers, Gryffine stroked herself slowly. She gasped and arched with pleasure, moving in time with Luc's breath, and then faster, and faster still. Luc brought her with his breath as she touched herself, in one long, deep pull that reached through Gryffine's throat and gathered her chest and spine, and penetrated deep into her loins. She climaxed in a shuddering rush, and cried out her pleasure, feeling Luc's answering shudder and gasp of fulfillment from afar.

Alea and Marisseaux had taught them well.

There was so very much they could do to one another without touching at all.

Gryffine exhaled through pursed lips, pushing at Luc Tournet with her breath, urging him to go away. "Rollows, my love. Rollows..."

* * *

Gryffine stood before her manse, tugging her grey lambswool dresscoat closer, adjusting her red scarf against the brisk autumnal wind. The season had changed already, earlier this year than last, and Rollows was going to be chill. The trees were bright in their change, half the leaves already down, and it had been nearly a month since Gryffine was last home. She gazed around the yard, at the reds of the tumulo-vine, and the cheery yellows of the oaks, at the everycolor medley of the turning maples. Her yard was a riot of color, but Jessup had kept it well, waiting for her to come home. Every bush was still carefully pruned, the leaves upon the grass and pathstones only a thin fall that indicated they'd been raked recently. The pears from the tree at the left corner had been gathered, and only a few still remained to ripen upon the boughs.

Gryffine took a deep breath, stepped up the front stairs, and pulled the bell like a stranger. She heard Jessup's footsteps coming down the hall, heavy with his height but still somehow dancelike. He would have been at breakfast, probably having coffee. Jessup was not an early riser when left to his own devices, and she'd heard from Marnet that he was working the dinner and late shifts now that he had no one to come home to. Marnet had urged her to go see Jess, that he was in shambles. That this spark was gone, and no amount of booze or merriment could bring it back.

Gryffine fidgeted with her scarf, dreading and yet desperately wanting Jessup to open the door. She heard the latches click back. He'd not even been outside today. The door opened a crack, and then was flung wide. Jessup froze, staring at her with his lovely dark eyes. Stunned, it seemed, or perhaps befuddled. His black curls were a rumpled mess, his face and body thinner than she remembered, and his jaw was unshaven in the extreme. He was shirtless still, as he often was in the morning, and shivered as the chill wind rushed in through the door.

"Jess. May I come in?"

He blinked, as if confused at his very own name, then stepped back, motioning her inside. Gryffine stepped carefully into the hall, navigating around him, fearful and also hoping that they'd touch. But Jessup kept himself away, dancing around her just as she did around him, to shut the door and latch it. He shuffled his feet and tousled his hair a moment, staring at her, then seemed to remember something.

"There's coffee in the kitchen. And eggs. Will you have breakfast?" There was a plea in Jessup's dark eyes.

Gryffine nodded, relief flooding her. She'd not even known if Jessup would let her in the door after she'd left like she did a month ago. And to be invited to breakfast gave her hope. "I'd like that."

Jessup turned and walked down the hall, leading the way as if it were truly his own manse now, and she the visitor, and gestured to a chair corner to his at the kitchen table, much like they used to sit at breakfast. Gryffine unbuttoned her dresscoat and sat, unwinding her scarf and settling it over the back of the chair, taking off her red leather gloves and setting them aside. Jessup produced a plate with an egg scramble, which was woefully absent of anything but eggs, far unlike his usual ornate style of cooking. He fetched a cup and poured Gryffine coffee, then sat, holding his own full cup but not drinking, only staring at her with dark eyes full of pain.

Gryffine salted and peppered her plain eggs, and had a few bites to be polite. They were dry and awful, burned on the bottom, and Jessup clearly was eating only for bare sustenance now, rather than pleasure. His thinness reflected that, Gryffine saw, the bones of his ribs more prominent than before, though his muscle seemed hardly lessened, only more rope-like.

He cleared his throat, and as if reading her mind said, "Forgive the eggs. I know, they're awful. I get distracted sometimes. Marnet won't let me cook for the past few weeks. I seem to burn everything I touch. Drinks are fine, though." He gave a small, rueful chuckle.

"Does Duriant distract you?" Gryffine pushed her plate away and reached for her coffee instead.

Jessup gave her a sharp look, a look that was not quite Jessup. "Sometimes. It's easier to reconcile him back, though. Now. The first few weeks were difficult. And Alea?"

Gryffine sighed and sipped her coffee. "The same. Mostly I'm myself, but her memories slip in now and again. And sometimes when I dream, the dreams are hers, of her time, her worries and fears. She pushes forward at odd moments, when I'm distracted."

"And now?" Jessup's dark eyes were more than curious.

"She's in the background. She's always watching and listening. I can't seem to stop that. But she's not... wearing me. Right now."

Jessup nodded, and then shivered, his handsome face falling into something between disappointment and relief. "Sorry. Duriant pushed forward for a moment there. He wants to speak with her."

Gryffine pulled back in her chair slightly, cradling her coffeecup. "I don't think that's wise."

Jessup gave a wry smile. "I know, Gryffine. I've felt enough of Duriant's emotions to know better than to let him have free reign. He's aggressive about her and I won't tolerate that around you."

Gryffine breathed a sigh of relief. "Thank you."

Jessup stiffened, then twitched. "Please don't do that. With your breath."

"Sorry." Gryffine fiddled with her fingers upon her coffeecup, stilling her breath to a calm, even rhythm. "Does he hate her? For what she did?"

Jessup shook his head, and had a sip of coffee finally. "No. He's angry with her still, but he understands why she killed him. He's hurt... but," Jessup's dark eyes flashed up to meet Gryffine's, "lustful."

"Dark's mercy..." Gryffine tried to control her breath. "And he's wanted her all this time? His own sister?"

Jessup nodded slowly, then crossed his arms over his lean chest, as if holding himself back. "He doesn't want me to tell you this... but, yes. Since they were children, he could feel her breath. Every day he's wanted her. And it's only grown, Gryffine. I've felt his memories. It's like a drug to him. He was a careful and solicitous brother for a reason."

Jessup pursed his lips and let it out slowly, a very Jessup thing to do when he was upset, and the very motion comforted Gryffine in the extreme. "Duriant wanted Alea," Jessup continued, "but he also wanted to live. He knew what pursuing her would cost, the scandal of it, and personal risk. He has a temper but he's not rash, Gryffine. So he couldn't understand it when she wanted to die with Marisseaux. To Duriant, life with Alea in it was more precious than anything else, even if he could never do what he wanted. And for her to not choose the same... he was furious. After Maris and Alea were engaged, killing Marisseaux was all Duriant could think about. He *planned* it, Gryffine. He knew he could kill Marisseaux in a duel, and that Maris was too proud to stand down or ask for a second. And that Maris wouldn't let Alea kiss him while he was dying. Marisseaux was too proud to compromise his one perfect moment, and Duriant knew it. What he *didn't* know... was that Alea would pick up the sword and stab her own brother through the heart with it afterwards."

Alea surged forward within Gryffine suddenly, and Gryffine couldn't stop it. Her hand flew to her lips. "Oh, Duriant...! How I've pained you!"

She watched Jessup struggle for control as she wrestled Alea back down, and Jessup's face flashed through anger, and obsession, and then was carefully neutral, and then angry again. And finally neutral. He let his breath out through pursed lips, and cocked one eyebrow, very Jessup.

"Easy, Gryffine." Jessup reached out for his cup, and carefully sipped his black coffee. "Tell me, what did you come here for today? Just to talk about them?"

Gryffine cradled her own cup, Alea subdued within her once more. "Not just. I came to talk about us."

"Us?" Jessup looked up, and his dark eyes were entirely himself, vulnerable and winsome and trusting, though scared and hesitant to hope.

"Yes. Us," Gryffine murmured. "Just because I've needed some time away doesn't mean I've given up, Jess. I just... needed a quiet place. To gather my thoughts."

Jessup smiled ruefully, but there was a bit of humor in it at last.

"Dotorre Fausten has been very chivalrous about turning me away from the door. Did you know he usually offers me a scone and coffee on the front porch?"

Gryffine almost laughed. "I didn't know."

"He does." Jessup actually grinned a little. "He's a good man."

"Yes. He's been very kind." Gryffine curled her hands around her cup, feeling the comfort of her manse, and the coffee and Jessup's smile, even as wry as it was. "My time has been my own, and he does not press me to talk at meals or when we play chess in the parlor, though I can tell he's very curious. It suffices that I know I am Gryffine, and that I recall my own life now, I suppose."

Jessup nodded. "So why are you here?"

"I had a talk with Aeshe, a few weeks ago. The day I left here."

Jessup's eyebrows rose. "She hasn't allowed me in to see her at all. Unless I pay for a coffee, and even then, she won't talk to me."

"She knows."

"About Duriant?"

"About all of it."

Jessup settled back in his chair, his dark eyes incredulous. "You *told* her?"

"I didn't have to, Jess."

Jessup blinked. "She just knows?"

"Emlohaine knows."

Jessup let his breath out in a low whistle. "Dark's mercy. What doesn't that bastard know? What did he say?"

"He gave us a way to end this."

Jessup raised an eyebrow, wary. "Well that doesn't sound very good."

Gryffine sighed, and her sigh was tired. "It's not very good. There is tremendous risk…for all of us."

"All of us?"

"All six of us."

"I see." Jessup sipped his coffee, remaining carefully neutral. "So what did Emlohaine say?"

"That if we can do this, if we can end this… the cycle will stop."

"*Cycle?*" Jessup leaned forward. "How many times has this debacle happened?"

Gryffine shrugged. "I went back to ask Aeshe that. She said four times. Once nearly every hundred years. You'll never guess what day Marisseaux and Duriant died, the day the wedding was planned for."

"Rollows."

"They didn't celebrate it the same way at that time," Gryffine murmured, seeing Alea's memories of Rollows flash by in her mind, "but yes. Rollows. And the curse resurfaces every so often in a new generation, so says Emlohaine, because of an intense yearning for perfection in my family line. Which allows Alea back in again. And where Alea goes... Duriant and Maris follow. Or sometimes Maris is allowed in first, and Alea follows. The Gypsun tale has some truth in it after all, and was probably based on stories about my family. My family line has been cursed for centuries, Jessup. Sometimes it is a boy born cursed with Marisseaux... sometimes a girl cursed with Alea, and then the other follows."

Jessup blinked. "So... so Marisseaux and Alea..."

"Were distant cousins. Yes. They didn't know it. None of the family did."

"Dark's tits." Jessup breathed, his dark eyes wide. "What a mess of a family! So you and this Luc fellow...?"

Gryffine nodded and swallowed. "Are the same. Gryffine Toulunnet. Luc Tournet. Alea Toulunne. They're far too similar to be coincidence. Luc's kin of mine.... Somehow."

Jessup whistled, leaning back in his chair, shaking his head in a sort of befuddled amazement. "And me? How was I cursed with Duriant? I'm full-blooded Gypsun, woman! I couldn't possibly be family of yours..."

Gryffine smiled a little. "Apparently, Duriant is not usually reborn within the family."

"Small favors."

"Indeed."

But Jessup was smiling now, his white teeth flashing in amusement, and he sipped his coffee somewhat rakishly, his mood considerably lightened back towards his old self. "So we're not related. That's good. No inbreeding."

Gryffine gave a short laugh despite the pain still between them. "It *is* good. I've thought a long time about this, Jessup. It's why I've needed to be alone so long. I've not been seeing Luc, though he comes to my door. I don't love him. I know what he is, and what I am, and I feel our bond like he's a part of me... but I don't *love* him. I don't even *know* him. But the part of me that is Alea loves Marisseaux within him, and that tie is strong, Jessup. Very strong. Too strong for me to resist."

Jessup's face had soured, and his anger had returned. "So you'll go be with him, then. Problem solved."

"No, it's *not*," Gryffine pressed, not willing to let Jessup go that easily. "That's what I came here to discuss. Emlohaine said that if Luc and I give in to each other, the cycle will only recur. Alea and Maris and Duriant will be born again a hundred years from now in new bodies, and you and Luc and I will simply die. Our memories will not pass on. We are all two souls, living within one body. No moment is perfect enough for Alea and Marisseaux. They had planned their one perfect, endless moment for *years*, Jessup. And nothing else will do. And Duriant had been planning his perfect future with Alea all the while, which was why he killed Maris. But Rollows gives us all a chance. My gift is mute on Rollows. And if I'm right... Luc's is the same. I discovered my rift on Rollows by accident, I don't think that's ever been known before. We can give them one night... one night together. And then we can get them to stop."

"How? What do you mean... give *them* one night?" Jessup was leaning forward now, elbows upon the table, his dark Gypsun eyes rapt but wary.

Gryffine swallowed, suddenly unsure. She fiddled with her now-drained coffeecup. "Have you ever heard of the power of the masquerade? The power to be whomever you want to be, however you want to be...for as long as you wear the masque?"

Jessup's dark eyebrows rose, incredulous. "You've *got* to be joking."

"I'm not. Emlohaine was not when he suggested it. For one night, we will *be* Alea, Duriant, and Marisseaux. And when dawn comes..." Gryffine swallowed, facing the truth of it at last, the bitter truth of all her preparations. "I'll kiss Duriant first..."

Jessup breathed out carefully. "And then Marisseaux."

Gryffine nodded. "How much can you turn away from my kiss, Jessup? How much can you hold yourself back from it, deny it, deny me, deny yourself? Let Duriant come forward into it, while you step away to safety?"

Jessup swallowed, and fear was in his dark eyes, but they also shone with a dire determination. "As much as I have to."

"Can you feel my pull, taste me, and still turn away? You have to be *unwilling* to kiss me, so much so... that you abhor it."

Jessup nodded, something steeling in his dark eyes. "If I have to. I'll do it."

"If you don't... you'll die," Gryffine breathed, terrified for Jessup like she'd never been before, and terrified for herself. "You and Duriant within you. I'll lose you... I can't lose you... I love you too much..."

Jessup's dark eyes brightened with passion then at her words, at her confession of love. He leaned forward, extending a hand across the table, cupping her cheek. "I told you. I'd do *anything* for you. That still stands."

Gryffine nodded, and pressed Jessup's hand to her cheek, feeling his warmth and his goodness and comfort. "You must live for me, Jessup. You *must* live. I can't do what I need to if you die. I can't live without you."

"And what will become of you?" His thumb stroked over her cheek, caressing it gently.

Gryffine swallowed, trying to hide her terror and failing. "If all goes well... I'll live. And Alea will be gone."

Jessup's dark eyes bored into her heart, and his murmur was soft. "And can you hold yourself back from Luc? From Marisseaux? Even with Alea surging forward like you know she will?"

Gryffine pressed Jessup's hand close. "I don't know. But I've been preparing." She touched the pearls about her neck, visible above her shirt-collar. "Emlohaine has blessed items for us, and they help, some. Aeshe has taught me how to set a sacred circle, and that will help, some. And the cathedral will help, some..."

Jessup's eyebrows shot up. "Cathedral?"

Gryffine swallowed. "I'm to see Padrenne Henri about it today. Acquiring the cathedral for a private ceremony on Rollows. It's not used on Rollows, there are no ceremonies until the next day, until Pentriant. Maris and Alea were to have a cathedral wedding. Saint Sommes was the only cathedral in the area at the time..."

Jessup made a sound like a growl. "No. Not with that madman around. He's *poison*, Gryffine."

"He won't be there when the time comes."

Jessup snorted. "Not very likely. If you're going over to see him now, I'm going with you." Jessup stood from his chair, rounding the table, but Gryffine stopped him with her outstretched hand.

"Please, Jess... I can't be near you just yet."

Jessup paused, his dark eyes flashing with an anger entirely his own. "But Henri... he's poison!"

"I've asked Dotorre Fausten to meet me there. I really should be going, actually. He's probably there already."

Jessup fidgeted from one foot to the other, clearly torn, his beautiful lean frame uneasy with tension and his dark almonne eyes distressed. "What am I to do?" He murmured at last. "How am I supposed to get through this without you?"

It was cruel, but it needed to be said. "You managed before, when I left you with the sweetness of Rollows upon your lips. Manage again. Please. Just a little while longer."

Jessup swallowed, but stood straighter. "And on Rollows?"

"Come just after dark. I'll be waiting for you inside the cathedral. If something goes amiss before then, I'll send word with Fausten. Your masque will be sent to you here at the manse. Wear formal attire."

"My masque?" Jessup smiled a little, bemused. "You found me a Rollows-masque?"

"I made you one."

Jessup's dark eyes tightened, too bright, but he nodded. "For you, anything. I'll be there, Gryffine. My life is nothing without you."

"Thank you." Gryffine tried to control her voice, but it broke anyway. Jessup rocked where he stood, and she knew he'd felt it. Him or Duriant, she wasn't sure, but she turned and squared her shoulders, fetching her scarf and gloves and pulling them on as she walked down the bright hall, opened the door, and left without looking back.

It was the hardest thing Gryffine had ever had to do, but it was necessary.

One look back, and then she'd be in Jessup's arms, and everything was ruined.

And it would all begin again in a hundred years.

***

CHAPTER 13

[handwritten: Time stood still.]

Gryffine clutched her red scarf close, more for comfort than for the warmth it provided, her gloved fingers resting upon the crook of Krystof Fausten's arm. The air seemed more blustery around Saint Sommes Cathedral, the open courtyards of the massive aiere-stone structure tumbled with fallen leaves. Leaves scattered across the flagstones leading up to the ancient stone stairs, but Gryffine had chosen her moment well, and the leaves far outnumbered the people going about their business in the early afternoon. There would be no mass until five o'clock that evening, and only a few scattered sisters and parishioners came and went now.

She could feel Alea's excitement heighten in the blustery wind, seeing the very same cathedral she and Marisseaux had chosen for their nuptials still standing, hale and lovely. The stones had been cleaned recently for upcoming Pentriant, the Second Day of Oblenite, and a holy day of fasting and penance for those of the Immaculate faith. They shone white and pristine, just barely tinged with the grey of soot and time. The spires pierced sharp and tall to their sumptuous heights and were yet festooned with their gargoyles and cherubs and dragon-head waterspouts. Saint Sommes was not the largest cathedral in the city of Julis, really no larger than a few barns put together, or two prodigious manses, but it was one of the most ornate. Built when the town of Sommes of Alea's birth had been flourishing, farmland had been steadily eaten up by city. And even in her time, Alea had sold some of her land so that the manses of the new wealth had crept in closer and closer.

But this part of her world was still here, and the part of Gryffine that was Alea was pleased. She tugged at Gryffine's mind like the blustery wind, urging her to go in, to meet with Padrenne Fellou and plan the wedding. Gryffine shoved her back somewhat.

Your Padrenne Fellou is long gone. My Padrenne is still here.

Alea felt some of Gryffine's trepidation, and sighed away.

"Ready?" Dotorre Fausten gave Gryffine's arm an encouraging squeeze, where he escorted Gryffine like a gentleman.

"Not really."

"Explain to me why we are here?" The dotorre glanced at her from behind his wired spectacles, his blue eyes sharp.

"To make peace, dotorre. I need some peace in my life. In my mind, with Jessup... with the Padrenne. With a lot of people."

"Do you think it will help, being here?"

Gryffine shrugged. "If all goes as planned, yes."

"And what are you planning, my dear?"

It was the first time Krystof Fausten had really pried into her affairs in the last month, and since he'd been so kind as to come with her today, Gryffine felt she owed Dotorre Fausten something of an explanation. "I'm planning an event. A celebration, of sorts. And I need Henri Coulis' cathedral to do it."

"Is that why so many parcels have been coming and going for you lately?"

Gryffine smiled wryly. "You don't miss much, do you?"

"Not much. I simply don't pry when it is not the right time. But you are pondering something that I sense is very dangerous for you, Gryffine. And I don't know the whole story of what happened the night you opened that hole beneath the coffin, my girl, but I know you were vastly changed by whatever spirit possessed you." He gazed at her askance from behind his spectacles. "And I'm not sure it's entirely gone."

"Do you believe in possession, dotorre?" Gryffine knew that it was not possession, this intimate bond with Alea who lived and breathed within her body and always had, only sleeping, but a part of her was curious anyways. The wind swirled as if in response to her query, lifting golden oak leaves and carrying them high into the air and scattering them across the pruned shrubbery.

"Every ancient culture has tales of possession, Gryffine." Dotorre Fausten's voice was low and thoughtful. "What man of science would I be if I discounted them because I cannot prove them? Oh, there are many kinds of madness, fugues, dissociations that a tortured mind can conjure. But what I saw in you that night was not conjured from some trauma. You simply opened a tomb, and touched something within that tomb, something you knew nothing about. But it *triggered* you, somehow. There was no trauma to that event, Gryffine. You've survived so much, but always you've come through. A bit solitary, but you're not mad. Not like your mother. And not like that man in there." He nodded to the cathedral, his lips pursing with distaste below his grey-streaked mustachio.

Gryffine smiled, glad that her friend was with her today, thankful that he had been true. "Thank you, dotorre, for everything. For taking care of my mother, for letting me stay with you these past months, for taking time out of your busy hospital schedule to do this with me now. You've been a better friend than I ever could have hoped for." Gryffine squeezed his bare fingers with her gloved hand.

"You're really not going to tell me, are you?" Fausten's mustachios turned up at the corner, a wry smile, but his blue eyes were searching behind their wire-rimmed spectacles.

Gryffine shook her head. "The less you know, the better. But I must ask you to do one more thing for me?"

"Anything, child. You know that." He patted her hand.

"Please take this." Gryffine produced a sealed envelope from her inner breast pocket of her beige dresscoat, and handed it to him. "It is my will and testament. It states very clearly what should happen to the manse and all my monies if I should die."

Dotorre Fausten blinked furiously, but he took the letter. "Are you going to die, child? Are you thinking about taking your own life?"

Gryffine shook her head. "No. I want to live, dotorre. I want to live, and I want to live with Jessup and live in my manse and make fat babies and throw lavish Rollows parties all year long. But if things go badly… in the next few days… please. Please see my will done."

"Is someone threatening your life?" Dotorre Fausten glanced at the cathedral doors, and his glare was protective and even angry, something Gryffine never saw from him.

"No, no!" Gryffine said hastily. "Nothing like that. Please. Ask no more questions."

"Are you in danger, child?" Krystof Fausten had turned to face her fully now, and there was a fatherly concern in his blue eyes alongside his professional care, and Gryffine mourned the way she had treated him. If she lived through this, she would honor Dotorre Fausten as a better friend than she had.

"I am in danger, dotorre. Just not a danger you could understand."

He was silent a moment. "From the possession? The woman Alea, she is still within you, isn't she? Do you need a Padrenne to pull her out? Is this an exorcism?"

Gryffine nodded. "Something like that. When this is all over, dotorre, I will tell you the story. Until then, please. Keep my will safe until it is finished."

He paused again as if he might speak or argue, then sighed. "I will keep it, and do your will. Are you ready to meet with Henri, child?"

Gryffine nodded, and together, they trod the long flagstone walk to the front steps of opalescent white stone, and then up the steps, and pushed in through one massive ironbound red-cedar door.

* * *

"Do you repent your sins, child of the Immaculate?"

"I do." Gryffine murmured the ritual answer. "How this sinner repents."

Padrenne Henri Coulis' droning, unctuous monotone was solemn as he took up his prayers once more, bringing his wayward child back into the fold. Gryffine was upon her knees on the purple velvet cushion before the altar, her hands resting in the silver bowl of blessed water upon the small scroll-iron table before her, and her head was bowed. Water was sprinkled upon the top of her up-pinned curls as Padrenne Henri walked a circle around her, clad in his best official robes of gold and purple and swinging a small censer as he went. He'd been delighted when Gryffine had approached him at the side of the pulpit where he'd been speaking to two sisters about the upkeep of the hall, to tell him what she'd come for.

To repent. To sluice her sins away and be Cleansed. To come to her marriage clean and forgiven.

Padrenne Henri had inquired about whom she was going to marry, and where and when, of course, but Gryffine had stalled on all of those points, insisting that she wanted the Rights of Cleansing right away, before she would speak to him more. It was duplicitous, showing him a repentant sinner ready to be cleansed, but it put her in his good graces, and when Henri believed he was saving someone, he was more than cooperative. He was fervent.

The part of her that was Alea approved of the Cleansing, of course. She'd had it done in the days before her own wedding, and it fit with her perfect plan. Gryffine didn't much care for Henri droning on and on, now saying an ancient prayer in High Lounienne that she didn't understand. But it soothed the piece of her soul that was Alea, and that was what mattered. And it attracted Henri, and that mattered nearly as much.

At last, it was over, and Henri Coulis touched his wetted forefinger to the center of Gryffine's brows making the circle and cross, then invited her to stand. "Please, step forward and lay your sins at the Immaculate's blessed feet."

Gryffine did as she was bid, stepping carefully around the small table with the bowl and approaching the massive aiere-stone likeness of the Immaculate at the front of the vaulted hall. Carven in the image of a man, the Immaculate stood before a massive oak tree with his arms upraised to touch the spreading leaves around him, and his bare feet twined in with the roots. He had chin-length curls like Jessup, and a serene face, and as Gryffine knelt to place her wet hands upon the opalescent stone feet of the statue, she imagined she was asking forgiveness of Jessup. Her prayers went out to him, and him alone, and she bowed her head, asking Jessup quietly to pardon her of all she was about to do. She brought her lips close, knowing it would do the stone no harm, and kissed one foot of the effigy, imagining that it was the warm flesh of her beloved Jess.

Gryffine paused there a moment, and when she finally stood she did feel somewhat cleansed, though whether it was Alea or herself that felt that, she didn't quite know. Padrenne Henri approached, his feverish eyes shining, and lifted a long white and blush-colored string of rose-beads over her head, and arranged it over her clothing. He grasped Gryffine kindly by the shoulders, and pressed a chaste kiss to her forehead with his paper-dry lips, a deeply satisfied smile upon his face.

"Welcome back to the fold, Gryffine Toulunnet. Your mother would be so *very* proud of you today."

"Thank you, Padrenne. May we retire to your study? There are a few arrangements I should like to discuss." He nodded cordially, then glanced at Dotorre Fausten, waiting patiently in the first row of pews. Gryffine shook her head. "The good dotorre will not be attending us. I wish to speak with you alone. Krystof Fausten will await us here."

Padrenne Henri nodded solicitously, and gestured for Gryffine to follow him, though he could not keep the fervent delight of his triumph from his step as she followed him out of a side-nave and through a door that led to cramped stairs and a narrow wainscoted hall. Henri went to the first door on the left, an ornate thing of mahogany, carven to resemble a summer woods with a stream, and ushered Gryffine into a room she knew all too well.

There was the prayer niche with the railing and the small statue of the Immaculate where they would sit upon their knees on bare stone for hours at a time, heads bent in prayer until Gryffine's neck ached and her knees screamed and her voice was raw. Here was the stool where Henri had tried to cleanse her by demanding that she not give in to the Beast's urges, which included holding her bowels and urine for hours. She'd ended up peeing all over herself and the stool. Gryffine noticed it had been recovered since her time as Henri's tortured pupil. There was the tiny child's desk where he'd made her write *I am not the Beast's own* over and over until her fingers bled.

She banished those cruel memories from her mind and turned to Henri Coulis' heavy wood desk, selecting the high-backed velvet chair across from Henri's own that her mother had always enjoyed the privilege of. Gryffine faced Henri over the desk as he took his place of power, and now the battle began.

He steepled his fingers beneath his gaunt chin, vivid grey eyes prying like a hawk. "Now. What can I do for you, Gryffine? You mentioned a wedding?"

"Yes, Padrenne. I am to be married. Three days hence."

"Three days? Upon *Rollows*, child?" Henri made a tutting sound with his tongue. "That's not a very holy day. The Beast and the Immortal Lust roam wild upon Rollows. It is the day of the Inferno, child, the First Day of Oblenite."

"All the more reason to sanctify it with a holy wedding under the sight of Our Blessed Immaculate, Padrenne."

He nodded his head, conceding her point, but then his grey, fevered eyes pierced her. "And the Infinite Lust that roams in your flesh, child? What of the Kiss of Death that we spoke of before? Has the blue-eyed Beast come for you? Are you to be his consort, Gryffine?"

Gryffine stilled her body, making her performance count, sitting up regally. "The only way to sanctify my flesh is with a holy wedding, Padrenne. Only then can the Lust within me be quenched and my kiss become the will of the Immaculate himself. I have turned away from the blue-eyed Beast, Padrenne. He has come for me, and I denied him. You've met the man I will marry, Padrenne. You'll recall his eyes are dark brown."

Padrenne Henri Coulis sucked his parchment-dry lower lip a moment, his fervent eyes concerned. "How do you come to know this, child?"

"I have spent a month in solitude, prayer, and fasting," Gryffine murmured. It wasn't far from the truth. She'd lost weight in the last month, grieving over Jessup and the dire event she was planning. "And the Immaculate has blessed me with a vision, Padrenne. A vision of how I may break this curse of Lust within me. And it can only be done through the sanctity of a wedding to renew my flesh in the life of my husband. Right here in this very cathedral."

Henri chewed his lip another moment, but his red-rimmed eyes had begun to shine with that fervent look he had when he spoke of divine visions and prophecies. At last, he spread his hands, bidding her continue. "And how can we help, child? I would give *anything* to see this dire Lust cleansed from your flesh. Your mother would be so proud…"

"The Immaculate has shown me that I must be married here. In the main cathedral," Gryffine murmured. "And that it *must* happen upon Rollows so that my flesh is made holy in time for Pentriant."

"Such short notice, child!" Henri suddenly fretted, tapping his fingertips together beneath his sharp chin. "How will we attend to the flowers? And the pipe-organist? And the choir! Ah! So much to be done... would you not rather have a day a few weeks hence? All Saint's Feast is coming at midwinter, and that is a very auspicious day, indeed."

Gryffine shook her head. "No, Padrenne. I require a private ceremony. The flowers that are already in the hall this week will suffice. No choir, no attendants of any kind, and not open to the public. Only the engaged parties are to be present. It will be very small, and very private."

Henri's ragged grey brows shot to the ceiling, making his gaunt, sunken face seem stretched. "Whyever so, child? Do you not want the Great Community to witness your nuptials?"

Gryffine shook her head. "All I must have, all the Immaculate showed me in my vision, is the witness of Our Holy Immaculate himself, and the man who is to marry us. That is all. Otherwise, the cathedral is to be empty. And my husband wishes it this way also." It was a lie, it was all lies, but it was the best Gryffine could do. In truth, she wanted a real wedding, with feasting and dancing and everyone she had ever known in attendance, the greatest fête this quarter of the city had ever seen. But she couldn't invite everyone she knew to a wedding and give them a funeral.

Gryffine wasn't as heartless as Alea had been.

Alea stirred inside her, angry at Gryffine's thought.

Padrenne Henri was frowning. "You do not wish me to do the ceremony?"

Gryffine shook her head demurely. "Though I wish to return to the fold, Padrenne... you and I have had... so many difficult times in the past. I wish to be married in the cathedral of my youth, but not... with so many difficult memories."

"I see..." Henri had steepled his long, gaunt fingers beneath his chin again. "And the Padrenne you have chosen instead? Do I know him?"

"You do not. His name is Luc Tournet. He's been away on mission for some time, in Afrienne. He is a very old friend of my soon-to-be-husband."

"And this husband of yours? Why all the secrecy, Gryffine?"

She fidgeted a moment with her tan lambswool skirts, doing her best to pretend it was real. "He is Gypsun, Padrenne. Surely you saw that at my manse, when you visited that day. He wants to convert to the Faith of the Immaculate from his heathen ways. His family is not pleased with our courtship, his own grammère a cursed Fatereader, and I dare not tell my own aunts and cousins. Hence why we tell no one, in addition to my vision. We wish to be married before our families can find out and ruin our blessed renewal at the Immaculate's hands."

Padrenne Henri was nodding along, his red-rimmed blue eyes deepening in their fervent cast, the prospect of bringing someone new into the fold blissful for him. And a Gypsun sinner would be a particularly stunning success for Henri Coulis. But there was still a piece that rankled. Gryffine wanted to use his cathedral without him, and he would not be there to crow at the moment of triumph.

"Well... and I suppose you and this Gypsun fellow have been courting a while?"

"We have known each other a very long time. Since we were children. But we have only been courting since the beginning of summer."

"Your mother never mentioned a Gypsun among your playfellows."

Gryffine shrugged, trying to make her lies nonchalant. "His father took him traveling often. But mother was friends with his parents Jacqueline and Aldus from when we lived in the country. They were a monied family, though they were Gypsun. Before we knew you. Before father went away to the war."

Padrenne Henri nodded again, then fixed her a level gaze. "There is a modest fee. Can you pay it?"

Gryffine nodded imperiously, like her mother once might have. "My fortunes have grown since my mother went into the Sanitarium, Padrenne. I *must* be married here, to achieve my Immaculate Renewal. And so it will be. Your fee is of no matter."

Padrenne Henri chewed at his lip and touched his steepled fingers together lightly. Their bargain was so close, Gryffine could nearly taste it upon her tongue. Deftly, Gryffine inhaled, pulling Henri close to her by her breath. And just as carefully, she let her breath out, allowing it to flow around him in a subtle sensation of ease and pleasure. Henri closed his red-rimmed eyes briefly, and Gryffine saw him sway. She breathed again, and again he swayed, a light smile touching his parchment-thin lips. Gryffine breathed a third time, and his lips parted slightly in a gentle ecstasy.

Then she waited.

At last, Padrenne Henri Coulis opened his red-rimmed eyes, and the fire of the Immaculate was in their crystalline grey depths. "I have felt the Breath of Our Immaculate Saviour, Gryffine. He has given me three signs, just now. Three touches of his Immaculate Breath, urging me to acquiesce. Very well. You shall have your hall upon Rollows, as it seems he truly wills it for your Renewal. But he is pleased you have returned to the fold, in whatever manner you have come, and that you have at last repented the Infinite Lust within you and seek to cleanse yourself."

"Thank you, Padrenne." Gryffine bowed her head, in a sham of penitence.

Henri extended his palm, placing it upon her forehead. "Pray with me, child. The Immaculate himself has blessed you. Pray with me and thank Him."

And together, they prayed. Henri, with all the fervency of his long, bitter years, and Gryffine with all her honesty and dishonesty, not believing in the Immaculate, but praying for salvation nonetheless. And when it was done, Gryffine pulled her cheque ledger from her inner breastpocket, and wrote the cathedral a sizeable donation. Henri's greedy old eyes lit. And then she demanded that the keys to the sanctuary be given to her the moment she arrived upon Rollows-eve, and that all doors remain locked and undisturbed until her wedding was quite over. Henri balked at that, but Gryffine breathed again and he shuddered, his fervency flaming once more, and he bowed his head.

"It shall be done. Your wedding is blessed by the Immaculate himself. Though it is strange and I do not understand, all shall be as you say, and as He wills it. You shall not be disturbed upon Rollows-eve until you emerge from the Immaculate's sight, wedded and Cleansed and confirmed by His Holy Breath. Be blessed, Gryffine. And walk in the Immaculate's presence."

Gryffine bowed her head, and lifted her stone rose-beads to her lips, like her mother had so often done. "So I shall do, Padrenne. Thank you." She rose from her seat and turned to the door, pushing out and through into the cramped, candlelit hall.

Her plans were set now, and there was but one thing left to do.

* * *

Gryffine sat alone, her back leaning against the mighty oak tree in Saint Sommes Park. Dotorre Fausten had left her alone in her room after supper, and she had snuck out the back door and through the yard and unlocked the gate like a naughty child. She shivered in the light autumn wind and watched oak leaves swirl across the dry grass, the bark rough and chilly behind her dresscoat. Part of her mind appreciated the danger of a woman out alone in the park after nightfall so close to Rollows, which began upon the morrow. More than once, Gryffine had heard a band of carousing revelers stumble by, already in their cups anticipating Rollows and roaring their opinions to the night. A nearby rowan-tree had played host to a kissing couple for a while, but they had moved on also.

And still, Gryffine waited.

At last, she felt what she'd been waiting for. A curl of breath, wreathing her ankle and sighing up her calf, stroking the arch of her foot and tickling behind her knee. Luc or Marisseaux, she wasn't entirely sure who he precisely was anymore, nor for how long, but he had become clever in his caresses. Gryffine leaned back against the oak as his breath wafted up her inner thigh and over her belly, pulling at each one of her ribs in turn and caressing up her neck until it reached her lips. They kissed for a long moment, and she felt him sigh in the shadowed darkness. His sigh slipped down her throat, diving to touch her heart with a single tendril, making Gryffine ache with longing.

"You're waiting for me," he murmured from the shadows.

"Yes." Gryffine opened her eyes, watching Luc's outline grow solid as he stepped from utter darkness into a bit of dappled moonlight, highlighting his flawless white skin and pale hair. His hands were tucked carefully into his overcoat-pockets, and he approached no closer, lingering at the side of a rhododendron tree a few steps away.

"Why do you wait for me, Gryffine, when you've shunned me nearly a month, kissing me so little, and from so very far away?" Luc's breath went curling up her skin, tasting here, pressing there, moving Gryffine to new ecstasies, though he moved no closer from where he stood. Gryffine's breath came faster, and she could not control it, not now. He was so close, closer than ever, and Emlohaine's blessed talismans against her skin seemed for naught.

"Don't do that, my love," Luc whispered, "do not heat for me… do not breathe for me so…" His whisper curled in through Gryffine's ear, touching deep inside her mind, flaring her to new heights.

Gryffine sighed, ecstasy moving within her, breathing hard now as her head fell back against the solid strength of the oak. "Then do not whisper thus."

"I can't help it, Gryffine," Luc Tournet moaned, his moonlight-silver eyes stricken and passionate where he stood, his breath pouring all around her now. "You are not a thing I can resist. I've tried. Gods, how

I've tried. But all my careful solitude is for naught around you."

Gryffine's breath was fast now, and she couldn't stop it, so she spoke with it instead. "Is that Marisseaux talking, or you, Luc?"

There was a long pause, and in it, the curl of Luc's breath suddenly stopped altogether. She saw him shift slightly in the dappled shadows, his eyes now hidden from the moonlight. "How do you know of Marisseaux?"

A slight smile touched Gryffine's lips. "Marisseaux was awakened first in you, wasn't he? When Aeshe told me... I knew it couldn't have been me. I was a willful child, Luc, and perfection was not something I bothered with until after Alea's gift was called to me. But you. You whose hands create such perfection in the grain of woods, you were called first, weren't you? Marisseaux awakened in you first, didn't he, when you were just three years old... and then he called Alea to awaken in me. A woman of our line. So I had the gift but not the memories, not for a long while, until I opened Marisseaux's grave."

"How long have you known?" Luc had shifted back to a shaft of light through the trees, and his blue eyes were steady in the moonlight.

"Almost a month. Did you have Marisseaux's memories when I first met you at the door of my manse?"

"Yes. I felt you up above at your window before you even opened the door. And when I saw you..." Luc Tournet gave a sad laugh. "Marisseaux and I have been joined more closely than you could ever imagine, Gryffine. I was three. My own self has developed in his way, in his own image. The work of my hands..." he gazed down at them a moment, then laughed again, almost a sigh. "Marisseaux was apprenticed to a carpenter. He created lovely, fanciful work. I'm not sure, and never have I been, what of my carving is his work and what of it is mine. It seems we are closer than ever when I carve, when I touch the grains of wood and think deeply about their perfection, about creating that perfect graven image. Now that you know all of it, now that you remember, and you feel Alea... what will you do?"

"Give them what they want." Gryffine murmured.

She felt him slide a step closer, saw Luc's perfect beauty illuminated by the moon and then vanish again into shadows. "That would kill us, Gryffine." His whisper curled along her jaw, stroking her throat. "Is it not better," he murmured, sliding a step closer, "to be like this? To touch like this... without hands... without lips... without risk... like we did so long ago as Marisseaux and Alea? Touching... but never risking. Keeping our souls back... until the perfect day we had planned." He slid closer another step, and Gryffine felt his whispers dive beneath her shirt and corset, cupping her shoulderblades and ribs, sliding down her spine and her belly until she shuddered.

"You tempt me to breaking, Luc..." Gryffine's whisper went out to him, and he shuddered, and stepped forward again.

"You tempt me to annihilation, Alea."

"Marisseaux..."

"Yes," he was close now, so close. He breathed once, and like an invisible hand had lifted her body, Gryffine rose to her feet, her back still against the stout oak tree, desperately drawing upon its strength.

"What are you doing...?" Gryffine murmured, closing her eyes.

"What I want to." Luc was very close now, his soft lips whispering over her cheekbone, but not kissing, not quite. "What I've always wanted to, even though you asked me to wait."

Luc's hand rose to cup her neck and jaw, and Gryffine sighed at his touch. His lips hovered at her neck, and she turned her face away, wanting and not wanting his bliss. She felt his lips brush her neck, teasing, tempting death and fate and a hundred years more. They parted, and his tongue licked out, tasting her, pressing her skin and drawing a firm line up to her earlobe.

Gryffine moaned and her knees buckled.

Luc caught her around the waist, pulling her close.

"I didn't know we could do that," Gryffine murmured, her heart floundering, unsteady in her breast.

"We can... and so much more, my love..." Luc whispered fervently at her neck, cupping Gryffine's jaw with one hand, pulling her neck to his lips, almost, but not quite. Holding her carefully against escaping. "Marisseaux and Alea know so many things... if you'd only open to her full memories. They've tried so much, lifetime after lifetime, learned from their mistakes and successes. Come with me. Let me touch you..."

Luc sighed at her throat, and his breath stole to Gryffine's lips and dove in deep and fast, choking Gryffine and flooding her heart. She shuddered in his arms, breathless, hopeless, consumed, drowning. He kissed her without lips, deep and fast and relentless, and it went on and on. Luc pressed her backwards against the oak, his body hard against hers, and Gryffine mewled a protest that wasn't really protest at all.

"Come to me," Luc murmured, "Nothing could be more perfect than this, my love... beneath the moon... in the darkness... under our tree. Come to me. Kiss me, Gryffine. Kiss me, Alea. Take my soul...and let me take yours to our perfect bliss..."

And then his true lips were at hers, and he was pressing close, pulling her in by the throat and his breath and his lust. Gryffine was sighing, mingling her breath with Luc's, pulling him in strong and deep, weaving her breath into a cord with his, a cord that pulled both of their hearts closer, both of their souls closer, aching for that perfection, the bliss that was promised.

But it was Alea who stepped forward suddenly.

"Not like this!" Alea whispered as she pulled back swiftly, and like a knife, it cut the cord of their breath's pull, which recoiled with a snap of pain for the both of them. Luc staggered back, releasing her, and Gryffine fell against the oak, breathing hard. Those sapphire eyes looked up, but Luc was gone. Marisseaux alone was in their moonlit depths now.

"Alea… why can't it be *simple*?!"

"You believed in our perfect union once, Maris," Alea had taken Gryffine's body now, and Gryffine watched from the back of her mind, shoved there as firmly as if she had been a small child. "Believe again. It has all been arranged, my love. The cathedral still stands. You and I can be wed at last! And Duriant has been found. He stands to witness for us, my love. Like he should have. He is *willing* this time. *Please*. The lady I share has found a way for us to achieve our Immaculate Perfection. The curse is not entirely hale upon Rollows, one day hence. We can be *together*, my love…" Alea reached out, cupping Marisseaux's face gently, "*truly*, in the flesh. Before we become one in heart and soul. Our limbs entwined, our breath entwined, alive and hale… for one night! Oh, please, Marisseaux… it is everything we ever dreamed!"

A fey light shone from Marisseaux's perfect sapphire eyes as he stepped forward into a slice of moonlight. "In the flesh? Are you *certain*?"

"Gryffine's done it many times…every Rollows…" Alea breathed. "*Please*."

Marisseaux blinked, and one hand raised to his temple. "I seem to recall this man, Luc, trying to tell me something of that. Something important about Rollows coming. Tomorrow?"

"Tomorrow. Just one night, my love. Come to the cathedral at midnight tomorrow, in your wedding attire. Everything is arranged. Our community is long gone, but Gryffine will stand as witness, and her Jessup, who holds Duriant within. Please."

Marisseaux reached out, taking one of Gryffine's hands. "I have waited so long for you. So many lifetimes. I can't wait much more."

"I know." Alea pressed his hand to her cheek. "Just a little longer, my love."

"And it will be over this time?" His sigh was a torment, an ancient soul longing for release.

"It will be over this time." And Gryffine was not sure who within her had spoken that promise.

* * *

CHAPTER 14

Gryffine stood alone at the altar, waiting.

For the first time, she could hear the revelry of Rollows all about her, could smell it in the air, could feel the vibrations of the drums and the fireworks and scatter-bones and the reverberating laughter and reedy flutes, but she was not a part of it, not this night. Tonight was a night for ceremony, a night that the revelrous masses outside the cathedral had long forgotten. Rollows was a night for Life to be made Death and back to Life once more, to cast off whom you once were, and prepare and revel in who you were about to be.

Gryffine smoothed her black dress, running her hands down the plain black silk, the black lace at her décolletage, and the lace at her shoulders that was not meant to stay put. Her gown sighed in clinging black silk to the floor, but what was seen was not the whole of it. Her sighing gown had no corset, and beneath it Gryffine wore nothing, in preparation for her bridegrooms this night, and her dress would not remain where it was for long.

Gryffine turned, gazing at her masque upon the opalescent altar-stone at the front of the cathedral. Black cormorant feathers arched back from the fine porcelain, that she'd not known how to shape until Alea had shown her. Gryffine's visage of the Eternal Consort was striped with silver at the cheekbones and above the brow, elongating the eyes and making them seem feral and desirable all at once. Little dots of silver edged the silver stripes, and each black feather had been tipped in silver paint. A wild mystery gazed back at Gryffine from the masque, and she knew it had to be so. Her lovers had to see what they wanted in her body tonight, in her flesh.

Whatever it was that they wanted most.

Or feared.

Gryffine reached out, lifting her masque from the embroidered purple and gold altar cloth of the Immaculate. She settled it upon her face, tying the wide velvet ribbons above her loose-pinned curls and setting the ribbons with pins. Whatever happened tonight, it had to remain in place.

Lives depended upon it.

She glanced briefly at the other two porcelain masques that waited, the black visage of Death with his gold-rimmed eyes and a single golden teardrop beneath the outer corner of the left eye. No feathers crowned the half-masque of Death, no other adornment. It was austere and pained, subdued and yet alluring. Jessup's curls were the only adornment for such a night, and Gryffine wanted to touch them without interference. And she needed to remember clearly, what was at stake. There was nothing fine and fancy about Death. Death would take her Jessup away from her, and Gryffine needed to remember it every time she looked in his dark eyes.

Every time she kissed his beautiful lips.

The other masque was sexual and passionate. The Infinite Lust half-masque was a wonder, even to her whose hands had made it. Inspired by Jessup's masque at the bar all those years ago, four sets of corkscrewing horns proceeded from the temples, with small rows of horn like the teeth of sharks at each cheekbone and proceeding from the eyebrows to the temple along the bone ridge. Golden with daring red stripes, Lust accused her and challenged her and called to her, and in its every line Gryffine had warned of danger. There was nothing smooth or sensual about this masque, not like Death. The Infinite Lust was a curse, and that curse was devouring, and this visage warned of giving in to being devoured.

Gryffine ran a hand over the Death masque once more, then over the pearls at her throat, the pearls at her wrist, and finally, the silver-filigree locket, newly polished, nestled between her breasts. She sighed and turned, picking up the fat stick of white chalk upon its white linen on the altar, and walked behind the altar to the foot of the Immaculate. There she inscribed a massive circle upon the pale stone floor, with the Immaculate as her only witness, the quiet of the vaulted cathedral a stark contrast to the booming drums of Rollows outside. Her circle traced, Gryffine returned to the altar. She set down the chalk, and picked up a bowl of consecrated water taken from the nave. She walked the circle again, sprinkling the blessed water all around the line of chalk, and then thoroughly within the circle. She returned to the altar, and gathered the last items. She set the ring of candles at regular intervals, just outside the chalk, then walked around on her bare feet, lighting the fat rounds one by one. They began to glow, filling the back of the altar with light, illuminating the Immaculate and making his great tree move with their flickering shadows in the dying dusk, as if stirred by the Breath itself.

Gryffine returned to the altar, and fetched the last items, an assortment of thick-woven blankets. With these, she padded the cold stone floor within the great circle, and then set an ewer of water within it also and a small platter of sweets. Wine there was not, for all needed their wits about them tonight, and the Breath was enough to pull them all into drunkenness. Gryffine tucked her ankles and sat upon the piled wool blankets in her tight silk dress, pleased to find the blankets made a thick, comfortable pad.

And then she waited.

* * *

Jessup arrived not long after the light had melted from the stained-glass windows and left Gryffine in darkness, but for her ring of candlelight. Drums were thundering outside now, the parade in full swing somewhere nearby, and as he opened the great door at the rear of the cathedral, the music and thunder swept in with the night wind. Gryffine shivered in her thin silk as she rose, stepping out of the circle and rounding the altar to greet him.

He was regal in his black Rollows-attire. Not one for pretense, Jessup had smoothed his curls back in a short tail, and wore only his clothes for a fancy event at the bar. Black well-polished boots, black trousers of a fine weave and neatly pressed, a black shirt of raw silk sans cravatte, rolled up at the sleeves leaving his forearms bare, and a finely-woven black silk waistcoat, of the kind that threw the light in a myriad patterns, as only the Gypsun could weave. A golden pocketwatch-chain extended to one pocket of the waistcoat, and he wore a single band of gold at one finger, his grammère's keepsakes.

"Gryffine?" Jessup approached slowly, entirely himself in his mannerisms, walking like a man in a dream up the center aisle, his footsteps quiet and dancelike in the echoing hall. His dark eyes searched her face as he mounted the three steps to the altar, but as he approached, Gryffine reached out and stilled him with her fingers to his lips.

"Shh. Tonight I am who you want me to be."

Jessup glanced at the altar, at the porcelain masques waiting upon it. "Which am I tonight?" His long fingers stole out, touching the golden tear of the Death-masque gently.

Gryffine reached out, touching it also. "Tonight, you are Death."

Jessup pursed his lips, and breathed out slowly. "I thought so. And you? He reached out, carefully touching the arching black cormorant feathers. "Who are you tonight?"

"I am the Eternal Consort," Gryffine murmured.

Jessup glanced back to the altar, at the other masque upon it. "And he is the Infinite Lust." He sighed. "So be it. But when this is over... you are mine. Heart, body, and soul."

"When this is over," Gryffine held his gaze, "I am yours. Heart, body, and soul. I swear it."

Jessup nodded, and said nothing.

Gryffine took a deep breath, and then began the ritual, stilling the nervous butterflies in her gut. "Tonight, you are no longer Jessup. Tonight, you will let Duriant come through you. But you, Jessup, are Death, and so you will remain until the night is over and dawn has touched the sky. Let yourself come through only as Death, and I am your Eternal Consort, not Gryffine. You must not utter my name, and I shall not utter yours. Not until the dawn is long past and our masques are removed. Do you understand?"

Jessup nodded, his dark eyes sober and hardened with determination. "I understand."

"Promise me," Gryffine insisted. "Before you become Death, promise me, as Jessup. Promise me you'll do as I say. Promise me you'll stay away, Jessup, *far away*, when dawn touches the sky. Promise you'll deny me, deny my kiss and my breath with everything you have, with everything you are." Gryffine's voice broke, as she unclasped the pearl bracelet from her own wrist and affixed it to Jessup's. "This is for protection. Whatever happens, remove neither masque nor bracelet, not until well after dawn. Promise me."

Jessup swallowed hard, his dark almonne eyes far too bright. "I promise, Gryffine. I *promise* you."

Gryffine nodded, and lifted his masque from the altar. But as she stepped around him to tie on the Death-masque, Jessup suddenly seized her hands, his manner entirely his own. "Gryffine. Whatever happens tonight... know that I love you. I always have. And I always will. *Always*."

Gryffine swallowed and nodded, fighting back her tears. "Words cannot convey what you mean to me, Jess. Live for me. I... I need you. I would gladly trade this gift and every ecstasy it brings for you. You are my home, and my Light. Live for me this night."

"I will. I promise."

Gryffine stepped quickly behind him before either of them could shed tears. She lifted the masque and settled it upon his face, tying it firmly about his curls above his gathered tail and then setting it with a few pins. Jessup reached up to adjust it to his satisfaction, and when

Gryffine stepped around to face him again, Death waited for her.

"Who are you?" She murmured, gazing up into those beautiful dark eyes, trimmed in gold and mourned by a single tear.

"I am your Death, lady," he murmured back, lifting a hand to stroke her neck. "Your Life, and your Death. Your Sun and your Moon. Your Light and your Dark. For the two are One. Who are you, lady?"

Gryffine lifted her fingers to touch his lips. "I am your Consort. Eternal, willful, and wild. Come to me Death, come to the circle and be as one with me now."

"Lady," Death sighed, stepping forward, "kiss me. Kiss me, and abandon all thoughts to Death, all flesh to Death, all passions to your Eternal Death. Come to the circle," he began to lead her away from the altar, the booming of the night heady in their veins now, just as it had been that fateful night long ago, "come feast upon the lips of your Death."

They stepped within the circle.

Death pulled his Eternal Consort close, his lips whispering over hers like sighs in the darkness. And then he was kissing her, deep and wild and slow to the drums of Rollows, and their kiss had no end and no beginning, only endless beauty and empty time.

* * *

Gryffine was naked upon the blankets but for her masque and her locket and pearls, cradled in the arms of her Death and her Life, her heart bound in the solace of his presence. Three times he had taken her already, three times they had been together, slow and then fast and then with all the languid passion of true lovers. Her ease was so absolute that for a time she had forgotten what the night was for, and simply resting in the arms of her Death was all she longed for, and all that filled her. The deep of the night had passed away as they lay in each other's arms, staring at the flickering candles as they burned low.

Gryffine stirred, and realized that she had been drowsing.

She glanced at the candles, seeing that they burned far lower than they had been. The scent of impending dawn was in the air now, and the booming of the Rollows-drums had long gone. It was still dark outside the high-gabled cathedral windows, none of their stained glass yet lit by dawn, but still, Luc Tournet had not come.

A vast sorrow filled Gryffine, clenching her heart, and Alea echoed it, mourning inside her.

But just when Gryffine thought all their plans were for naught, the door to the cathedral opened again. Gryffine's heart leapt to her mouth, and she felt her Infinite Lust's breath snaking through the vaulted arches and down the stone-polished opalescent aisles. His breath pulled at her bare arches and her palms like crucifixion nails, it wrapped her ankles and wrists like manacles of vines, and sighed about her neck like a collar of kisses. Alea leaped forward within her then, and Gryffine arched as the woman took her entire, gasping her pleasure and her pain of separation from her Infinite Lust. Alea abandoned Gryffine's perfect repose in the arms of Death, rising to greet her own true love.

He had come dressed in a dark robe, his pale skin and hair cowled and penitent. But when he shook back that cowl, his perfect sapphire eyes blazed for her, defiant of the rigors of time, and his alabaster skin shone like an angelus of the Immaculate. Marisseaux reached the altar in Luc Tournet's body and picked up the last masque left upon it, then settled it to his face, and the gaze of the Infinite Lust upon Gryffine was scorching as he finished with the velvet ties and stepped forward into the circle.

"I am Lust," he murmured, his breath snaking all around Gryffine's naked body. "Come to me, my Consort. Come to me. Be with me at last. And then wed me."

And without pause, she came, Alea stepping forward so completely that Gryffine was shoved to the back of her own mind, abandoned and trapped within her body, but still a part of it all. Gryffine rode their passion as Alea and Marisseaux entwined, kissing away their long starvation of each other in her and Luc's helpless bodies. She mourned as Marisseaux laid her back beside her incredulous Jessup, whose dark eyes now streamed with tears, staining the gold of his masque, fist to mouth as if it could keep him from screaming. Gryffine watched, she felt, she desired and succumbed as Marisseaux took Alea, deep and completely, and her heart broke as Jessup turned away, standing now at the very edge of the circle, gazing up at the stone effigy of the Immaculate, his shoulders shaking with silent tears.

But he did not leave the circle.

Gryffine surged as Alea and Marisseaux took one another with breath and body, heart and soul. She shuddered along with them, felt their diving breath as if it were her own, lusted and mourned her interlocking lips upon Luc's, his kisses devouring her flesh and hers in turn devouring his. But all the while, she watched her Jessup, watched how his shoulders shook, how he sacrificed for her. And when Alea and Marisseaux's feast was over at last with a mutual shudder and twin cries, Alea called to Duriant, reaching out to him as Marisseaux collapsed upon her, spent.

"Duriant, my love, my brother," Alea implored, "come. Do not fear this. I was wrong to shun you. All of us are supposed to be together, just like this. Come, brother. Come to us, Maris and I. We have loved you for so very long."

But Gryffine felt the truth deep within the body and mind she shared with Alea. She felt what Alea sacrificed to free Gryffine's beloved, to free Jessup from Duriant. She felt Alea's inner horror, her revulsion at what she was about to do.

Thank you. Thank you for this. Jessup is everything to me. Gryffine reached out within her own mind, as if she could kiss Alea upon the cheek like a sister.

And Marisseaux is everything to me. And if this is what it takes, for us all to be free at last... I will do as you have planned, Gryffine. And with that, Alea opened her arms to her brother Duriant within Jessup's flesh and masqued by Death, and to her surprise Marisseaux beckoned to him also, pulling him and wrapping Duriant in his sweet breath.

"Do not fear us, Duriant," Marisseaux murmured, plying and shuddering Duriant with his breath. "It was not only Alea that I loved. I tried to tell you... so many times... but you were proud. And your anger was righteous and swift. Please, come to us now. Be soothed, my own true brother. Be soothed. Let our breath soothe you."

"Be soothed, my brother," Alea echoed, but to Gryffine's surprise, Alea was using the moment to unclasp the pearl necklace from her own skin and affix it around Luc's neck, leaving only the silver locket behind upon her own skin.

Protecting Luc? Gryffine mused.

As much as I can. Luc seems a sweet man. He doesn't deserve our fate. If he can be separated from Marisseaux...

And Duriant had stepped forward in Jessup's flesh, wearing the masque of Death. He came back to the center of the circle with wonder in his dark eyes, sighing to his knees, first tasting the lips of Marisseaux tentatively, and then those of Alea. They sat upon the gathered blankets, kissing gently and touching, soothing the pain of their brother so long excluded. And Gryffine felt a tenderness build within Alea, as Gryffine enjoyed the body and the kisses of her own true love Jessup, something that eased Alea's horror and shame. And soon Alea abandoned everything to the moment, kissing her brother with a fierceness that he returned in every way.

And then in a rush of passion, Duriant inside Jessup's body had thrust her to her back. And then he was inside of her, gripping her thighs, thrusting into her and screaming out his passion and his vast need, so long held silent. And Marisseaux was kissing her mouth in Luc's flesh, his soft pale lips upon hers as she cradled his neck with one hand. Duriant was within her, and Alea's breath surrounded them all as she pulled her brother deeper and kissed Marisseaux at the same time, urging Duriant on with one hand to his thigh, releasing herself to the moment and the breath and every ecstasy it could bring. And when the moment was perfect, Alea pulled them all by her breath into one, infinite sigh, spooling out, on and on into the wild expansiveness of endless bliss.

Time stretched.

Everything stretched.

The breath danced through them all in a torrent of beautiful madness, heightening their desires, altering perceptions, shifting them all into a time centuries gone when they had loved so fiercely and lost, so much. It was perfect, this unity, this blessed trinity, Duriant buried within her and Marisseaux upon her lips, and Alea's breath pulled their souls close and their hearts closer towards completion. Alea tasted dawn upon her lips, and her mouth curved into a smile where she had locked upon Marisseaux so deeply and he upon her.

Alea was ready for her death.

But Gryffine felt Jessup reach out to her then, his ecstasy uncontainable in the height of their coupling. And Gryffine could not help herself, but surged through Alea, abandoning everything, needful of her true love Jessup, breaking off her kiss with Marisseaux with a gasp, breaking their holy trinity. Gryffine turned her head away from Luc and her lips met Jessups' in a fierce and holy bliss as they both surged to their climax, him rushing within her at his climax as her breath spiraled deep, claiming his heart.

Dawn touched the windows, the first rays of the sun kissing the edges of the morning-star at the front of the cathedral, high above the statue of the Immaculate.

And Jessup's breath died in his throat.

* * *

"No!"

Gryffine shoved Jessup off of her quickly as he crumpled, with the ferocious force of desperation. She keened as she rolled Jessup to his shoulder, his body lifeless, his rich caramel skin dull with a pallor Gryffine had never seen in him. His dark almonne eyes were staring through the eyes of his Death-masque, his lips open slightly as if surprised, but there was no breath that issued through them, and no beat of his heart beneath Gryffine's hand as she rolled him desperately to his back. Gryffine froze in panic, her mind halted, all her plans crumbling, everything she had worked so hard for and thought out so well abandoning her in a single moment of utter despair.

Her hands clutched Jessup's masqued face as she knelt beside him.

"No... no...!" Gryffine's moans went on and on, resounding in her lonely ears. "You weren't supposed to die... no...! You are my Death and my Life... my Dark and my Light! No... Jess..."

"*Do not say his name.*" Luc's words were harsh and clipped beside her. "Careful. Do not call him back."

"What?" Gryffine roiled in confusion, feeling her beloved motionless beneath her frantic hands.

"Feel... taste... just with your breath..." Luc murmured, watching Jessup intently, his masque of Infinite Lust yet in place.

Gryffine blinked, unsure of what he meant, but then Alea pressed forward, questing outward with her breath. Gently, she dove within Jessup's throat, easing so carefully within his heart that it was the merest brush of fine silk, and Gryffine felt at last an answer. The slightest movement filled Jessup's chest, the shallowest breath. The slowest heartbeat suffused his chest, weak and faint. But signs of life were there, and even as Gryffine and Alea felt them, Jessup gasped more heartily and his staring eyes flickered closed. Gryffine felt Alea questing into his heart, breathing it, feeling it slowly, painfully recover. And then she quested deeper, looking for the soul within that heart.

Pained and confused and oh so very small, the answering touch was Jessup.

And not Duriant.

You were right, little sister, Alea mused within Gryffine's mind, *Duriant has been freed. Your beloved lives, though I know not when he'll return. There was enough of Duriant within him at the last for my brother to be taken and not your love. Come, do as we promised each other. Set me and my own beloved free.*

Gryffine breathed out, a deep and shaking relief flooding her that Jessup lived, albeit faintly, and that he was entirely Jessup once more. And then she breathed again, surrendering herself in her promise to Alea. Gryffine stepped back within her own mind, allowing Alea to rule her entire. And by the time it was done, Alea commanded her mind and body once more.

"Come, Maris," Alea spoke. "Our Endless Bliss is at hand. Will you marry me, my beloved? After this night of revelry... will you be mine at last?"

Marisseaux stepped forward in Luc's perfect sapphire eyes, though in truth he had never left, and he took Alea gently by the hand. "For you, I would do anything, my love. Let us be wed at last."

And on their knees, naked upon the blankets, they cradled each other close. They quested out with their breaths, wrapping each other in sighs of passionate bliss. Gryffine stepped back further within her own mind and flesh, uttering a prayer deep within, and gazing at the masque of Death that was Jessup from the corner of one eye. And his beautiful black curls, quiet upon the blankets. And at his chest, seeing now that it rose and fell, rose and fell, slow and serene, and stronger than before.

Alea closed her eyes.

Her lips touched Marisseaux's.

And upon the tide of their kiss, in the light of the dawn, Gryffine felt the pull of Alea and Marisseaux's endless moment, the seduction calling her, more beautiful than anything she had ever known. It was a river in flood, a tirade of the sea, ripping her from safe shores and flinging her from the rocks to be drowned, drowned, drowned in Luc's smooth flesh and his soft lips and his firm hands. The tide pulled, washing Gryffine helplessly towards her annihilation. And Gryffine struggled, trying to pull back from it, Jessup's dark eyes fixed in her mind.

But the pull was too strong, and she was drowning, drowning, drowning.

Someone was there suddenly, pushing her, denying her, commanding her back as he shut out Gryffine's heart and her kiss with a stern ferocity. But Gryffine felt herself swept into an undeniable tide anyways as her body knew no boundaries and her mind exploded out into the world.

And her vision fell black as the breath was stolen from her throat, and she choked, and her heart clenched to a sudden ceasing.

* * *

CHAPTER 15

"Gryffine?"

Gryffine gasped to awareness, her body arching as the pain of flooding back into her flesh hit her like a rip tide. She screamed, a rawness ripping her throat, primal and wild. Something inside her felt cavernous, and she keened, pain prickling through every limb and vein and bone.

"Shh... it'll pass, it'll pass..." Jessup's soothing baritone calmed Gryffine's spasming nerves, his soft lips kissing her temple, her porcelain masque and his already removed. Jessup's strong arms held Gryffine close to his front, rocking her gently where they sat.

"It'll pass, Gryffine, it only lasts a little while... I felt it, too..." Jessup murmured, and his utter kindness and devoted love broke Gryffine's heart wide open. She clutched Jessup close, needing him like she'd never needed him before, feeling his love and brightness fill her void, fill that place that was hollowed within her.

"Jessup..." Gryffine croaked, her throat raw like it had been filled with sand.

"Yeah, it's me," he murmured, kissing her again. "Gods of the Dark and Light, I thought I'd lost you. You were cold for so long..."

"Cold?" Gryffine shivered in Jessup's arms, realizing how true that was, though she was bundled in blankets upon the stone of the floor, still within the white circle of chalk and candles. Shivers took Gryffine and her teeth chattered, snuggling into Jessup's clean warmth, though he was already dressed. All the candles were out, she saw, their fat cylinders burned to nearly nothing, and as Gryffine glanced at the high windows of stained glass in the gables, she saw the sun lipping its way down their faces. The multihued star above the Immaculate was full and blazing, its glory shining far back into the hall and illuminating the cathedral with a golden glow.

"We have to get you out of here," Jessup murmured, concern deep in his voice. "You're freezing. We have to get you home."

"Luc?" Gryffine managed, fearing the answer.

Jessup paused, and in that pause was everything Gryffine needed to know. Her eyes tracked to the side, to see a man lying mostly covered by a blanket within the ring of now-spent candles and chalk. His masque of the Infinite Lust had been removed, and set carefully to the side. His alabaster skin was so pale, paler than Gryffine had ever seen it, and the blue shades of death tinged his closed eyelids and lips.

"We have to leave, Gryffine," Jessup murmured urgently. "It's long past dawn. I locked the doors, but someone has been knocking."

"Let me up." Gryffine staggered to her feet with Jessup's support, and together they padded to the front door of the cathedral, Gryffine wrapped in blankets but still naked beneath. The knock Jessup had spoken of came again, tentative and in triplicate.

"Who is it?" Jessup called low through the heavy ironbound door.

"Krystof Fausten. And Aeshe!" A female voice hissed that they both recognized instantly. "Let us in or be caught and hung for this mess!"

Hastily, Jessup unlocked the red-cedar door with the heavy iron key, and Aeshe slipped in, bundled in scarves, followed by Krystof Fausten. Aeshe promptly slapped Jessup across the face, hard, and then seized his face in her teensy hands and shook him like a wayward puppy, tears running down her face.

"I thought I'd lost you! *Never* do that again, Jessup Rohalle! *Never*! And Gryffine! Come, we have to clear all this away...! The world is stirring, and it *cannot* know of such events as have happened here! Least of all the Church of the Immaculate... they would never understand... hurry! Hurry!"

And Aeshe's fluster and fluttering multicolored scarves caught them all, and set them to hastily packing all traces of the night back into the baskets Gryffine had brought as she stepped aside to dress, and scuffing chalk and wax of the tapers from the stone. But Gryffine caught Krystof Fausten's gaze as he hunkered to mourn the man beneath the blanket. When Gryffine came to him, he wiped his tears from behind his spectacles with a pocketsquare, and shook himself.

"I will see to him. Jessup, a hand?" Dotorre Fausten gazed at Gryffine, his keen blue eyes accusatory, and sad. "Your manse? May I dress him there? It is but a short ways, and my cab-man is waiting. He is a personal friend and utterly discreet."

Gryffine nodded, relief and gratefulness flooding her. "He belongs in the sepulcher. We will lay him there, and proper funeral rights shall be held. He was kin. And he was brave."

Dotorre Fausten nodded, then sighed, covering Luc's dead face with the blanket. "Ready, Jessup? One, two, three, hup!"

In a matter of minutes, all traces of the night had been scoured from the vaulted hall.

Gryffine left the key in the lock, and threw up the cowl of her dark cloak, hurrying down the stairs in the early morning hush after her loved ones.

* * *

Gryffine hadn't even had time to realize that Alea was gone, but some part of her felt it, deep within, like a gaping wound that hadn't yet closed. The manse was sad and busy all that morning of Pentriant, the Second Day of Oblenite, the day of holy penance and cleansing.. They dressed Luc's corpse, sent a runner-lad to Rennet to inquire about Luc's kin, if any could be found, they made breakfast and coffee and tidied the manse for a funeral.

The business of death was not new to Gryffine, but this she went about with a willing heart. She sat now with Luc Tournet, the man she had known too little and too late, by the stone dressing-altar down in the sepulcher, now lit from corner to vaulted corner with candles and wreathed with incense. Gryffine held Luc's cold hand, tracing his deep carpenter's calluses and the blue lines of veins in his alabaster skin. They were good hands, kind hands, and she wondered what kind of man he would have been had he not been taken by Marisseaux so very young.

"Would you have been a painter, or a musician with your tender soul and these fine hands?" Gryffine murmured, wondering at a life too little lived, and too short.

Leaning over, Gryffine pressed a kiss to Luc's cold blue lips, lingering, remembering something of his life, the little she'd known of it. She remembered their companionable walk in the park, the ease and gentleness of her hand within his, breathing in the night, before Alea had encouraged Marisseaux to truly come forward. She remembered their talk of Life and Death, and how sundered this gentle man had been having taken even a single one. Gryffine recalled Luc's careful denial of her the first day they met, though he had already known who and what she was and it had cost him everything to do so, his misery palpable from the rafters, and his look of anguish as he left her porch.

"In every way, you tried to spare us this pain, this suffering, didn't you?" Gryffine murmured to Luc's cold corpse. "You knew Marisseaux was waiting for me. You knew how you would change once I remembered Alea and Maris stepped forward to claim you. And you fought it, every moment. For us. Just for us."

Gryffine admired his pale lashes a moment, his high cheekbones, the austere and haunting planes of Luc's face. "You were a hero today," she murmured at his lips, stroking his face gently. "I could never have done this without you. I don't know how it happened, but I know you gave your life to save mine. I was drowning, Luc... drowning. And I felt you push me. Just a little, but it was enough. You pushed me back from the flood, and dove in yourself." Gryffine smoothed his pale hair gently, feeling tears prick her eyes.

"Thank you." She pressed a kiss to his cold lips again. "Thank you."

Gryffine felt a presence at the cellar-doorway to the sepulcher, and she looked up, knowing it was Jessup. At last, they had a quiet moment together, away from the funeral bustle upstairs. Jessup stepped forward, wrapping her in his arms, his chin falling to her shoulder. Gryffine pressed back into his chest and let her head fall back upon his shoulder with a sigh.

"Is she gone?" Jessup murmured quietly.

"Yes. Alea is gone. You?"

"Duriant is gone, too." Jessup paused a moment, then nodded at the dressing table. "How did we survive but he did not?"

"He pushed me back," Gryffine spoke simply. "I was drowning, and he pushed me back. He gave his life to save mine. But I think, really... he was too entwined with Marisseaux. Their personalities had influenced each other for so very long... I don't know if anyone could have survived that much of themselves being torn away." She paused, needing to say what was next, and fearing it.

"Jessup... I... what happened last night..."

"Shh..." Jessup stroked her ebony curls back from her face and kissed her neck and jaw gently. "It's over. It's all over. We all did what we had to. I don't hold it against you, Gryffine. I never could. In a way... my pain was what saved me. My jealousy... watching you two together... it kept me away when Duriant stepped forward. But I could feel you there, Gryffine... every curve of your body, every sigh, every kiss... I could *feel* you there, with me...and it was too much. If I could have just stayed back a moment longer..."

"No... no." Gryffine soothed Jessup now, reaching up to stroke his stubbled jaw. "I needed you, Jessup. I was in your flesh and you were in mine, and we called to each other, and that was all. That was all."

She felt him take his long, slow breath, and let it out through pursed lips. At last, Jessup nodded, and kissed her delicately upon the jaw, and nuzzled her ear. "And your breath?"

Gryffine blinked. In the tumult of the morning and everything after, she had forgotten it. She took one long, slow inhalation, waiting for the feel of the curling, sensual touch. It didn't come. She let her breath out as seductively as she knew how. Jessup didn't even flinch. There were air currents in the sepulcher from the open door, and the candles flickered lightly, but of the surging breath of the world, Gryffine could feel nothing.

And it was beautiful.

"Anything?" Gryffine murmured to Jessup, hope rising in her heart.

"Not a thing." Jessup turned her in his arms, cradling her close, wonder and passion and devotion shining in his dark eyes. "Kiss me, Gryffine. Just you, just me. Just us. *Kiss me.*"

Gryffine leaned forward, an excitement like she'd never known flooding her, but hesitated at the last moment, her lips barely brushing Jessup's. Caution and the pain of Death had been a part of her soul for so very long, the iron cage that held her, bound her, and suffocated her, that a part of Gryffine's mind could not comprehend that it would not be that way forever.

She hesitated with a moment's panic, terrified that it was not Rollows.

Jessup wound his arms closer about her, his soothing fingers caressing Gryffine's spine, and making her ache for him. "Kiss me, pretty *demonne*..." he murmured, teasing his lips over hers, his tongue licking out to taste her, like he had done with markou upon his lips so many years before.

Something within Gryffine broke in that moment. Some gate that had been locked flung upon, some gaudy Rollows-lantern that had been darkened suddenly lit. And she surged forward, wanting him, needing Jessup with a sweet ache that was all her own. She placed her lips upon Jessup's, and then she was tasting him, and he answered back, tasting her in turn and winding his strong hands tighter about her body, pulling her close.

And as they touched, as they breathed each other in and tasted each other, there was no pull of fate, no diving and drowning and endless bliss. Just a simple kiss, sweet and loving, a kiss that stole Gryffine's heart and promised it to the man before her forever. They kissed a long while, only the natural lust of a man and a woman kindling between them, warming Gryffine's belly and chest as she molded close, enjoying every last inch of it, and ready for so much more.

Jessup pulled away and gazed down at her, a tender fire in his dark eyes. "Marry me, Gryffine. Today. With all our friends and family together, here in our home. Let's put the funeral off another day. We were robbed of Rollows last night, but now we can have Rollows every night of the year. Marry me. Love me. Create a life here, with me, of joy and revelry. Life is so fleeting, Gryffine, and I don't want to spend a moment of it without you…"

Gryffine's heart filled with joy, and she reached up, pulling Jessup down for another kiss, fierce and passionate with life, and love. And in the place of hallowed Death there sprung a new Life, made of two souls choosing to spend their short spans in bliss, and sadness, and peace, and pain, and kindness, and whatever the rest of such a life together might bring. And this kiss etched itself upon Gryffine's memory, there to live forever in her mind and heart and soul, even if there was no perfection to the moment, kissing in the flickering candlelight next to a corpse.

But Gryffine didn't care.

Tonight was Rollows. Every night was Rollows.

And on Rollows, Death danced side-by-side with Life.

From Life to Death, and back again, to Life.

* * *

EPILOGUE

Time passes, as all things do. Death to Life, and back into Death.

He interred her in the sepulcher where the bones of his first beloved lay, a bitter reminder to what once was. But the Child of Light is not sad. He visits her dead, lovely form everyday, always placing a single yellow day-flower in her hands upon her breast. Gradually, her lively, ebon-haired beauty wilts in the sepulcher of stone, and then decays, and he comes to see maggots beneath her flesh. But still he places his flower everyday, and then walks the park, a tall man in black finery and a now-subdued but still handsome white smile with his dark almonne eyes that speak of a merry life well-lived.

The neighbors know him. Once there were gay parties at their manse, celebrations of Life in the ever-present face of Death. Once there were children, reckless and wild, shrieking and laughing about the manse before they moved on to the wider world. Once she lived, dancing with him until all hours of the night, hand-in-hand upon their summer patio and kissing like true lovers do among the light-bugs, even as they grew old and gnarled with time.

Once her laugh filled their home, her breathless laugh a thing admired by all who came to know her and be welcome at their manse, which were many.

And still he comes to see her, and then to the park, through rain, sleet, snow and sun. And gradually she becomes bones, and gradually so does he, and at last the tall man in black finery comes no more.

Ages turn, and the manse is sold. Ages turn, and the city changes, but never too much. The household sepulchers seem macabre oddity, but nothing to be feared, just dead bones. Until one day a family moves in, and their little boy begins to venture into the sepulcher in secret, drawn by the bones. Every day he goes down for a while to stare at the crystalline bones in the darkness, the ones with the strange objects. A porcelain bowl, painted blue. A withered wooden pipe, nearly decayed. Two beautiful strings of pearls, a tarnished silver locket, and a sapphire ring.

And one day, despite the sepulcher's gloom, there is a little yellow day-flower rising from the dust and bones, where none had grown before. And so the little boy slips through the bars in the sepulcher fencing and stands transfixed, staring at the bones.

And his mother finds him down in the gloom, and reaches through to him, beckoning, and saying, "Come away!" But he does not. He reaches through the wrought-iron, and touches the little yellow day-flower, and then caresses the bones, as if he remembers something about them.

And what's left of the bones siphon away to a shimmering, crystalline sand beneath his fingers. And frightened, the boy runs back through the bars to his mother, who gathers him up and coos in his ear, petting him and soothing him and kissing him as mothers do. And the boy is relieved to be safe in his mother's loving arms, and he reaches up his lips to kiss her upon the cheek.

And she laughs and coos to be so beloved by her boy, and she carries him away, back to the sunshine and the Life and a whole world full of little yellow day-flowers.

And that's how the curse was broken.

Or so some say.

***

This book is available in print at most online retailers. Please remember to leave a review for *Three Days of Oblenite, Book One: Breath* at your favorite retailer!

ABOUT JEAN LOWE CARLSON

Jean Lowe Carlson is a Naturopathic Doctor and writer of both fiction and non-fiction. A keen observer of the natural world and human behavior from a young age, Jean received a B.A. in Biology and B.Mus. in Opera from Oberlin College in 2003 and went on to earn her medical doctorate in 2011 from Bastyr University. An avid study of yoga, pranayama, energy healing, homeopathy, Reiki, Craniosacral Therapy, and Emotional Freedom Technique (all of which she uses in her daily medical practice) Jean pulls from her deep knowledge of human psychology, energy interactions, and naturalistic awareness to paint vivid scenes and emotionally complex interactions between her characters. Jean maintains a blog on Esoteric Buddhism (Tantric Practice), produces health newsletters for her clinic, and weaves her daily experience into compelling adult fantasy fiction. Her writing is a mixture of the lush worlds of Jacqueline Carey with the intrigue and vivid characters of Robin Hobb and the dark thrill of Clive Barker's *Imajica* novels. Jean lives with her delicious husband Matt in Redmond, Washington, and desperately wants to get a cat. Miao!

CONNECT WITH JEAN LOWE CARLSON

Facebook: https://www.facebook.com/jeanlowecarlsonauthor

Web site and new publications: http://jeanlowecarlson.com/

Blog for new excerpts: http://jeanlowecarlson.com/blog/

Visual world of Three Days of Oblenite:
https://www.pinterest.com/jeanlowecarlson/

Name and place pronunciations on YouTube:
https://www.youtube.com/channel/UCovv9664IFh3vL-sKe2KVLA

PREVIEW: TEARS

Three Days of Oblenite, Book Two

"Our Immaculate, who art free of Lust, cherished is thy soul…"

Whispers filled the Cathedral of Saint Sommes, arching high into the vaulted ceilings with their stone ribs like the belly of some great, soothing beast. Through his closed eyelids, Phillip d'Auvery could see the comforting flicker of candles in their tall branches to either side of where he sat. The cathedral was dark now, he could see the change in the light despite the fact that he'd not opened his eyes for hours. His belly rumbled, protesting its usual mealtime.

Phillip ignored it, focusing once more upon his everlasting soul.

His lips moved by rote, whispering along with the others in the shadowy hall. The branch to his left flickered as someone stole in by a side door and sat a gracious distance away upon Phillip's pew, settling into silence as they arranged their skirts and then came to a penitent position upon the cushioned kneeler. Phillip heard the rustle of fine fabrics, and the sweet scent of almonne and jasoune-blooms wafted past his breath.

His dark brows frowned slightly, his lips murmuring on.

Markou and perfume and a fancy dress.
Probably just stopped in between supper and post-Rollows parties.

The final phrase of his prayer ended and Phillip sighed, adjusting his shoulders and neck with a slight twist until one of the bones cracked all but inaudibly, and then settled himself once more. His knees ached from his long hours of prayer. His back and neck were stiff, his fingers and hands tingled now from lack of movement. His lips were dry and his throat parched from whispering since morning without water, but all those discomforts were trivial to the condition of his soul.

Phillip sighed and put the woman's indiscretions and his judgment of her aside. Not everyone observed all the tenets of Pentriant, the Second Day of Oblenite. Unlike Phillip, more casual parishioners had been trickling in and out all day, the crowd of the morning mass thinning as the day wore on through the afternoon into evening. These were followed by the influx of industrial and factory workers who came in just after five o'clock, those who didn't get time off for the Day of Holy Penance, and whose schedules could not be helped. But Phillip set his own schedule as a member of the Carpentry Guild, choosing jobs as he liked and attending to them when he liked.

And for Pentriant, Phillip d'Auvery always set the day aside, plus a few days after.

His Immaculate Soul was far more important than cupboards and beams.

Phillip d'Auvery picked up his prayer again, his lips whispering it out to the flickering darkness, and in the near-emptiness of the great Cathedral of Saint Sommes, the hours crept by.

* * *

"Our Immaculate be with you, ever in your hands, ever in your heart, ever in your soul, child."

Phillip sighed, a deep sigh of sweet relief and cleansing, his vigil finally at an end. The midnight hour had been struck by the tolling of the bells in the tower, and one by one, those who were left in the long red-cedar pews had come to the conclusion of their final prayer and approached the altar at the front. They knelt upon the cushion there and placed their hands in the silver bowl of water, as Padrenne Henri Coulis walked around them with his censer, cleansing them at last with the traditional closing of Pentriant.

Phillip knelt upon the red velvet cushion now at the front of the cathedral, one of the last to approach the altar at the end of the night. The Padrenne was concluding his circumambulations around Phillip and his blessing. He came to stand before Phillip, and Phillip knew the man's Immaculate love and devotion by his benevolent presence. He heard Padrenne Henri Coulis dip his fingers in the silver bowl where Phillip's own hands rested, then felt the official closing of Pentriant as Padrenne Henri traced two gentle lines of water over his closed eyelids and down his cheeks to his clean-shaven chin.

"The Tears of the Immaculate be upon you," Padrenne Henri murmured kindly. He took his wet fingers and made the cross-and-circle at Phillip's brow. "Be cleansed, my son, of your suffering, and arise with joy. Your Vigil of Pentriant has ended at last."

Phillip took a deep breath and sighed, hearing it waft away to the silent presence of the Immaculate himself, twined benevolently into His Holy Tree behind the candlelit altar. "Thanks be to His Immaculate Soul," Phillip murmured, traced the circle and the cross upon the center of his chest with one cleansed hand, then opened his eyes and rose. Henri Coulis met his eyes briefly and gave a tired but benevolent smile, and a flicker of a smile touched Phillip's lips also. Then he stepped aside, making way for the next soul to be fully cleansed of their suffering.

He moved carefully back down the steps at the altar, nodding to a few faces he recognized who were yet waiting for the Padrenne, and then turned towards a door upon the left side of the cathedral. Phillip made his way through and up the cramped stone staircase to the narrow wainscoted hall of the cathedral's Holy Servants offices, and entered the first door upon the left without knocking. The Padrenne's offices were tidy and plain, befitting a man of his station and devoutness, and Phillip selected his usual overstuffed chair across the desk from the Padrenne's and sat, settling in to await Henri Coulis in quiet meditation.

At last, the iron latch of the door clicked open, and the ancient wood groaned inwards, and Phillip heard the rustle of Padrenne Henri's fine garments, the black robes and white stole used only for this particular day. He heard a sigh, and then the crack as Henri Coulis popped his own back. A rustle of the fabrics came as the vestments were hung up properly in a cupboard. Phillip heard the Padrenne take a seat in his usual chair behind the desk, and Phillip opened his eyes at last.

"Phillip." Henri Coulis' red-rimmed grey eyes were exhausted, but his thin lips held a kind and satisfied smile. "How may I help you tonight?"

"I would like to conclude my Pentriant in the old way, Padrenne."

Henri Coulis nodded, his eyes kind and unsurprised. It was merely a formality between them, after so many years. Padrenne Henri knew that Phillip d'Auvery held to the old ways, like his mother had before him, one of very few who still did.

"Very well. Give me a moment to prepare. You may strip to the waist, remove your boots and socks, and anoint yourself at the basin in the prayer niche. Then please kneel upon the bare stones before the Immaculate, my son, and settle into silent meditation. I will attend you shortly."

"Thank you, Padrenne." Phillip inclined his head.

"As the Immaculate wills it, my son."

Padrenne Henri made an offering gesture towards the prayer niche and Phillip rose, turning away from the desk and walking to the niche. He settled upon the plain wooden bench by the wall and removed his boots and socks, then hung up his grey wool fall-weight coat upon the peg. His trim black waistcoat followed, and then he stripped his black shirt off over his head rather than bothering to undo all the buttons.

Phillip's lean muscles were tired and ached from the day, and his abdomen seemed thin and hollowed from fasting. He adjusted his neck and shoulders again, rolling them out a little as he took his place upon his knees before this smaller statue of the Immaculate in the prayer niche.

The Immaculate's arms were open and welcoming as he knelt upon the cold stone floor, the effigy's face kind and slightly sad. Phillip's knees protested with twin surges of pain, but he consummately ignored them, settling before the effigy. He leaned forward, dipping his hands into the bowl of water to the side, and rubbed the water over his face, hands, neck, chest, and through his short ruff of unruly black hair. Then he rested his forearms upon the stout wooden railing that housed the statue. Phillip clasped his hands and closed his eyes. He allowed his head to fall forward and his neck to relax, his forehead coming to rest upon the wood railing with his elbows.

He left his rose-beads around his neck, their miniscule weight comforting.

With long, slow breaths, Phillip d'Auvery prepared for his final Cleansing of Pentriant, and urged every muscle in his body to loosen. He heard the Padrenne approach at last, and fought the urge to tense. Henri Coulis took up his usual place directly behind Phillip, the quiet step of his bare foot a whisper in the chamber as he took his ready stance.

"Are you prepared to come to the Immaculate, my son, and to be Cleansed of your sufferings at last, upon this Most Holy Day of Pentriant?"

Phillip swallowed, fighting his tension, urging his body to be calm and loose. "I am, Padrenne. Cleanse me of my sufferings, and bring me to the Everlasting Joy, the Infinite Bliss of His Holy Soul. So Be It."

"So Be It," Padrenne Henri murmured.

The crack of the lash startled Phillip as it always did, as it curled over his back and snaked around his ribs. There was always a moment, the first moment, when his body responded to the sound, tightening with surprise, before the pain came.

But then it came.

A searing of pain, a bright line of misery, a flash of horror and anguish and then the surge, the blossoming of every dark touch and miserable need of Phillip's flesh and his soul. Phillip gasped at the pain, all pretense of manhood abandoned. It devoured him, blistered him, dived within him and scourged him, knifing like hot fire through every part of his poor corpse and his everlasting soul.

He had a moment to breathe.

The Immaculate gave him that small concession, at least.

And then the lash fell again.

Phillip screamed, the sound torn from his throat like the beasts howling in the night, like all the desperate sinners who cried and died in torment, whose pitiful pain mimicked his own. It sent him reeling. Their suffering abounded within him. Phillip breathed it in and keened it out. Every night of passion abandoned into misery, every mother aching for a child long gone, every curl of madness and anguish and every twisted, obliterated heart that cried out into their own endless Inferno.

And then the lash fell again.

Phillip d'Auvery broke with a sob, and began to weep.

Tears beaded upon his dark eyelashes and dripped down his hanging head to his nose, dropping upon the cold stone of the floor and striking upon the wood of the stout railing. And as they fell from his lashes, Phillip felt the Ecstasy of the Immaculate begin to flow through him like wine.

Tears streamed freely now, and the lash fell a fourth time. Phillip screamed, rocking forward upon his elbows at the railing, absorbing the pain, taking it all in, holding it close within his heart, transmuting it. Bliss filled him, eternity filled him, life itself filled him and he gasped from the pure pleasure of the Immaculate building within, scouring away his sufferings at last. Abandoning himself to its deep succor, Phillip shuddered with livid pain and infinite pleasure. He lifted his head, the breath of his Immaculate surging through every pore. Drinking it in, he opened his throat and cried out for the Great Mercy.

The lash fell a fifth and final time.

Phillip d'Auvery fell back upon his knees and sat upon his bare ankles, his elbows falling from the wooden railing. His chest opened and his head fell back, baring his throat in surrender, his hands resting palm-open at his sides.

Open to the Eternal Bliss, he wept in silence.

Open to the Light and the Life and the Joy, he wept in silence.

Broken open, his back streamed blood from the lash and his naked throat gasped. The pure ecstasy of the Immaculate dived down his throat and in through his closed eyes. It penetrated his chest and thrust deep into his aching flesh.

As the tears streamed down his jaw to his neck, the world opened up suddenly. The ecstasy rolled out from Phillip's flesh in a burgeoning wave. Phillip heard Padrenne Henri fall to his knees with a short cry. And then he felt the Padrenne's benevolent hands upon his bare shoulders as Henri Coulis was taken by the Immaculate's ecstasy also.

So it was, with Phillip d'Auvery.

***

PREVIEW: KINGSMAN

The Kingsmen Chronicles, Book One

Eloel slipped through the morning-heavy darkness like an eel through a rainbarrel. Cowled, with his head bowed, he looked like any Jenner's Penitent making midnight pilgrimage to the Mercy Wall, except that he was headed in the wrong direction. His footsteps were light and quick, and if one looked closely, they might have seen that his feet blended with the darkness of the dew-wet paving stones, rather than the peek of toes one might have seen from a Penitent. Doeskin tall boots as soft-cured as slippers made no sound as he passed over the cobbles, turning down a tight alley whose name he did not know, the location marked only by the wooden plaque of an alehouse creaking in the early-morning wind.

He didn't remember any names for the streets and alleys he whisked through. He had always been weakest at maps, remembering only the proper turnings and distances for his feet. Eloel had always relied on touch, on sound and smell, and it was at these tangible things that his training had excelled. He navigated the dew-slick streets by instinct, dodging late-night drunks unseen in gutters by a tingle to his feet here, avoiding a low-hanging sign in the midnight blackness by a pressure near his face there.

At last, his fingers stopped him upon the palace gate-wall. Thin black gloves covered his hands, but left the pads and gripping surfaces free to feel, to sense, and to climb. The soft boots upon his feet made no sound as Eloel dug into holds by the same instinct that kept him moving in the darkness. He was up and over the time-roughened bluestone of the wall in a matter of seconds.

Everything in Lintesh was time-roughened, and a climb of such a height was nothing to Eloel in the King's City. Built straight out of the southern face of the Kingsmount, Lintesh had been hewn straight from the blue byrunstone rather than constructed, and those who had shaped it hardly had time to polish and carve, leaving that to the elements. Lintesh was a marvel of roughened edges and simple holds for a climber such as Eloel, and fancy had no place here. The Kings of Alrhou-

Mendera had been practical men, and the King's City was as practical as the mountain itself.

The palace courtyard was layered in hush, offering deep shadows and soft mossy quiet as Eloel passed through, angling for the eastern garden-keepers' door that he had memorized before he left Alrashesh. As Olea had anticipated, the garden was drowned in the night-whisper of ferns, and the arch of the gardener's entrance led beneath the palace to a recessed ironbound door that proved no match for Eloel's picks. His touch was softer than goosedown. The lock clicked, he whispered in and through like the nightwind, and the door sighed shut behind him.

Eloel's breath sounded heavy to his ears, frightened and rushed. Sweat slicked his hair, though the night had been cool. Had he taken the time to smell his underarms, he would have discovered the same rankness of his First Seal. This was far worse.

Everything rested upon him, now.

Eloel glanced down. His hands trembled in the darkness, like the nightwind blew through him rather than sighing through the cracks in the ironbound door. He breathed one measured breath, just as he had been taught. The wind that trembled through him stopped. Eloel moved forward down the soft-echoing byrunstone.

* * *

Two rights and then a left, darting across three halls of armor-statues, the twisting and turnings of the palace bowels were a maze to be reckoned with. Hewn from the foot of the Kingsmount, these passages had been orchestrated to hopelessly confuse any invader, and it was this part of the task that Olea had quizzed him upon, over and over again. He had to be right. Everything rested upon him.

Shuffling footsteps sounded to the light of an approaching torch, soft silk slippers and heavy embroidered robes. A Lord and Lady walked, arms linked, through the bowels of the palace. Their conversation dropped to a murmur as they saw him, and then ceased altogether.

Rhoushenn Palace was a place of secrets, and everyone within it kept them well.

Eloel placed one foot behind the other, and dropped into a moderate bow, two fingers to his lips in the manner of a Jenner. He felt more than saw the Lord and fine Lady relax in their dressing-robes, and as they passed, each murmured, "Penitent."

"My Lord. My Lady. Blessings be upon you."

They nodded again, and then they were past, and Eloel moved on. If they had looked more closely, they would have seen that his black tunic was tight-bound at the sleeves rather than loose. If they had looked more closely, they would have seen that the young man before them wore what looked like a long robe, but was really a black leather jerkin, quadrant-split from hip to knees for fighting, with blackened steel buckles. Or they might have noticed that his black Jenner-cowl was not the rough weave of a Penitent, but an oiled hood that flowed seamlessly into his leather jerkin, a garment made to keep off the rain. But they believed as they wanted to believe, and they saw a Penitent walking his Mercy in the early morning hours.

If they had looked more closely, they might have noticed that he wore the garb of a Kingsman rather than a Jenner. But no one noticed such things these days. Kingsmen were all but extinct.

Or nearly so.

Sweat beaded upon Eloel's forehead, and he hurried on, his heart pounding his own death-knells in his chest.

* * *

The high-vaulted Assembly Room was not hard to find. The ancient doors, Eloel had known beforehand, were always open, the grand underground space an alehouse now for the weary lower-class and servants of the palace. No one really kept the alehouse, except the Master of Spirits, whom Eloel had been told came 'round nightly to tally the various kegs. Hopt-ale there was, mellon-blume wine, Yegovian cider and various other spirits either produced by palace lands, or the industrious and altogether dry-palated Jenners, who hired local men and women as tasters for their productions. Other spirits of fine caliber were traded for from Valenghia and Praough, known for their grapes and fruit-wines. Eloel navigated around the spectral stands of kegs, both massive and modest, without the tails of his longjerkin even so much as brushing one, when a sound in the darkness stopped him suddenly, and then a flicker of light confirmed it.

Someone else was here, and they shouldn't have been. Not by this hour.

Senses tingling with care, a cold sweat slicking his chest now, Eloel edged forward along the shadows of a stand of kegs taller than himself, dropping eaves upon the conversation ahead. Around a single candle upon the roughshod bar, four figures stood. Crouching a little less in his shadows, Eloel could see a map spread out between them, their heads down as they conversed in low murmurs. Scouting the route to his destination, Eloel cursed internally. His destination, through a vaulted passageway behind the bar, was blocked by the nighttime agitators.

The highwall that was his objective was beyond a vaulted section behind the bar, and Eloel either had to ascend the staircase to his left, and hope there was access to the highwall, or pass right next to those gathered around the candle. The vaulted piece was actually a natural stone bridge, an edifice of the once-safehouse at the heart of the palace. The stairs likely led to the bridge, to a second-story within the stone, but Eloel had no idea if there was access to his destination from the second level. Even to gain the stairs, Eloel would have to squeeze around the bar, passing only three lengths from a fat man in a very small jacket with an ample behind.

Eloel edged forward out of the deepest shadows of the barrels and out of safety, keeping low, and his nostrils caught the dry-sour scent of Yegovian cider. His father had allowed him a tot here or there in honor of training well done, and Eloel had enjoyed a full pull after this Fifth Seal at age eighteen. But spirits were frowned upon for a Kingsman, and Eloel generally abstained. He wrinkled his nose and edged forward just out of the candle's flare, creeping behind the man with the massive buttocks at the edge of the bar.

"Ho, there! Penitant! Halt!"

A rough-gnarled voice ripped through Eloel's darkness. He froze mid-step, heart thundering in his ears. Heads turned, faces scowled, one man drew a knife in a rush with a curse. But the titter of a woman seemed to put them at ease. Blonde hair peeked from beneath her dark thieves' hood, and her curvaceousness rounded the bar in a mockery of gracious refinement, reaching out for Eloel with dark-gloved hands.

"Oh, but Yurgas! He's so young!" The woman chortled, the dry-sour scent of cider reeking from her as she sidled close to tempt him, the jasoune-bloom of her perfume stronger then any true jasoune-bush could ever produce by the dead of midnight. Breasts heaved purposefully above her tight corset as she uncowled Eloel and put a soft glove to his face. Eloel wasn't taken by her charms, but what he was, was frozen in place and breathing hard, panicked.

"So young for a Penitent!" Merry blue eyes gazed up to his height as she considered him, mistaking his flushing for the blush of a celibate. Her hands slid down his neck, stroking over the black leather of his jerkin at the high collar. "You're built like a heron, lad... so slender and tall, and with such lovely dark looks... such a waste in a Jenner!"

"Here lad," a gruff man chortled from behind her. "Have a pull and go. Bar's closed."

A thick glassware tumbler was slid across the polished stone of the bar, straight to Eloel's fingertips beyond his black fingerless gloves. His face flushed crimson to the roots of his cowl-mussed black hair, and he could feel his cheeks burning at his discovery, and at their mocking.

"Just a smell," Eloel murmured, trying to play the ruse that they, like so many others these days, duped themselves with when faced with the truth of a Kingsman standing before them in the flesh. Grey eyes flashing guiltily to the four, he laughed nervously and picked up the tumbler, like a Jenner might if discovered coming down to the Deephouse for a forbidden drink in the dead of night. But Eloel's eyes flicked uncertainly to one seated in the shadows beyond the candle's light, the one who had marked him and spoken first. The one whom Eloel felt watching him far too closely.

Eloel's skin tingled, telling him to run.

"Just a whiff," Eloel murmured again, raising the tumbler as if to smell it.

"Not so pure after all, are we, young Penitent?" The woman laughed, then lifted her hand to his, urging the tumbler towards his lips. "Have a sip. Just one."

Why not? Might be my last.

Eloel contemplated it a moment, gazing at the amber liquid reflecting the wan candlelight, then brought it to his lips, and tossed it back entire. He grimaced, then set the thick tumbler back upon the bar. Low whistles and merry jeers greeted his stunned and buzzing ears as he fought to not cough or choke from the fumes now plaguing his insides and screaming up his throat.

"Three whole pulls! Jenner can keep his liquor!" One man laughed.

"Ain't no Jenner."

The place where the cider had passed in liquid flame now cooled in terror, deep into Eloel's belly. His ruse was forfeit. He could feel it, searing all over his skin like molten glass. Eloel fought the urge to flee, forcing himself to find the man in the darkness and pin him with his father's commanding grey eyes as the bulky thief stood. Eloel saw the man hesitate, just for a moment. But Eloel was young, and though he had his father's eyes and his father's frame, he hadn't lived his father's life. He wasn't Rhakhan, not like Urloel.

Eloel wasn't even a Kingsman. Not yet.

The big man overcame his uncertainty, seeing only a scared lad once more. A well-trained lad, but scared and young all the same. He approached the flame.

"Sure he's a Jenner," the woman tittered uncertainly, "poor thing's just mussed from the dew, that's all."

The man in the darkness drew closer, and Eloel could see his hulking mass now, his height even with Eloel himself, though his bulk was thrice what Eloel might one day become. Eloel had the height of his father's line, of den'Alrahel, but like his twin sister Olea, he was whip-slender from his mother.

"Ain't no Jenner. He's a Kingsman. Young, but a Kingsman, mark me."

Without warning, the big man lunged. Eloel slipped sideways in the tingle of instinct that was his strange birthright, then avoided a flying fist. Lithe as a heron, he launched himself into a twist that landed him upon the bluestone wall behind the bar, in which he found a number of ancient iron fittings, perfect grips for the tips of his fingers. He scurried upwards guided by the minutiae of sensate instinct, not pausing to gauge a route or watch the ascent of the big man behind him, whom he could feel climbing clumsily, his motion peppered liberally with curses. A knife went whizzing through the air, and a tingle through Eloel. He dropped his right hand from the wall. Steel glinted and clattered stone right where his hand had been. Eloel matched his left, still moving upwards as easily as the little eloi-lizards for which he was named.

Curses sounded, as loud as the marauders dared in the deep of the palace underground. Eloel did not look down. He moved up and over the natural byrunstone bridge, angling left and finding it merged into the highwall that was his objective. He scurried upwards, climbing the stone diagonally, making for the farwall in the deep southern corner of the ancient cavern. There, nearly at the top of what was a two-hundred-length climb, he scoured the stone with his fingertips.

It would only be a hand's gap at most, anywhere up in this corner.

And there it was.

The gap Ghrenna had described to him, one hand high and three hands wide, was a perfect natural oval in the stone. Eloel reached in with his left hand, clinging to the stone with his right. His fingers brushed the box inside, smooth-polished cendarie with an etched metal hasp. He fished it to the edge, ears straining for the breathing of the two men now climbing below him, still twenty lengths behind his ascent and having trouble with the holds. Eloel snugged his fingertips under the clasp. Ancient, it snapped off the box.

He flicked open the lid.

A small metal object rested upon the moth-eaten black velvet. The padding crumbled as he reached in to touch the filigreed piece, which seemed to be an ornate clockwork of some kind with the design of the Jenner Sun upon it. Many-layered and fitting together all-of-a-piece, it was roughly rectangular, large as two fingers together and made of a variety of precious metals. But as his fingertips brushed the object, it fell to pieces, clockworks and gears falling away from each other as if whatever magic that had held them all these long years was utterly undone.

An involuntary cry escaped Eloel's throat.

This wasn't it.

Eloel's head reeled and his chest compressed, as if trapped beneath the crushing depths of a highmountain lake, and he was drowning.

This isn't it. But the box, the niche, it's all where Ghrenna said it would be, it's all here! But this... this is not it!!

A boot scrabbled for purchase ten lengths now below him. Eloel startled. He scoured the cliff-face with his dark-adjusted eyes. There was no other niche, no other possible hiding place. This was the only one in the byrunstone highwall, and this was the box, and this was what was supposed to be in it.

But it wasn't.

Quickly, he gathered all the pieces of the miniscule clockworks into his hand, stuffing them down into his belt-pouch by the agility of his clever fingers. Gazing higher, he saw the natural cut through the top of the bluestone cavern. He could smell the night-breeze where it sweetened to dawn outside. Fast as his hands and feet could take him, muscles of his long torso and thighs bunching in perfect coordination, Eloel hurried up, slithered through the crack, and was out upon the high roof of the King's palace.

***

Eloel wasted no time upon the high-gabled roofline of Rhoushenn. He could hear the heavy breathing and scrabbling of his pursuers, who had proved surprisingly agile up the sheer highwall.

Everyone in Rhoushenn Palace kept their secrets, and he had just happened to stumble into one.

Eloel vaulted over a few ancient boulders that had dislodged from the mountainside ages ago and fallen upon the palace roof, then hurried over the side of one dome. Backing over toes first, he found the handholds he needed in the rough-hewn rock where the carving-out of the palace proper met the uncarved grey-blue byrunstone of the Kingsmount. It was hundreds of feet to the ground, but Eloel didn't need to look. He never needed to look. He found his way down by the instinct of his feet, a tingle in his left foot leading him left, a pulse in his right foot leading him back to the right, until he found a nice long vertical crevasse that got him nearly to the ground. He dropped the last five lengths, and then he was on grey-blue pavingstones of Lintesh behind a weaver's shop. Dawn had not yet crested the eastern side of the Kingsmount as he sped away into the city, the hopefulness of the lightening sky unnoticed by his despairing heart.

***

A dark-cowled shadow melted to his side as Eloel ran, a shadow nearly as tall as he, keeping easy pace. The shadow darted through narrow alleyways and beneath awnings and leaped stone benches with far more grace than Eloel himself could ever manage, despite his gifts. Eloel caught the flash of longknives in her hands, at perfect ease there as she ran. Olea was like that. She was the natural runner, the natural fighter, the one with talent at weapons to match their father. Eloel had his gift, effective but unorthodox at weaponry. Eloel's twin was as fine as her blades, honed into an effortless articulation from long practice. She sidled close enough to whisper as they ran, never losing pace, her breath unruffled.

"Did you get it? Was it there?"

"No," Eloel did not break his stride to shake his head. "It wasn't there. The box was, but not the bluestone ring. These were there instead. Do you have your pouch? Can you stow them while we run?"

He fished out the miniscule clockworks, making sure each piece made it safely into Olea's waiting palm, somehow steady even as she ran alongside. After all were received, she eyed them, dark brows furrowing, then stowed them away in the tiny silk-thread *gerundahl* around her neck, and tucked it safely under the open front of her black shirt and leather jerkin. "We'll discuss this later. Run. There are five men following."

"Five?" Eloel lost a step to glance behind. He saw no-one.

"Trust me," Olea's wry smile was amused, but the tension in it betrayed her. They were all tense. Far too tense than any of the Seventh Seals had any right to be. They shouldn't have needed to sneak into the King's City. They shouldn't have needed to invade Rhoushenn palace like thieves. Once, the Alrashemni Kingsmen had been respected, listened to as trusted advisors. Once, everyone had known their garb and lords and ladies alike had bowed.

Once, they had been a symbol of justice in Alrhou-Mendera.

Once, a Seventh Seal would not have been allowed either gerundahl or ohriquet.

Eloel unbuckled the collar of his jerkin and tugged his shirt lacings open to get more air as he ran, lengthening his stride to match Olea, who ran with the effortless confidence of a gazelle. If others had been looking this night, they would have seen the Inking of the *ohriquet* upon Eloel's chest, the Kingsmount crowned with five stars, the topmost star just visible where Eloel's black shirt-lacings began. He rubbed at it absently as he ran. It still burned, the skin yet raw from when Suchinne had inked it upon him. Eloel knew he didn't deserve it, none of them had earned it yet, and these Inkings had also been Suchinne's first. It was not a tidy marking, the stars' points of uneven lengths, the shading of the mountain not quite right.

But Suchinne might be the best Inkwoman they had, now, if they couldn't stop the Summons.

Please, let them still be there. They mustn't go... There must be some other way.

The thought spurred him on, and Eloel's fleet steps skimmed over the pavingstones, then raced under the already-open Watercourse Gate, the guards still sleeping soundly from pith-crest in their ale. Eloel and Olea sped on, out into the leafy verge of the Elhambria Forest.

* * *

This book is available in print at most online retailers. Please remember to leave a review for *Three Days of Oblenite, Book One: Breath* at your favorite retailer!

Made in the USA
Charleston, SC
20 May 2015